MONSTER GIRL DOCTOR

1

Story by
Yoshino Origuchi

Illustrated by
Z-ton

Seven Seas

MONSTER MUSUME NO OISHASAN
© 2016 by Yoshino Origuchi
Illustrations by Z-ton
All rights reserved.
First published in Japan in 2016 by SHUEISHA Inc., Tokyo.
English translation rights arranged by SHUEISHA Inc.
through TOHAN CORPORATION, Tokyo.

Seven Seas books may be purchased in bulk for promotional,
educational, or business use. Please contact your local
bookseller or the Macmillan Corporate and Premium Sales
Department at 1-800-221-7945, extension 5442, or by
e-mail at MacmillanSpecialMarkets@macmillan.com.

Seven Seas and the Seven Seas logo are trademarks of
Seven Seas Entertainment, LLC. All rights reserved.

Follow Seven Seas Entertainment online at
sevenseasentertainment.com

Translation: David Musto
Adaptation: Ben Sloan
Copy Editor: Marykate Jasper
Book Layout: Karis Page
Cover Design: Nicky Lim
Proofreader: Julia Kinsman
Light Novel Editor: Jenn Grunigen
Production Assistant: CK Russell
Production Manager: Lissa Pattillo
Editor-in-Chief: Adam Arnold
Publisher: Jason DeAngelis

ISBN: 978-1-626926-5-47
Printed in Canada
First Printing: December 2017
10 9 8 7 6 5 4 3 2 1

CASE 01:
The Centaur of the Arena

"Ummm... Are you reaaaally going to do this?"

It was a small room.

Partitioned off with a thick cloth screen, the interior was a sterile white. Everything from the sheets to the beds themselves was all properly prepared, and the room overflowed with an air of cleanliness.

Inside, a man and woman faced one another.

The woman had already taken off her outer clothes from the waist up. The only thing she wore was her cow-hide bra; her hands covered up her voluptuous chest. With her cupped breasts and her beautiful figure, a somewhat strange atmosphere hung in the air of the cramped room.

She looked distressed. The man spoke to her gently.

"Yes. And I'll need your help to complete the treatment."

"Buuuut it reeeeally is embarraaaassing..." The woman had a slow and elongated style of speech, but her anxiety could be heard distinctly in her voice.

"Yes ma'am, but this is something that everyone has to do."

"Buuuut my husbaaaand..."

"If I can finish this properly, then I'm sure your husband won't be worried, either."

The woman thought this over for a few moments, but finally

seemed to make up her mind and lowered her arms, exposing her breasts. The way she cast her eyes down gave the impression that she was frightened in some way.

"Um, if possible, please be geeeentle."

"Please don't worry—it won't hurt."

The man, acting as calmly as he could manage, extended his hand straight out to the woman's voluptuous chest. He lifted one enormous, weighty breast as he touched it.

"Ah...!"

"D-did I hurt you?!"

"I-It's okaaaay... Just surprised me a liiiittle."

"In that case, I'm going to continue, okay?"

The man looked absolutely serious as he began to thoroughly rub the woman's breast.

"*Unh*, ah! There, it hurts!"

"I'm sorry—please try to bear with it just a little longer."

"*Uhn*... Ah! *Hah*..."

Her heavy breathing began to sound like she was both gasping in pleasure and—conversely—enduring a painful examination. The man massaged her breasts even further and seemed to be checking the woman's reactions to his touches.

"I-I'm sorry, please forgive me. Let's see here. Does it hurt?"

The man apologized, but his hands didn't stop. Similarly, while he looked flustered, he continued to properly observe the woman.

"Ah, no! That's—*hunh*!"

Pressing her hand against her mouth, the woman desperately tried to endure the pain without letting her voice slip out.

The man closely observed her condition while she endured his examination.

At long last, it was over, and he removed his hands from her breasts. The high-quality cowhide underwear that the woman was wearing seemed to be meant for someone much smaller and had slipped down, letting the tips of her breasts peek out from underneath.

Her breathing still heavy and rough, the woman fixed her disheveled clothes. She slipped her cotton clothing over her underwear, but her cheeks remained flushed red. Even with her now dressed, the atmosphere in the room remained suspect and uncertain.

"Now, then…"

The man shifted his attention once more.

The focus of his gaze was the woman's face. Poking out from her sandy hair were large, curved horns and a pair of pointed, cow-like ears.

"Next are your ears."

"M-my eeeears? But uuuum, are you all done with my cheeeest?"

"Yes, thank you. Next, I'll need you to show me your ears.

"My eeeears? Buuuut they are a little sensitive, sooooooo…"

The woman averted her eyes, looking uneasy. Her ears twitched as though responding to her unease. Their skin was so thin that even the blood vessels running through them were visible to the naked eye. They bore a striking resemblance to the ears of a cow and vividly demonstrated that she was not human.

"That aaaand…my husbaaaand…"

"Yes, I understand. However, I believe that being thorough will be the best way to put your husband's mind at ease."

"*Uuungh…*"

For a moment, the young wife hesitated, her ears twitching and trembling.

At long last, however, she seemed to have readied herself, and suddenly turned her head towards the man. She presented her energetic ears and curved horns in front of him.

"P-pleeeease."

"Okay, then, please bear with me a moment..."

The man's words were polite, but he looked tense. As he felt her ears, his face was stiffer than when he had touched her chest.

"*Nnnh!*"

The woman let out a yelp.

The cry was very different from the voice she had made when her breasts were being touched—so much so that the man instinctively yanked his hands from her ears.

"S-sorry, are you okay?"

"I'm fiiiine. It's juuuust, the stimulation was a liiiiiittle strooooong..."

"I'm sorry, but it's necessary. Can I continue?"

"I-I'll try to bear with iiiit."

The man again touched the woman's ears.

"*Un... Hnh!*"

He brought his face up close to the cow ears and her visible blood vessels, examining them minutely. Although the man had been touching the woman's body for some time now, he still paid serious, meticulous attention to her reactions to his touches.

"*Ah! ...Hnh!*"

"I-If it hurts, please tell me."

"It's not that...it hurts, buuuut... *Ah, hah, ah-nh!* I'm sorry, deaaaaaar..."

The man thought that it was likely the woman herself didn't understand what exactly she was apologizing for.

She called out to her absent husband. Nonetheless, the man continued to examine her ears, deliberately ignoring what she was saying. He pulled them up and down and shined a light through them, but if someone had been looking in at the two of them, they would have had a hard time figuring out exactly what was going on.

"*Nh! Unh... Hnh!*"

"F-forgive me, I'm so sorry. Please just bear with it a little longer."

"I-I can't take it... I'm... I caaaaaaaaaaaaaaaaan't!"

Then, finally.

"*Unnnnnnnhhhhhhhh!*"

The woman made an exaggerated leap into the air. Her shoulders twitched and convulsed, and she tried desperately to cover up the moan of ecstasy that threatened to spill out.

"A-are you okay...?"

The man couldn't help being flustered by the woman's extreme reaction.

For a moment, she could only breathe heavily, but before long she turned towards the man with watery eyes. Her upturned gaze was enough to make the heart of any man alive swell with feelings for the woman.

"I-I'm fiiiine. So, umm..."

"Oh, yes. Thank you for sticking through my examination. I've figured out the source of the pain."

"Reaaaaally? That's gooood, but ummmm—"

The woman gave a quick sideways glance towards the man.

"You're a dooooctor after all, so can you please conduct the examination in a more dignified maaaanner? It's embaaaarrassing for me if you are so...*flustered.*"

Her words thrust into the man— Glenn Litbeit—like a dagger.

"...I am ashamed of my behavior, please forgive me."

In the face of the woman's groaning, frowning face, all he could do was bow his head in apology.

This was a clinic whose specialty was treating monsters.

As a doctor that specialized in examining non-human patients, it was Glenn Litbeit's place of work, and he took his duties there extremely seriously.

× × ✖ × ×

A tightening of the chest, with pain.

Some days the acute pain was strong enough to make walking difficult.

Experiencing this chest trouble, the young minotaur wife—Silsha Tessius—had come to the clinic, and it was almost time for her one day of outpatient care to be completed.

Minotaurs were a species of monster that had many distinctive characteristics similar to cattle. The male minotaurs had heads exactly like those of a bull. Their bodies were generally tall and muscular. Female minotaurs had faces quite similar to humans, but their horns and ears were just like those of a bull, and it was said many of them also developed large breasts.

Glenn concentrated his examination on the patient's chest and ears. By palpating her breasts, he was able to conclude that she had no lumps or tumors. On the other hand, her ears were tinged red and had become enlarged, as though they were slightly swollen. Glenn believed that this swelling was the cause of her ears' sensitivity. A female minotaur's ears becoming red and inflamed were symptomatic of only one possible condition.

Namely—

"You are pregnant."

At Glenn's assistant's quiet words, the Tessius couple—sitting together now that her husband had joined her in the room—were stunned.

When his wife began to experience pain, the husband had jumped to worse and worse conclusions about whether it was a sign of a more serious illness, so the results of the examination were a great relief for the newly married couple.

"The chest pain is a symptom of pregnancy. Congratulations." Glenn's assistant, Saphentite, gave this blessing with a smile on her face.

With her white skin and red eyes, Saphentite Neikes gave off a cold, indifferent first impression, but after seeing her gentle, friendly smile, it became immediately clear that her seemingly unfriendly appearance was misleading.

She was a lamia, and an excellent assistant. As she addressed the couple, she swung her tail back and forth, performing miscellaneous tasks he had assigned her.

"Follow-up observation will be necessary, but the chest pain will subside before long. If there are times when the pain is truly unbearable, please boil this herb and drink the decoction."

The medicine tucked away in the cloth bag had been mixed together by Saphentite with herbs from the garden. She had thorough

pharmaceutical knowledge and oversaw the dispensing of free prescriptions at the clinic.

Saphentite couldn't tell if the Tessius couple was actually listening to her as they hugged each other and shared in their delight. Glenn was also happy to bring the case to a close without condemning someone to a serious illness.

Glenn and Saphentite saw the couple off as they took the medicine and left the clinic. With the good tidings in their hearts, the young minotaur couple were all smiles as they faded from view.

"I'll go flip the sign, Doctor."

Saying this, Saphentite turned the sign at the entrance over to "closed." There were no more patients left for them to treat, so their work for the day was now over.

Glenn began cleaning up the examination room. This small section was separated with a curtain, but the clinic itself was reasonably spacious. More importantly, since it was used for medical treatment, cleaning and sterilizing the space was important work. To put it bluntly, it was more than just the two of them could handle.

And so—

"Time to tidy up!"

"Cleaning time!"

Lightly running across the floor were a group of fairies that helped them out.

The fairies were employed by the clinic, and were paid a fee of one serving of milk for a day's work. No matter what they tried, Glenn and Saphentite couldn't handle it all themselves, so they hired the fairies to take care of the routine, everyday chores. The small beings couldn't personally assist with any of the medical treatments, but they were invaluable when it came to the various chores, and as such were a very convenient group to have around.

Now that they had seen the couple off, Saphentite let out a sigh, relieved that the day's work had come to a close.

The assistant was a monster covered in white scales. Being a lamia, her lower body resembled the tail of a snake, and had a charming radiance to it. An albino, her skin was white with scales, and she had red eyes that gleamed like rubies. Coupled with her silver hair, she struck a mysterious figure, but because she worked in a medical clinic, her beautiful white face made her seem like the perfect person for the job.

On close inspection, a somewhat pink and purplish color could be seen shining deep within her white scales. It was a strange tinge of color, and it only served to enhance Saphentite's mystique.

She had been working as Glenn's assistant ever since the clinic had been opened. She was a capable person and indispensable to him.

"Thank you for your hard work, Doctor," he said, expressing his gratitude.

"Oh, yeah..."

Glenn felt a sting behind her words of acknowledgment.

Saphentite also began to clean up, putting away paperwork and medical supplies with her serpentine lower body. Her dexterity was impressive as always, and the operation of the clinic would be hard-pressed without her. However...

Saphentite's red eyes weren't staring at Glenn, but somewhere off into the distance. Glenn had been with Saphentite for a long time, and he could always sense when she was in a bad mood.

"Um... Is something wrong, Saphentite?"

"No, Doctor. Not really anything in particular."

Saphentite extended her slithering tail and took the bundle of herbs that Glenn was holding. She was clearly upset.

"But?"

"I'm not mad. I'm not upset in the slightest."

Her silver hair was nearly transparent. Through it, Glenn could see her looking toward him. Her vivid red eyes penetrated through and shot daggers at him.

"That's right...Doctor. Even if I hear lewd voices that sound like a man and a woman making love coming from the exam room, and even if during an 'examination' the doctor touches the patient in a wretched and shameful way, that doesn't give me any reason to be upset. Indeed, I am simply worried about the future of the clinic going forward, that's all."

"That was...umm... Sorry..."

"If it's something to apologize for, I'd rather you just act more appropriately from now on."

Saphentite's stare was ice cold.

Everything he had done was part of the patient's medical treatment, so Glenn shouldn't have anything to be ashamed of, but...

"Honestly, if this is how things are going to go, then there was no point in leaving that octo-woman—excuse me—no point in leaving Miss Cthulhy in the first place. Yes, we relied on her for help in the beginning, but this is *Dr. Glenn's* clinic. Please be aware that you need to be a doctor that everyone can trust."

"Y-you're right. I am really sorry."

Even at times like this, they were still in their roles as doctor and assistant, but originally, both of them had been students at the academy. Studying under the professor of medicine Cthulhy Squele, the two had achieved good marks in each of their respective fields. Their instructor, Cthulhy, also played a large role in helping them open up their clinic in the town of Lindworm.

Saphentite had been the first to start studying under Cthulhy, and as such she was a senior pupil compared to Glenn. The two of them operated the clinic together, but to tell the truth, there really hadn't been any change to the power dynamics of their relationship. Glenn was often scolded and lectured by Saphentite.

"As a human, Doctor, you are the only one who can examine and treat monsters, you know."

"Yes...I know. I'll try harder." Glenn nodded. He was seventeen years old, and while his timid personality made him look even younger, he had exceptional personal achievements to his name.

Although he was originally from the main metropolis inside the human territory, on the eastern edge of the continent, he still had an interest in monsters. Due to his extraordinary passion for the subject, he had transferred to the monster academy. There he studied under the authority on monster medical science, Cthulhy Squele. Even among the brilliant, talented boys and girls that Cthulhy had collected from all over the continent, Glenn showed exceptional promise.

Saphentite took pride in her genius for pharmaceutical studies, but Glenn Litbeit was head-and-shoulders above her.

Not only were monsters wide-ranging in form, the ecology behind those forms was extremely varied and diverse. They were all classified as "monsters," but though they shared that same label, between lamia and minotaurs there were those whose bodies were so different that they could almost be said to be another species entirely. As such, the illnesses they faced were just as distinct.

Treating and examining just the single race of humans took an enormous amount of knowledge. Glenn, however, not only examined various diverse species of monsters, but was also prepared to provide treatment and perform surgery on patients when necessary.

In a town where humans and monsters lived together like Lindworm, once could say he was an indispensable talent to have available, but...

"From now on, I'll make sure to do things properly."

"Of course. Tomorrow is the arena's health examination. This is a very important job that Miss Cthulhy forced on—*entrusted* to us, so no matter what, you need to see it through to the end."

"That's right... I understand. I'll make sure to do it properly."

Unfortunately, Glenn couldn't help that he was still a rookie with very little life experience. He was a timid and unreliable boy, enough that it was natural for his assistant Saphentite to fret over him.

That said, he was actually quite capable; since the clinic had opened, he had given countless consultations to the monsters living in the town and diagnosed their diseases and disorders. The biggest issue was that Glenn himself still hadn't come to grips with this fact.

"One more thing, Dr. Glenn."

"Yes?"

"I've said this many times, but please don't call me Saphentite. Call me Sapphee, like when we were at the academy."

Whether it was to hide her embarrassment or for some other reason, her tail swung back and forth.

While Glenn used to refer to her that way, since opening the clinic he used a more formal manner of address in order to make clear their positions as assistant and doctor. However, Saphentite had always been displeased with being referred to that way.

Ultimately, it seemed that *this* was the primary reason she was upset today.

However, she hadn't stopped referring to Glenn as "Doctor," which he didn't feel was fair. On top of that, he didn't want to be called "doctor" by a woman who was his senior, but Saphentite didn't show any indication that she would make this change.

"I understand, Sapphee."

"There you go. Now then, Doctor, shall we prepare for tomorrow?"

Finally looking directly at Glenn, he saw that his exceptional lamia assistant was smiling. Her expression was still stiff, but it was much softer than it had been up until then.

"Preparations!"

"Help!"

"Where's our milk?"

The fairies fluttered about, thin wings flapping. The price of their services was cheap, but because of this they were strict about their service contract. If they were made to work past what they had been scheduled to do, then they would be furious. Such were their conditions.

"I've prepared the milk for you. Now, then, there is just one more thing to be done."

"Okay," the fairies said. Glenn had answered as well, his voice mixing in with the fairies'.

In this town of Lindworm, where there were few people able to diagnose and treat monsters, the Litbeit Clinic had finished another busy day.

× × ✕ × ×

Once upon a time, over one hundred years ago, there was a large war.

The Vivre Mountains cut through the heart of the continent, serving as a border between the humans and monsters who waged war against one another. The humans fought with both superior numbers and technology, as well as with the proper leadership to command it all. The monsters, although fewer in number, overwhelmed the humans with their diverse range of abilities, and used ingenious schemes the humans were unable to cope with as they met them in battle.

Why exactly had the war started? The cause of the dispute was forgotten in the chaos of history. There were a number of plausible explanations, but none of them had sufficient evidence to back them up. What was certain was that the fighting bred more fighting and became a spiraling, swirling source of calamity for both sides.

It commenced with an enormous battle, two massive military hosts confronting each other head-to-head on a vast prairie.

But the long, continuous war steadily began to drain people of their will to fight. Grudges lingered over the deaths of relatives and loved ones, but as the scale of the war gradually grew smaller and smaller, the number of people who felt such pain and harbored such animosity began to decrease with it. On top of that, the longer the fighting continued, the more fearful each army's monarchs and generals became of their fortunes being lost.

As the long war came into its final stages, the only battles that popped up occasionally were small skirmishes out in the remote areas--and these hadn't even resulted in any casualties. At long last, the humans and monsters formed a mutual cease-fire agreement on the condition that they wouldn't invade each other's territory. That had been ten years ago.

"I mean... There wasn't really any reason to keep the war going, anyway," Glenn murmured as he rocked back and forth in his carriage, looking out at the view of the town.

From his carriage, he could see the scene of the marketplace. A human fruit vendor was selling apples to lamia children. A cyclops craftsman caught the attention of a young housewife and promoted his wares, extolling the sharpness of his kitchen knives.

This town where human and monster lived together was where Glenn worked as a doctor—Lindworm.

Located at the foot of the Vivre Mountains, it had once been a prosperous fortified city within human territory. Even now, after the signing of the cease-fire agreement, generally the monsters lived in the monster part of town while the humans lived in the human part. It was thought to be the only city where humans and monsters existed together peacefully, as if such harmony were normal.

"What brought that topic on so suddenly?"

"Oh, it's nothing. I was just thinking how now that peace is here and the war is over, all sorts of people are living together. That's all."

As a doctor specializing in monster medicine, Glenn was frankly delighted by the peace that had come. In fact, the carriage that Glenn was riding in at that very moment was a symbol of that very peace. There was an emblem of two crossed spears painted on the side of the carriage—the emblem of the Scythia Transportation Company.

The Scythia family was a prestigious centaur family, so in other, more precise words, what Glenn was *actually* riding was a carriage hauled by a centaur.

"How's the ride in our carriage, Doc?"

"It's comfortable. Thank you."

"That's right—it's great, isn't it?" Acting as both carriage horse and driver, the centaur gave a hearty guffaw as he pulled the wagon.

Glenn thought to himself that this must be a good life for centaurs these days. The equine monsters who had once been well-known mercenaries, charging through grasslands to do battle, were now carriage drivers. Their new occupation at the transport company was, to them, the perfect fit for their skills.

"Everything hasn't been settled for good, you know, Dr. Glenn," Sapphee said, poking her head out of the carriage. "You can see the arena now," she added.

"The arena," Glenn mused. "During the war it was used to execute monster prisoners of war, right?"

"Yes. Combining entertainment and public executions, it is the place where prisoners were forced to kill animals, or even other members of their species. All because Lindworm was a fortress town on the front lines of human territory." Sapphee made a somewhat pained expression. The prisoners of war that were killed there had been monsters, which meant there were sure to have been other lamia among those who died there.

"But the war ended," she went on, "and the reason for Lindworm's very existence—not just that of the arena—was questioned."

With the fighting done, the facilities used in the war had served their purpose, and became unnecessary—along with all of Lindworm. The troops stationed there began departing, suddenly putting the merchants and shopkeepers in dire straits. There were many people who sold food, bowls, and other daily necessities to the soldiers. The prisoners of war in the arena were also put in a rough spot. Even if they returned to monster territory, as soldiers they no longer had a job.

Then appeared a single dragon who was given the moniker the "Draconess."

With its original function coming to an end, she rebuilt Lindworm. She encouraged many monsters to migrate to the city, sustaining the town's population while protecting the livelihood of its merchants and shopkeepers. In order to accommodate the variety of ways of life each monster had, she created a new city development plan. The actualization of that plan had brilliantly turned the town into a place where monsters could easily live.

The arena was a perfect example.

She recruited fighters and established detailed regulations for their fights. Furthermore, she made sure that gambling occurred under the strict regulations she put in place. The arena once used for executions had been transformed into a place where those former military men could use their skills in combat to entertain an audience.

These days, everyone knew how difficult it was to get seats for fights between high-profile warriors. It had a reputation as being a place where one could see powerful strength and skills clash.

"It is thanks to the Draconess that Lindworm has grown these past ten years. I hear that many of the mercenaries started a new life as fighters in the arena. Even with the war over and their livelihood as soldiers gone, in Lindworm they can continue on as fighters. They don't use real weapons either, so there's little risk of death, too."

CASE 01 : THE CENTAUR OF THE ARENA

"Yes, I know," Glenn said. "What are you trying to say?"

"I mean that with the rapid growth, there are still some things that have yet to catch up... Dr. Glenn's workload is going to increase with it." Sapphee mixed a sigh in with her words, and Glenn laughed dryly.

Just because the war was over and a large number of monsters had flocked to Lindworm didn't mean the number of monster doctors grew with them. In all of Lindworm, there were only two places monsters could go for medical consultation.

One was Central Lindworm Hospital, which was run by Glenn's teacher Cthulhy. The second was the Litbeit Clinic that Glenn operated.

The Central Hospital had more facilities at their disposal and could manage difficult surgeries—but handling such a large-scale hospital meant that the staff, including the medical director Cthulhy, was busy. The wait time for patients was long. Therefore, patients that were experiencing trouble that didn't necessitate a trip to the big hospital all headed to Glenn's clinic.

This wasn't to say that their clinic wasn't busy, just that they managed to scrape out enough time to humor elderly ogres who used leg pain as an excuse to come and gossip—and, from time to time, they were given work to do by their teacher Cthulhy.

Cthulhy was unable to attend to the routine medical examinations of the fighters who appeared in the matches at the arena, so their work that day was an example of one of the jobs that fell on Glenn to complete.

"Honestly, making us close the clinic for the day and sending us out on a trip to the arena... That octo-woman doesn't consider our situation at all..."

44

"I know, but you don't need to say it like that, Sapphee. Dr. Cthulhy is busy, too."

The fighters in the arena were constantly getting injured in their matches. Very rarely, fighters lost their lives due to accidents that occurred during a fight. In order to prevent situations like that from happening, it was necessary to have a doctor who could examine and diagnose monsters.

"I know, but still." Sapphee looked as if she didn't accept Glenn's justification. Though they were both distinguished pupils of Cthulhy's, the two really did not get along well.

For Glenn's part, he optimistically thought they were simply close enough friends that they felt comfortable quarreling with each other.

"Anyway," Saphhee went on, "there's nothing we can do but agree to her demands. Today's examination will be focused on the rank-three and rank-four monster-fighters. According to the documents we were given, it seems many of them are centaurs."

"Centaurs, huh..." Glenn looked at the carriage driver, whose face streamed with sweat as he pulled the cart forward.

They were born to be cavalrymen. While it was said that outstanding cavalrymen were of one mind between horse and rider, that was purely referring to humans. From birth, centaurs were able to run as fast as a horse, and with just a small amount of military training, they were able to lead others into battle splendidly.

During the war, the centaurs had charged across the open plains with spears in hand, the most dangerous threat to the human forces. Though Scythia Transportation showed that they were settling into the transportation industry these days, their roots traced back to their life as warriors. For a species born into battle, it made sense that a large number of them would then take up a new life as fighters in the arena.

"We will be taking their height and weight measurements, and conducting medical inquiries into the patients' health," Sapphee said. "Will that be okay?"

Glenn nodded. "Yes. That's fine. There isn't anyone who needs immediate treatment, right?"

"It seems anyone in that condition is being sent to the Central Hospital," Sapphee said, with the look of a calm, cool-headed assistant. "Our job is to interview the fighters and discover any injuries or signs of illness that have outwardly exhibited themselves."

Discovering ailments in advance and treating them appropriately during the early stages was also part of a doctor's job, though it naturally required a lot of knowledge and skill to do so. What would happen if, by any chance, a critical symptom was overlooked? It would likely have a major impact on that patient's life.

"We're going to be there soon, Doc. Can I drop you off at the main entrance?"

"No. Please take us to the back."

"The authorized-access-only entrance, huh? All right."

The main entrance had a crowd of audience members milling around; getting into the fighter's waiting room from there was quite difficult. Glenn gathered up some documents and an assortment of tools necessary for the medical examinations and prepared to get down from the carriage.

Although they had traveled a rather long distance from the clinic, and the centaur driver was covered in sweat, Glenn glimpsed an invigorating smile on his face and couldn't help but be struck with admiration at the centaur's ability to run so far.

Finally, they came around to the back of the arena and rolled to a stop. Glenn got down from the carriage first and immediately turned to help Sapphee do the same. Sapphee, however, used her lower serpent's body to smoothly slide down the ramp of the carriage and didn't really need Glenn's help at all.

Even so, Sapphee looked somehow happy as she held onto Glenn's hand.

"So you'll be doing the check-up for the fighters today?" the centaur driver asked, unloading the large bags from the back of the carriage. Since some of the equipment stored inside was fragile, Glenn wasn't especially keen on leaving its care to a stranger—but the centaur was surprisingly careful and neat as he picked up and carried the bags.

"Yes, that's right."

"In that case, you'll most likely end up meeting our princess. We'll all be counting on you to take care of her," the sturdy centaur said, as he took down a bag crammed full of medical examination equipment.

Princess?

Glenn hadn't heard anything about the existence of a centaur royal family, but before he could ask the driver to clarify, he had already started pulling the carriage, heading quickly toward the main road.

"What was he talking about...?"

Before he could raise any more questions, his hand was caught by Sapphee's long tail. With her urging, practically dragging him along, Glenn moved towards the arena.

✷ ✷ ✖ ✷ ✷

The location for the routine medical check-up was the training grounds in the back of the arena, where the fighters practiced.

The training ground had a smooth surface stripped of weeds, and there were a number of target dummies scattered about for the fighters' training purposes. All told there were around fifty of the fighters gathered together there.

All of them were middle-ranked fighters. They didn't have any of the clumsy, awkward injuries of the rookies, and they were able to engage in intense battles day-in and day-out. Many of them were clad in a kind of simple, sparse armor that was most likely not used for real battle, but instead made specifically for matches in the arena. Others held the wooden weapons they used during their battles.

There was a diverse range of monster species among them. However, just as the advance documents they received had indicated, it seemed that a lot of them were centaurs, a monster characterized by the upper body of a human and the lower body of a horse. From their shape, it was natural for them to be taller than humans—tall enough that Glenn had to raise his head and look up at them.

Length-wise, lamias were longer, but because they often coiled their bodies and folded their long tails, centaurs appeared larger. Sapphee, with her slender shoulders, looked even smaller in comparison.

The powerful centaur fighters were enveloped in some kind of tense, strained atmosphere. Among them was one figure that stood out from the rest.

"Welcome!"

With a well-projected voice, a single woman stepped forward. Her rich blonde hair gathered together in a bun, she gave a fresh and invigorating impression. She seemed large even for a centaur, and

Glenn couldn't meet her gaze without lifting his head. Her turquoise eyes stared directly at him.

The armor she wore was light, but with its checkered pattern and superior craftsmanship, it was different from the rest of the fighters. The crest on her chest also advertised that she had the social status to spend money on adorning her armor. The unique design clearly stood out in the arena.

Her lower body was just like any other centaur, but even Glenn could tell the way her black coat lay meant it had been meticulously brushed. She was clearly a fighter based on the armor she wore, but whether it was the styled blonde hair or her diligently maintained coat, it was clear that strict attention was given to her grooming and appearance. It was as if she was an actress of the theater.

"Welcome to the Great Lindworm Arena! My name is Tisalia Scythia, and I'm a rank-three fighter here! I would like to thank you for taking time out of your busy schedule to perform our check-up in Dr. Cthulhy's stead... Oh, you're surprisingly young for a doctor, aren't you?" The blonde centaur's greeting ended in a rather surprised tone.

Whether it was her exaggerated mannerisms or her unexpected voice, the impression she gave was less of a fighter and more of a stage actress.

"N-nice to meet you. My name is Glenn Litbeit, and I will be examining you all today. This is my assistant—"

"Saphentite Neikes."

Wriggling her snake lower body, Sapphee bowed.

"I had heard that you were Dr. Cthulhy's pupil, but to think you would be so young... Incidentally, how old *are* you, Doctor?"

"Seventeen."

Surprised and intrigued cries rose up from the crowd. At first, Glenn thought they were suspicious of such a young doctor, but it seemed this wasn't the case with the fighters. Instead they all stared at him with unreserved curiosity.

"You're all being quite rude!" Tisalia said, and the lively group of fighters obediently answered back, "Sorry."

"Honestly... I apologize, Doctor. They just think it's rare for a human to be a monster doctor."

"Miss Tisalia, have you had a long career as a fighter?" Sapphee asked.

Judging just by Tisalia's behavior, it seemed that she had taken on a leadership role among the fighters. But Tisalia shook her head in denial.

"No. After all, I'm still rank three. I'm in the middle ranks of the arena."

"Yes, but... Even still, everyone seems to have a great amount of respect for you."

"Well, that's obviously because of who I am!" Tisalia puffed out her chest. Glenn had heard that Centaurs often had big busts, but it seemed Tisalia's was even bigger than the average for a horsewoman. More than that, with how tall she was, Tisalia's hefty chest was directly in front of his eyes.

Whether he liked it or not, his eyes were drawn to her bosom.

"Oh, my."

Noticing Glenn's gaze, Tisalia grinned.

"My, my, my! Well, I suppose it'd be impossible *not* to be charmed by my goddess-like body!"

"N-no, that's not—that wasn't my intention at all!"

Glenn desperately denied what Tisalia had said, but it was undeniable his gaze had been fixed on her chest. Next to him, Sapphee's snake eyes glared at him intensely.

"Anyway, that wasn't what I meant. This is what I wanted you to see."

She showed off the emblem depicted on her breastplate. Displayed there was a crest Glenn had seen before—two spears crisscrossing each other. It was the same crest that had been displayed on the centaur carriage that brought Glenn and Sapphee to the arena moments earlier.

"Oh, I see... In that case, Miss Tisalia is— ".

"That's right! Heiress to the sole transportation company in the city! I am the one and only daughter representing Scythia Transportation—the company that can bring anything anywhere, with our motto *From Parcels to People*! I'll be expecting the respect that befits my status! *Ha ha ha ha*!"

She gave a loud boisterous laugh, holding her hand up to her mouth. The gesture suited her well.

Glenn now understood. When the carriage driver had mentioned a "princess," he had been talking about her.

The Scythias were a prestigious centaur family. During the war, they were said to be veteran warriors active on the battlefield. These days, they operated a transportation business in Lindworm, which included a wide variety of operations—from simple home delivery to caravans capable of transporting large amounts of goods and people. And she was the only daughter of this giant transportation company.

Glenn now realized why she was referred to as a "princess." Even if the Scythias weren't a royal family, to the centaurs of Lindworm, Tisalia was undoubtedly worthy of the title. Indeed, thrusting her voluptuous chest out and laughing boisterously, she had the air of someone who forced others to obey her. That she had become a kind of a manager at the arena was most likely due to this personality of hers.

"Well, now—our greetings have dragged on a little, but I'll ask that you begin the health examinations shortly. Kay! Lorna!"

"Yes, my lady!"

"We're here, my lady."

At Tisalia's call, two female centaurs attended to her on either side.

While theirs weren't as high quality as Tisalia's, the two of them shared the same armor and emblem on their chest. Presumably, they were handmaids-cum-bodyguards who served Tisalia. Their presence at the arena meant they were most likely fighters, as well.

"Please line them up like always. Now, Doctor, you'll be here."

"O-okay."

The disorderly atmosphere that had been there since Glenn and Sapphee arrived evaporated.

Under the directions of Kay and Lorna, the disorganized mass of fighters came together in a line as if they were all trained soldiers.

"There have been many medical check-ups here, so we've become quite used to it." Tisalia said this to Glenn as if it were nothing, all while facing the fifty other fighters and shouting out quick orders.

"I have no doubts about your skills, Doctor," she went on. "After all, Miss Cthulhy was the one who suggested you for the job. I'm counting on you to make sure everyone will be fit and sound for their matches."

"...I don't think I'll compare to Dr. Cthulhy, but I will try my best," he said.

Tisalia gave another boisterous guffaw before joining the line, her hooves sounding as she moved. Her arms and legs were well-balanced, and seemed like the limbs of a true warrior. She had good posture, perhaps due to her properly trained upper body. Covered in a coat of black hair, her lower body had four legs that anyone who was knowledgeable about horses would find enchanting.

"Who'd have thought someone like that would be a fighter here, huh?" he said.

"Agreed. I was expecting nothing but violent ruffians, myself." There wasn't any restraint in Sapphee's choice of words.

When Glenn thought about it, however, the way the area was now was—perhaps—the natural way of things. It was, after all, no longer a place where people killed one another, but rather, one where fighters competed using their skills in combat, performing for cheers from the audience. The beauty of their appearance and the elegance of their technique in the ring were both something that the female fighters had to be aware of.

"Well, then—let's get to work, Dr. Glenn. And please work properly, without letting yourself become entranced by someone's breasts."

"I-I wasn't entranced or anything, seriously," Glenn feebly protested.

Any further objections of his were silenced easily by the snake's glare.

* ✖ ✖ ✖ *

CASE 01 : THE CENTAUR OF THE ARENA

The medical check-up was completed without issue.

Everything was thanks to the three centaurs: Tisalia in her role as a peacekeeper, and her two handmaidens, Kay and Lorna. Forming a line, all of the fighters accepted Glenn's examination with indifference, and because of it, Glenn's job also proceeded quite smoothly.

There were many centaurs among the fighters, so Glenn assumed that in some form or another many of them were connected with Scythia Transportation, and that was one reason Tisalia was able to lead the group as she did.

But on the other hand, during the examinations...

"Doctor, I know you are quite young, but I wonder if you are fond of horsewomen such as myself?"

These words from Tisalia kicked off quite a scene.

"B-by 'fond of,' what do you mean?" he asked.

"Well, I am the heir to the Scythia Transportation name. Eventually, I will lead the centaurs of Lindworm and shoulder the burden of our company's future. With that being the case, first I will have to marry and have children. My parents are enthusiastic about my interviews with potential partners, but none of the men I've been introduced to have been a good match."

Glenn had her take off her armor and was holding a stethoscope to her chest. Although it was over her light underclothing, he was still touching her voluptuous breast—but perhaps because it was for a medical examination, Tisalia didn't seem to mind.

Meanwhile, her small talk continued without end.

"I want an excellent person of talent. While we Scythias are a famous warrior clan, I'm not interested in a strong and sturdy partner. I'm, well... I'm somewhat more inept when it comes to matters of education and culture. I'm wondering if there isn't someone who could make up for that deficiency of mine."

From the sound of it, it seemed studying was her weak point. Glenn desperately pushed away the thought that floated into his mind. While her lower body was that of a horse, thinking that her brain was similarly equine was extremely rude.

"That's right. Someone like, say... someone who is so brilliant they've been diagnosing and treating monsters from a young age, perhaps."

Tisalia gave a sidelong glance at Glenn.

It appeared that within less than a day of knowing each other, he had been included among her marriage interview prospects. If anything, Glenn was more curious about the men who *didn't* suit her fancy.

"Excuse me?"

"*Aaah!*"

A sudden cry rang out.

The reason was obvious: a tail had wrapped around her lower body. Even Glenn's eyes widened at the sudden affront. The culprit hardly needed to be said. There was only one person present who possessed white snake scales.

It was Sapphee.

"Miss Tasilia. The measurements around your waist have increased quite a bit compared to last month. Forgive me for saying this, but I recommend that you lose some weight."

"We were having a very important conversation! More importantly, can you *not* measure me with your snake tail?! *This* is what you need to measure! *This* is where a centaur's waist is!"

Although she was angry, Tisalia was true to her words and showed off her waist on her upper body. Of course, since centaurs had two stomach areas on their bodies, Sapphee hadn't technically been wrong in her measurements.

"Are you telling me as a nurse you don't even know *that* much?!"

"I'm not a nurse. I'm a doctor."

"It doesn't make a difference!" As she shouted, Tisalia tore off her clothes, exposing the exact boundary between her horse lower body and her human upper body. Glenn didn't know where his eyes should be with her exposing her own stomach with no reservations.

"Now take a look, snake woman! Look at this gorgeous waist line! I dare you to say it's grown an inch!"

It was true that, possibly thanks to her habitual training and discipline, Tisalia's abdomen was quite firm and tight. Combined with her striking breasts, Glenn thought the curves of her body were all the more entrancing.

"Dr. Glenn is still only a novice doctor. It's thirty years too early for there to be talk about any sort of marriage interviews."

"I'll be an old man at that point," Glenn protested.

"The sooner one marries a horse the better!"

"I'm not sure about that one, either," he said.

Aside from this exchange during Tisalia's examination, the check-ups finished smoothly. Glenn and Sapphee finished cleaning up their equipment and filling out the necessary documents before the sun went down. Without coming upon anything that suggested serious illness, it was safe for them to say that generally all of the fighters were in good health. On the other hand, there were a number of them who had injuries currently being treated—was another distinct

characteristic of the fighters in the arena.

There were quite a few of them that Glenn wanted to forbid from participating in any matches for a while. But when he considered that these battles were their livelihood, he couldn't bring himself to tell them not to fight over some minor injuries.

For example, there was a centaur that had twisted his right front leg, but he was still going to fight in a match the next day. In the end, Glenn had decided on treating it with a simple knee brace. The centaur's injury itself wasn't anything major, but there was plenty of reason to worry that, with the arena being the place it was, it could lead to other, more serious injuries in the centaur's future matches.

Dr. Cthulhy had been in charge of the medical examinations up until a month prior. Judging by the records she kept, she didn't interfere in the lives of the fighters too much with her check-ups. She gave injuries the minimum amount of treatment they required, and there were only a few examples where she told the patient to cancel his fights. All of them were instances when the patient was clearly suffering a serious injury or illness.

"I guess I should follow her example..."

On top of being there on Dr. Cthulhy's behalf, Glenn also thought this was the logical course of action.

"Dr. Glenn, I've finished with the cleanup," Sapphee said, having been asked by Glenn to gather up the various documents. Despite his worrying, Glenn had also just finished gathering their things together to return to the clinic.

"Okay, thank you... I'd like to properly thank Miss Tisalia and say goodbye..."

However, the princess of the Scythia family had said she had some business to attend to and had entered the arena—and as expected, Glenn didn't have the courage to follow into the colossal structure after her.

The fighters that remained at the training grounds were sparse. Having gathered together for the examination, it seemed they now had their own matches to arrange and train for, and those who had finished the check-up left the training grounds.

"Well, if she's not here, then there's nothing you can do about it. We've finished all of our work, so you can just tell someone and be done with it." Sapphee's words were sharp. Glenn was certain that her previous quarreling with Tisalia, including the incident involving her marriage interviews, were still having a lingering effect on her mood.

However, Glenn agreed with what she said. All he needed to do was have someone pass on a message to Tisalia. He just needed to find someone who was close to her, like the two attendants she had at her side earlier, but—

"Excuse me."

Just as he thought this, they appeared to greet him.

"Doctor."

"Do you have a minute?"

It was the two centaurs, Kay and Lorna.

"Oh, yes. Thank you for your help today. We were able to finish the examinations smoothly because of your assistance."

"Thank you for your work, Doctor"

"Our mistress was also quite pleased. Gratitude."

They bowed their heads politely. As to be expected from the handmaidens of Tisalia Scythia, the lone heiress to a commercial empire, they seemed to have a certain dignity unlike that of an average attendant's.

Their evenly cut hair and chestnut coats looked very similar. Glenn couldn't figure out which one was Kay and which one was Lorna. They didn't seem to be sisters, but it felt like they were intentionally copying each other's aura.

Appropriate for the arena, they were both now dressed in light armor, but without a doubt a maid's apron outfit would suit the both of them just as well.

"So... Doctor."

"We don't mean to be rude, but we have something do discuss with you."

"Discuss...?" Glenn said.

Kay and Lorna nodded in agreement.

"What were the results of Mistress's exam?"

"Is she not suffering from some sort of illness?"

"Illness...?" he echoed.

In his diagnostic opinion, there had been nothing to suggest any illness in Tisalia's check-up. She didn't seem to be suffering from any injures, and there were no signs of dormant illness, either. Of course, Glenn was still inexperienced, so it wasn't entirely impossible that he might have overlooked something, but—

"Tisalia Scythia is in exceedingly good health." It was Sapphee who spoke. "There are no significant changes in her body weight, just as she said herself. I believe it is because she has a healthy lifestyle, habitually training her body and getting exercise. At the very least, looking at it from our position, there is nothing in the slightest that would suggest to us that she was ill."

"Oh..."

"I see..."

Kay and Lorna were visibly disappointed by Sapphee's words. Looking down, their gazes swayed back and forth, apprehensively.

What Sapphee had said was true—there were no findings to suggest that Tisalia was ill. However, Kay and Lorna's expressions were something that Glenn had witnessed many different times before. It was the uncertain, anxious look a patient or a patient's family gave when their loved one suffered from a grave illness.

"Is there perhaps something that you are worried about?" Glenn said to the two attendants, thinking that they would stay silent otherwise. "Please tell me anything. Even if she is in good health...if she or those close to her are worried that she might in fact be sick, then we can't say that she is truly healthy." He paused, then said, "Miss Kay, Miss Lorna, Miss Tisalia is an important person to both of you, correct?"

"Y-yes."

"Of course."

"In that case, please tell me everything. If, afterwards, I can once again assure you as a doctor that she isn't sick, then I'm sure that will give both of you peace of mind."

Kay and Lorna looked at each other.

At the same time, Glenn thought back to Tisalia, and the fact that her attendants loved her so much. He had only known her for less than a day, but he thought she truly was someone who stood a head above those around her—a real leader to others.

After both nodding their heads, Tisalia's two attendants began to talk.

"Now then, let us tell you..."

"Actually, the Mistress has—"

✕ ✕ ✕ ✕ ✕

The moon was visible.

The town of Lindworm was nestled at the foot of the Vivre Mountains, and from their heights flowed a constant cold wind, so that even if the day was warm, the temperature at night would drop surprisingly low. But despite the chilly evenings, the view of the moon among the steep peaks of the Vivre Mountains was famous. The beauty of the clear moonlight in the cold air made for one of the continent's most picturesque locations.

They say that nothing can compare to the yellow brilliance of the harvest moon in the town of the dragon. The mountains were always visible from Lindworm, and the sparkle of the moon was a sight that anyone in the town could enjoy.

"I see you're still awake," Sapphee said to Glenn as he stared out at the moon from the clinic.

"Sapphee... You can head off to bed. It's already pretty late, after all."

"That's what I should be telling you. I thought perhaps you might be here and decided to check... What are you doing? Staying up like this is bad for your health."

Sapphee and Glenn each had their own bedrooms adjoined to the clinic, but they were sparsely furnished, so the two of them rarely returned to their own quarters. Whether they still had work to finish or simply something on their minds, they would often stare out at the moon from the clinic's window.

It seemed that Sapphee had guessed what was on Glenn's mind. She could only do this, he supposed, because of their long friendship together.

Indeed—the two of them were childhood friends.

Before Saphentite and Glenn became pupils at the academy, they had already been acquainted with one another. In fact, when they were very young children, the two of them had lived under the same roof together.

Later, when they were reunited at the academy, Glenn remembered how shocked he was at how much Sapphee had changed. The sickly young girl he remembered had developed into an intelligent and talented woman.

"Even since this afternoon, it's been on my mind."

"Miss Tisalia, right?

"Yeah. Kay and Lorna really seemed to be worried. I've been wondering if there isn't something we could do."

"Something we can do?"

Our Mistress can't win a single match.

Hearing these words from Tisalia's two handmaidens naturally brought a complicated look to Glenn's face. After all, Tisalia hadn't shown a single crack in her unwavering confidence.

It was hard to believe that the woman he'd seen laughing with spirits higher than any of the other fighters could actually be in the midst of a slump. And yet, according to what Kay and Lorna told Glenn, for the past few months her win rate had been dropping noticeably.

Tisalia wasn't the kind of fighter to ever skip out on her daily training. And being born into a warrior family meant that her martial arts talents were obvious to anyone who saw her fight. To Kay and Lorna, it seemed that she had to be suffering from some kind of serious illness—why else would someone like her continue to lose over and over again?

"If you were to ask me," Sapphee said, "a drop in wins is something that could happen to anyone. No fighter is invincible. Being in a slump isn't all that rare, right? So long as it isn't being caused by some illness."

"If that's all there is to it, then it's fine," Glenn agreed.

If it was a normal slump, then it was nothing he needed to be concerned about. But if by chance he was overlooking some ailment of hers... That possibility was extremely frightening to him. If he overlooked some sort of illness dormant inside of her despite these signs presented to him—well, depending on the kind of disease, Tisalia's life could be in danger.

Protecting the lives of others was Glenn's duty as a doctor.

"But the possibility that that's not the case is what's scary," Glenn said as he looked up at the moon.

He expected Sapphee to call him a worrywart, but all she did was let out a sigh. She might have been fed up with him, he thought, and her exasperation was inevitable, but—

"Would you like to have a drink, Doctor?"

"Huh...? By drink, do you mean liquor?"

"Yes," Sapphee said. "If you don't have any preference, I'll prepare a medicinal drink from liqueur and herbs. It's weak, so it won't affect you tomorrow, and I think it'll help you clear your head."

Glenn wasn't very good with alcohol. However, he thought that it might be slightly more effective at clearing his mind than staring vacantly up at the moon. His decision made, Glenn asked Sapphee for a glass.

"In that case, please hold on just a moment," Sapphee said and left the room.

Glenn thought to himself as he waited. Relying on the moonlight, he strained his eyes as he looked at the documents in front of him. Paper was still a valuable commodity, but in the clinic it was a necessity. These were the medical files he had been given by Dr. Cthulhy. They contained all the findings from Tisalia's scheduled check-ups through the previous month.

In short, her condition was normal. No symptoms of any illness or other ailment had been found in Tisalia—and if that had been Cthulhy's diagnosis, then Glenn could scarcely think it was wrong. After all, it was congruous with his diagnosis as well. Tisalia was not sick.

In addition, there was no record of any serious prior illness or injury. Without any other special records in her file, it was safe to say that she was both healthy now and had been in the past.

But on the other hand...

Health was something that would be affected even by something seemingly trivial. The two who served Tisalia, Kay and Lorna, were certainly the ones who would know if she was in a slump. It was logical for Glenn to take them at their word.

Perhaps it's that there is a primary factor even a doctor might overlook, he pondered. *Maybe that's what's causing Tisalia to sink into poor health? Moreover, maybe the fact that nothing is written down in the documents simply means that her ailment originally wasn't worth writing down in the first place?*

"Something not recorded... Hm?"

"Here you go."

Glenn thought he'd glimpsed some sort of light—when he looked up, there was an outstretched hand holding a transparent red glass. It was a high-quality type of glass made in Lindworm. It was filled with ice and liquid.

"S-Sapphee...You used ice?! That's for treating patients' fevers!"

"I only used a little—it's fine. Besides, we can gather more from the Vivre Mountains."

"Well, yeah, sure! But that's a two-day round trip to the summit!"

In the clinic, the ice blocks they scraped from the mountain summits were kept in an ice room in the basement for safekeeping. Of course, they were lent ice from the ice vendor for their treatments, but it was to be used only when necessary, not for their everyday life, and certainly not for a drink.

"The herb liqueur and the chill of the ice will help you work out your thoughts. It's only a little, Dr. Glenn. Please don't be so strict about it."

"But..."

"Drink."

Smiling—or rather, looking sidelong at Glenn, Sapphee even managed to look slightly alluring. Although she seemed to be teasing him a little, the consideration she had for him was clear. He couldn't refuse her kindness, so he gulped down the drink.

A fresh, mint-like flavor sank down his throat. It barely tasted of alcohol, and the refreshing sweetness made Glenn feel like his brain had been revitalized with a dose of nutrients.

"It's good," he said. "Thanks."

"Did any good ideas come to mind?"

"I guess. Yeah. Tisalia probably isn't sick, but there still might be something wro—"

"*Ngh, gulp, glug*!" Glenn's thought was interrupted by the loud sound of chugging.

"Huh, wait a sec!" he cried, as Sapphee drank her own tall glass of alcohol. He hadn't noticed she even had one, as it was her tail holding the glass, rather than her hands. A loud gulping noise rose from her throat as she skillfully lifted the smooth glass.

"Hold on—what are you drinking? Jeez, it reeks of alcohol! This is Firedragon Whiskey. Why are you drinking something so strong?!"

"Kay and Lorna gave it to us. As a thank you for performing the check-up."

Glenn thought it was extremely intemperate to give alcohol to a doctor in thanks for a check-up. Perhaps it was some sort of centaur custom.

Lindworm's famed Firedragon Whiskey—a distilled liquor said to be strong enough to make one breathe fire. Drinking something like that was sure make one tipsy in an instant.

Sure enough, with just one gulp Sapphee's cheeks had turned red. Her smile began to change, growing soft, as if relaxing.

"Don't worry about me," she said. "Did you figure out the cause of Miss Tisalia's current condition?"

"I can't really say it's anything obvious. But Dr. Cthulhy didn't have anything written in any of her files. That's why I think it's not any kind of sickness."

"In that case—"

"But even if it isn't an illness," Glenn went one, "there comes a time for a doctor to act."

Tilting her head to the side, Sapphee didn't seem to understand his line of reasoning. Her snake tail set down the glass it was holding and started coiling itself around Glenn's arms. Sapphee was a woman who liked both drinking and making others drink, and this was always how she acted when she was inebriated. She quite literally wrapped others up in her drunkenness.

Coiling her serpentine lower-half around others was Sapphee's bad habit.

"There's a place I need to go tomorrow," Glenn said. "If possible, I'd like to go see Tisalia at the arena. Will you come with me, Saphentite?"

"Honestly," she said. "Bringing me along as you go off to see another woman? What are you thinking?"

"I'm pretty sure I'm the one who wants to ask that question, but..." He trailed off as Sapphee coiled herself further around him.

The end of her snake tail was loosely wrapped around his right arm. It wasn't enough to prevent him from drinking, but the feeling of her snake belly on his skin was pleasantly cool. Her tail continued to wrap around his neck. With gradually strengthening force, it began squeezing Glenn's torso gently.

Since it was normally coiled or folded up, the true length of Sapphee's body often went unnoticed—but in truth, it had a considerable amount of length to it. Coiling herself around a human's entire body was easy.

Using her alcohol-aided strength, she didn't hesitate to do things she wouldn't normally do.

"I refuse," she said. "After all, you'll just get recruited into a marriage interview again."

"Even still—" he protested.

"Maybe you've gotten a little full of yourself after that horsewoman princess made eyes at you? You're quite the unprincipled man, aren't you, Doctor? To make things worse, I was even warned by Cthutlhy that she wouldn't forgive me if I ever laid a hand on you!"

The grip of her coils rapidly grew more intense. The strength she used to squeeze Glenn's body grew stronger with her complaints. It was said that jealousy was characteristic of lamia, but Sapphee was being slightly more harsh than usual. Glenn was sure without a doubt that the strong, distilled liquor she had imbibed was at fault.

"I won't allow any more rivals!" she said.

"What are you talking about, Saphentite...?" Glenn retorted. "You know we're just going to treat her, right? It has nothing to do with any kind of marriage interviews."

"Hmph! I can't trust you!"

Glenn jolted as Sapphee tightened her grip, almost spilling the drink that she had gone to the trouble of fixing for him.

Even he understood that Saphee wrapping him up in her drunken stupor was her way of acting selfish and spoiled. No matter how long they had been together, secrets—or things unable to be said—built up to the breaking point. Even if their relationship was normally characterized by her lecturing Glenn, there were still things that she couldn't let off steam about.

Perhaps it was *because* of the nature of that relationship that she couldn't relax. Sapphee had it hard, too, after all. As an assistant, all of the miscellaneous matters around the clinic were left up to her. Glenn understood the burden that he was putting on her. And now, to find a solution to Tisalia's slump, he was trying to take on a job they hadn't actually needed to be involved with.

"Hey, Sapphee?"

"Yes, Doctor?"

However. Simply by changing the way he referred to her, Sapphee broke into an easy smile. Glenn wondered if calling her by her nickname had really made her that happy. He also wondered whether she was acting drunk just to get Glenn to call her by her nickname— or if it was all thanks to her drunkenness.

"I'd like help," he said. "Will you assist me tomorrow?"

"But of course. I would follow you anywhere." Her expression changed effortlessly, a reflection of her calculating personality. She released Glenn from her coils. Drinking like she just had wasn't very good for her health and Sapphee herself seemed to understand this. In truth, she hadn't had any alcohol at all recently, but had apparently wanted to cut loose today.

All in all, she was a charming assistant. That said, the clinic had grown with Cthulhy's support. If she had known her two students were whispering sweet nothings to one another in the clinic, she would have flown into a tempestuous rage. Thus, Glenn couldn't exactly say that having Sapphee coil around him was in any way desirable.

The clinic was, after all, a sacred place of medical care and treatment.

"Take it easy, okay...?" Glenn said, wondering if his words of warning had properly reached her.

At his frank advice, Sapphee gave a profound smile. Whatever she was thinking was inscrutable—even to someone who had been with her as long as he had.

Glenn wasn't sure how to respond to her expression, so instead, he finished off the rest of the liqueur in his glass. He felt like the herbal fragrance had cleared his head a little bit.

* * ✖ * *

Tisalia didn't win the next day, either.

The sole daughter of the famous Scythia centaur family bit her lip, but only because the training grounds were empty.

She was the princess of a proud clan. Even among the centaurs—who were generally considered to be a tribe of pure, equestrian warriors—the Scythias were particularly outstanding martial artists. They had once made a living charging through battlefield after battlefield as mercenaries, under no one's thumb, receiving enormous sums of money in exchange for their services. The war had shunted them across numerous lands, and—depending on the period in question—had pitted close relatives against each other.

Tisalia's grandfather and great-grandfather had both died on the battlefield. Even her grandmother was fierce, and—although she was a woman—had charged across the battlefield clad in armor and helm.

It went without saying that in the clan's long history, many of its members had died on the fields of battle. For the members of the Scythia clan, however, this was not a tragedy. Falling to the arrows, swords, and spears of the battlefield wasn't disgraceful. For the Scythia, battling with one's life on the line, having it come to an end in the midst of a fight, was in fact the ideal way to meet their end. Dying anywhere but the battlefield was a disgrace.

Thus, when the longstanding war between the humans and monsters came to an end ten years past, the Scythia had been forced to make a decision. How would live their lives now? When the war was over, what were those who lived on the battlefield going to do?

As the head of the clan, Tisalia's father had provided the answer to these difficult questions. He had decided that they would set up a business in the new, still underdeveloped city of Lindworm. Using their talent for transportation, they would circulate goods and services, and thus make their clan's name known.

As such a change meant throwing away their weapons, there was a large backlash among the clan members. When it was decided they would move to Lindworm, many members of the clan abandoned Tisalia's father.

Are you telling us to become mere cart-horses?

Where is your long-held pride as a warrior?

Such were just a few of the criticisms her father had faced.

But at the end of it all, her father succeeded. They carried people, pulling carts, and bearing packages on their backs. With their dependability and agility, Scythia Transportation gained the trust of Lindworm. It quickly became a large company without which the city couldn't survive. Having achieved such renown, no one who dared refer to the Scythia as mere carthorses.

Her father carved out a path for the clan to follow through the time of peace, and showed his brilliant leadership in doing so. Though they were no longer fighting a war, it wasn't a stretch to describe his accomplishments as the work of a military general in action.

"But..." Tisalia murmured, still chewing her lip in frustration. Her father was successful, which was utterly fine. Indeed, as the only daughter of the head of the clan, she would on day have to lead Scythia Transportation as his successor.

But if she did, what would the Scythia family, proud of their former military fame, do? Having found a way to thrive in the new era of peace, was it really okay for them to abandon their past so easily? Now that a fair wind blew, was their history and past honor no longer necessary?

Absolutely not. Tisalia wanted to cherish their former glory. The Scythias were a clan of martial prowess, and she wanted their name to ring out across all of Lindworm. Moreover, she wanted to expand her family's business and secure their everlasting prosperity.

Ensuring these things was her duty as the princess of the family. It was why she had become a fighter. Her parents were both busy running the business. Holding a spear in her hand was fitting for someone like her, who needed to acquire more experience and educational refinement.

As such, winning in the arena, rising to the top rank, being inducted into the hall of fame, and having her name eternally etched into the monuments of the arena—all of these things Tisalia Scythia was staunchly aiming for.

"I lost again today," she said and readied the replica spear she used in the arena.

Alone, she galloped around the training ground. A circular target. The concentrically drawn lines showed where she should aim. Sounding her hooves, she aimed at the target and thrust out her spear.

She couldn't win.

It was the same as yesterday, and the day before. Her match record seemed to be dropping by the day. She hadn't won a single match in quite a while. Even though her whole clan and all of her fans in the arena were cheering her on, this awful showing was all she could give them.

Even she had no idea what was wrong with her. One thing she *did* know was that no one wanted to see her looking depressed about her match records, like she was now. Chewing her lips in frustration and being on the verge of obvious tears was not a look that suited the princess of the Scythia clan.

A princess was someone noble and proud, someone who was burdened with the past and the future of their family. Princesses absolutely never cried, never backed down, and never gave in. That was how Tisalia wanted to be, which was why she was now brandishing her spear alone in the training ground. She didn't want anyone to see her tears. Given her usual boldness, she didn't want to show any weakness.

Such was the determination of Tisalia, both a princess and a fighter.

Tck.

The spear tore straight through the target with precision.

The wooden target snapped neatly in two and crumpled to the ground.

But—it was wrong. Something was off. She couldn't express what it was, but something had been off the instant she brandished her spear. The moment she put her strength into it and reached out her four legs and aimed with her sharpened weapon, a sense of discomfort rose in her body, only to leave just when she seemed close to grasping what it was.

That was how she would lose again. A warrior of Tisalia's caliber could predict how the match would play out before it even started. In her current condition, she knew it wouldn't make a difference—not even if she were flawless.

"Why..."

The hand that held her spear trembled.

Kay, Lorna, her parents, and the hard workers of Scythia Transportation all had confidence. She couldn't let herself get stuck here—not if she wanted to properly pay them back and show that the military might of the Scythia clan was still hale, or make their name resound across the continent. And yet...

"I have to train harder. Much, much harder."

The target was back in position. Tisalia's greatest weapon was a spear thrust delivered at top speed. She repeated the exercise over and over again, carefully examining where she was falling short.

Determined, her hooves resounded as she drove them harder against the training ground.

"Hm?" Someone was standing nearby—she could see their shadow.

Strange, Tisalia thought.

There shouldn't have been anyone at the training ground, not at the moment. Tisalia had chosen this time to come and train hard in secret. Why then was there someone standing there, as though they had been waiting for her? Who was it?

"...Dr. Glenn?"

It was the young doctor that had been in charge of Tisalia's check-up the day before.

There, with a gentle smile upon his face, stood Glenn Litbeit.

✕ ✕ ✕ ✕ ✕

Glenn felt guilty for interfering with Tisalia's secret, special training.

Tisalia stared at the two attendants next to him with a look of surprise. "Kay! Lorna! How dare you!"

"Our apologies—"

"—Mistress."

The two attendants meekly bowed their heads to Tisalia. She had been keeping her training a secret, but naturally her two attending handmaidens were fully aware of the situation. They couldn't interfere at all with her private efforts, and had been silent about it until they had informed Glenn.

"Please don't scold them," he said.

"...Dr. Glenn."

Kay and Lorna had accommodated Glenn's unexpected request to see Tisalia. Naturally, the two understood Tisalia's feelings about her training and her losses. However, they must have felt that Glenn's treatment was more important, as neither of them had shown any hesitation in leading him back to the training grounds.

"Well, now... I suppose I've been found out, haven't I?"

"We are your attendants."

"We are aware of how you feel, Mistress."

"I am truly blessed to have such excellent attendants... Now then Doctor, what is your business here today? Did something come up in your examination yesterday?"

There wasn't any sense of despair in Tisalia's eyes, but Glenn quickly recognized that she was forcing herself to look this way. Concealing her emotions, she only showed others what she wanted them to see. Tisalia was haughty and overbearing, yes, but she was also someone who could control herself.

"No, you're healthy. Thanks, I'm sure, to your normal, everyday lifestyle."

"Well, then."

He went on. "But the reason you aren't winning your matches is clear. I've come today to inform you of that reason, and if necessary deal with the problem."

"You told him everything, didn't you? Kay? Lorna?" Tisalia said and sighed. The two attendants apologized in unison, though it didn't seem that she was looking to press the issue any further.

"Now then, Doctor," she said. "What is the cause of my slump?"

"Right. The cause is your hooves."

"H-hooves...?"

Glenn picked a sword, which had be resting at his feet. It was no normal sword, however, but a colossal, boorish blade—not at all becoming of a gentleman like Glenn. Its tip was bent at a sharp angle, making it appear more like a sickle than a sword, though it was much too exaggerated to be useful for farming.

"Ah!" Tisalia exclaimed. At the sight of the brusque blade, even she couldn't help flinching—but that wasn't all. There was another reason behind Tisalia's faltering.

"As you know, a centaur's lower body is quite equine in nature," Glenn said. "As a species, centaurs themselves have no ties to horses, but it is thought that in order for them to rush over open plains in a fashion similar to horses, they have evolved into a similar form. All of this was taught to me by my teacher."

"A-and what is that supposed to mean?" Tisalia said.

"It's simple. Horses have hooves which—much like human nails— grow. For those living on plains and grasslands, the part of the hoof that grows get worn down naturally. But living in the city, where running freely is not usually an option, can cause their hooves to grow too long. On the other hand, race horses sometimes wear down too *much* of their hooves."

Glenn continued his detailed explanation, but to be quite honest, his information should have been obvious to a centaur. It should have been apparent that growing out and cutting down one's hooves would have an effect on one's movement.

Glenn took a quick glimpse at Tisalia's hooves. They had clearly grown too long. There was too much extra at the tip of her hoof. Her city life, despite her time as a warrior in the arena, did not provide her with the proper amount of exercise. Walking on the clear and level city streets just wasn't enough to keep her hooves naturally honed to a healthy length.

"Shoeing prevents this from happening," Glenn said and took out a horse shoe. The basic idea was that the shoe was made to match the shape of the hoof, to which it was was affixed with nails. This protected the hoof, and maintained a steady gait in the horse. In short, it was an essential tool for domestic horses.

Of course, it was a necessary tool for not only centaurs but for any hoofed monster. In the worst case scenario, the lack of horseshoes could even make going about ones daily life a chore. Living her life in the city without horseshoes must have been a great hardship for her up until now.

"Miss Tisalia, you are in good health," Glenn said. "There are no major injuries or illness in your past, and there isn't a single record of any treatment within your documents."

"Right? That's exactly right! I've always paid close attention to my health!"

"There isn't any account of being shoed, either," he added.

"Tch..." She averted her eyes.

She hadn't been sick, so there hadn't any mention in her history about not being shoed. A typical centaur had their horseshoes attached by someone familiar with the shoeing process. Glenn wondered why he hadn't noticed the absence of the record.

If he had compared her files with those of another centaur, he surely would have noticed. For instance, both Kay and Lorna had been fitted with horseshoes. However, because Glenn had been preoccupied with Tisalia's condition and had only looked at her documents, noticing that she had no records relating to horseshoeing had been difficult.

Glenn readied the sword.

"Now then Miss Tisalia," he said, "let me put your horseshoes on. With just this small change, your movements during your matches should become noticeably better."

"N-no, that's quite all right," Tisalia said. "There's no need."

It was exactly the answer he had expected, which proved Glenn's suspicions right.

"I'm—I am the princess of the Scythia clan. My body is precious, bestowed upon me by my ancestors. Even if it's only the tips of my hooves, needlessly damaging them is out of the question!"

"I'm sorry, Miss Tisalia."

Seeing Tisalia's pale expression, Glenn could only apologize. Without her knowledge, Kay and Lorna appeared on either side of her and restrained both of her arms. It seemed Tisalia hadn't noticed their approach until they were already upon her. The two attendants were seasoned fighters themselves, after all.

"Y-you two..." Tisalia said.

"We have already spoken to the two of them about the shoeing today, and received the appropriate payment for our services," Glenn said. "Miss Kay and Miss Lorna asked us to do this by any means necessary."

Glenn had asked the two attendants whether her slump could have been because of her lack of horseshoes, and they affirmed his theory. They asked Glenn to shoe her—to fit horseshoes on her hooves—if he could.

He had received their payment for the service and the necessary craftsmen were already ready and waiting behind him. There also, holding a colossal pair of tongs, was Sapphee. Next to her with various instruments at the ready were the craftsmen of Kuklo Workshop, a large establishment that was one of the prides of Lindworm. At first glance, they seemed to be nothing more than a stout group of one-eyed men—cyclopses—but in contrast to their appearance, they were excellent artisans, very skilled at delicate work.

Glenn had gotten the one-eyed craftsmen of Kuklo Workshop to agree in advance, arranging everything so that they could forcibly put the horseshoes on Tisalia after catching her during training.

"Now then, Miss Tisalia, let us get started," Glenn said.

"*E-eeeep...*" the princess cried. Her eyes were already tearing up. It was plain to see that she hated being shoed.

Glenn knew very well the type of people who made this face. As a doctor, it was something he was familiar with. In other words, her expression was just like that of a child, trembling in fear at the sight of the tools needed to treat a cavity.

Now that he thought about it, the tools he had gathered before *were* a bit frightening. They included a giant blade resembling a scythe, a pair of metal tongs, nails, and an iron hammer to nail them in. There were also a number of large iron tools, all crude and frightening looking—enough that it wouldn't have been strange to mistake them as tools for torture.

"I-I can't stand pain! It's scary!" Tisalia said.

"Mistress!"

"Don't say such childish things!"

Shouting and struggling with tears in her eyes, Tisalia had already succumbed to her fear and lost her pride as a princess. She tried to slip out of Kay and Lorna's grip. Her extreme, primal fear had been the reason for her avoidance of the process, as well as the reason she didn't wear any in the first place.

Holding the long sword, Glenn approached Tisalia, emphatically childish in her hatred for the process.

"Don't worry," he assured her. "It will be over quickly. If you don't move, it won't hurt at all."

"N... nooooooo!"

The wails of the proud warrior princess echoed across the open training ground.

× × ✖ × ×

Tisalia was terrified of pain—but in truth, the work of an experienced farrier meant that the patient felt almost no pain at all. There were a number of monster species that used horseshoes, and even Glenn was generally well versed in the required technique. Indeed, it was a skill that one learned early on when treating monsters.

Even with that being the case, it appeared that the reason Tisalia remained teary-eyed was because she had a good understanding of exactly what getting shoed meant.

"This is such an inappropriate showing... How insolent to come between a woman's legs!" she said. "I'm no longer fit to be a bride! Mother...Father...please forgive me for being unable to give you an heir!"

"You can still be a bride," Glenn said. "This is just medical treatment, after all."

First, he slipped between Tisalia's legs. Whether she was a centaur or not, there wasn't any woman that would feel good having a man slip in between her legs in such a manner. Tisalia covered her face as he began.

First, he bent her front left leg. Upon checking the end of her hoof, Glenn found he was right—it had grown long. First, he needed to cut it down to a normal length, and for that purpose he took the scythe-looking blade—known as a sickle hoof knife—and adjusted the shape of the hoof.

When the blade hit the tip of her hoof, Tisalia shivered in surprise.

"*Nh*...Ah, um, Doctor...That's a sensitive area, so be gentle. Gentle, okay?"

"Don't worry, I'm used to doing this."

"*Hnh*..."

The feeling was much like cutting one's nails.

There wasn't any pain from trimming the ends of the hoof, though deeper inside there was a concentration of nerves. Shaving the hoof too much could hurt the nerves and cause intense pain.

"*Anh*...Ooh! I-I can't bear it!"

"D-does it hurt?!" Glenn asked.

"I-it just tickles. Hurry, get it over with quick!"

Tisalia looked toward him with teary eyes. He wasn't sure if her red cheeks were because she was embarrassed, or of some other reason. Indeed, her reactions started to make Glenn embarrassed as well. He had to remind himself that this was just medical treatment—nothing more than treatment.

Typically, after shaving a hoof down, he adjusted it more minutely. He used not just the hoof-knife but a file as well to neatly adjust the hoof's tip and also removed anything that had wedged itself in the gap in her hoof.

"*Eek!*"

Tisalia shuddered again. Both Glenn's work and the work the cyclops were doing beside him must have come into her view. The one-eyed men were in the middle of making her horseshoes. The process was quite straightforward: first, the curved iron horseshoes were placed into a special furnace and heated up. Then, when that was finished, the shoes were placed on trimmed down hooves and the final minor adjustments were made.

The ends of hooves were like a fingernail. Trimming them with a blade and putting a hot horseshoe on them caused the centaur no injury. Even so, few people would have been able to passively watch a burning hot iron approach their body.

"It's not going to be hot, right?!" Tisalia asked. "It's okay, right?!"

"Mistress!"

"Please stay still!"

Tisalia surely must have known that it would be hot, and could not settle her fear. She looked on at the hot iron, face twitching.

Glenn had a good working relationship with the cyclopses of Kuklo Workshop. Whether it was needles, forceps, or scalpels needed for surgery—or things like stethoscopes that required a difficult manufacturing process, the one-eyed artisans of Kuklo Workshop had the ability to arrange anything for him.

For them, horseshoe adjustment was a simple, straight-ahead job.

They pressed the horseshoe against the hoof several times, each time making precise adjustments to the horseshoe's shape. Once the horseshoe adjustment was finished, at long last it was time for them to fix the shoes to her legs.

"*H-hmph*, g-give me everything you got! A princess of the Scythia clan has nothing to fear!" Tisalia was gradually beginning to grow desperate.

"Okay. Well, then."

"*Eek!*"

Appearing to have mustered all the bravado she could manage, Tisalia's face again twitched in fright.

Glenn took out the nails and the hammer used to drive them into her hooves. The horseshoes were fitted with six nails. Had an unskilled farrier been at work, there would have been a risk of damaging the nerves and causing injury, but Glenn was past the point in his career where he made those kinds of blunders.

"I-I hate this! I can't take it anymore!" Tisalia cried out.

"Mistress!"

"That's completely different from what you just said!"

But it seemed she had reached the limits of her tolerance.

Tisalia began to struggle violently and shamelessly. At her feet, Glenn's head twitched and jerked at the stomping of her hooves.

With her struggling, it was impossible for the shoeing to continue.

Indeed, as an arena fighter Tisalia had doubtless squared off against a multitude of opponents. Although they used wooden weapons, they fought each other as seriously as if they were on the battlefield, and with that came a certain degree of risk. Glenn wondered at the tolerance of someone who was fine in an arena match but couldn't handle horseshoeing.

"Miss Tisalia, it will be okay!" he said. "It doesn't hurt!"

"Still! You intend to assault me, do you not?! Nails—how barbaric!"

"They're needed to affix the horseshoes!" he protested.

"Completely uncivilized! You're going to do something like that, to me?! Someone! Anyone!"

"*Hnk!*" said one of her attendants.

"Mistress...! Please...don't struggle!" the other cried.

Her struggling was so fierce it looked as though she was going to break free of Kay and Lorna.

There was nothing dangerous about the shoeing process itself. However, if the tools and hot iron weren't handled properly, they were quite capable of causing injury. It was possible that Tisalia's struggles could possible cause her injury.

Glenn wondered what he could do about the situation and knew there was really nothing left to do but physically restrain her with rope. Just as he came to this conclusion, something whip-like streaked past and twirled itself around Tisalia.

"*Hnh?! Augh! Ungh?!*"

"You've gotten quite noisy, Miss Tisalia."

It was Sapphee.

Despite the centaur's large frame, Sapphee's long tail coiled

around her and restrained her with remarkable ease, in the same way she had carefully constricted Glenn's body the night before.

Large snakes hide in dense forests and sometimes even swallowed horses whole, Glenn thought. It was the sight of Sapphee's white snake tail coiling across Tisalia's black hide that caused the association to spring into Glenn's mind. Restraining patients was an important part of the treatment process—although Glenn had a hard time figuring out why Sapphee had shoved the end of her tail into Tisalia's mouth.

"*Guhg! Hngugh!*"

"It seems somewhat likely that my tail will be chewed off," Sapphee said. "Please work quickly, Dr. Glenn."

"*Ungh! Gugmufngh!*"

Tisalia seemed to be saying something, but Glenn couldn't understand what. Beyond that, the awkwardly movement of her mouth drenched Sapphee's tail in saliva and even dripped down onto the centaur's large chest.

If Glenn was being honest, the scene in front of him reminded him of something else entirely—something completely unrelated to any sort of medical treatment.

Tisalia continued to shake her neck in defiance as saliva dribbled down from her mouth. "*Mhugnh! Fnugh!*"

Thinking that someone might get the wrong idea if they happened to see them, Glenn quickly set about his work.

With the six spots on her hoof fixed with nails, Glenn's work on the first hoof was completed. So, too, then was the shoeing process for that hoof—protecting the natural growth with a hoof of iron. It was a process little different than the shoeing of a horse, as a centaur's legs were quite equine in nature. While it was dangerous work, a farrier well-versed in the process could complete the process without causing any pain to the patient. This was all the more true for a doctor of Glenn's expertise.

"*Haa... Haa... H-ha...*"

Tisalia caught her breath now that it was all over. It seemed having the end of Sapphee's tail in her mouth had been considerably hard on her. Her face was still red.

Never one to go easy on someone, Sapphee feigned ignorance at Tisalia's suffering.

"*Haa, haa...* N-now, i-is it over?" Tisalia gasped.

"No, the right leg is next."

"I...can't do it...anymore... I don't have...the power to stand."

"Please put up with it just a little while longer. It'll all be over soon."

Tisalia had lost her energy to keep struggling, so Glenn comforted her and continued on with his work.

✖ ✖ ✖ ✖ ✖

A few days passed.

Glenn and Sapphee once again were paying a visit to the arena. However, this time it wasn't for a medical check-up. As a thank-you for the treatment they had given her, Tisalia had personally prepared tickets for them to watch a match in the arena. Their seats were first-class, with the best view of the action.

Glenn wondered exactly how much it would have cost had he purchased these tickets himself. The fact Tisalia had gotten them these priority seats made it clear how much gratitude she felt towards Glenn.

The match was just about to start. The princess was in the middle of the arena, quietly looking down. She seemed to be in the middle of focusing her mind on the match ahead.

"You worked quite hard, Dr. Glenn," Sapphee said.

"Oh, yeah... That's right, it was quite tiring."

Getting horseshoes onto Tisalia as she struggled hadn't been a normal, straightforward job. It would have been nigh impossible for Glenn to try and shoe Tisalia on his own. Kay, Lorna, Sapphee, and the craftsmen of Kuklo Workshop—it had only been possible thanks to the support they had all given him.

"But that octo-woman... I mean Dr. Cthulhy seems to be growing senile. If she knew Miss Tisalia wasn't wearing horseshoes, it would have been much easier for her to have put them on herself. With those eight legs of hers, I'm sure she would've been able to keep Tisalia's struggling in check."

"I imagine Dr. Cthulhy thought that it wasn't a good idea to interfere too much," Glenn said.

"...What does that mean?" Sapphee said.

Essentially, Glenn thought that his teacher was rather hands-off. It didn't seem likely that Cthulhy had missed the cause of Tisalia's slump during her regular medical check-ups. This meant that, ultimately, Cthulhy had decided that until she was told to do so by the patient or her family, treatment wasn't necessary. That was how such things played out. The patient had been against it, so Cthulhy hadn't shoed her.

Still, for Glenn, it would have been easier for him to take over if she had at least written that information down in Tisalia's file. Either way, it wasn't good for doctors to meddle and interfere in everything.

Considering his teacher's personality, this seemed likely to be her reasoning. To her, there was no need to treat a patient who didn't want to be treated themselves, and Glenn felt there was probably some truth to that.

In the match area, Tisalia confronted her opponent. She wasn't in the light dress she wore at the training ground. Instead, she had donned a helmet and more armor around her chest. This was Tisalia's armor, what her natural form looked like. Glenn couldn't see her face, but he felt her dignified air reaching up to his seat through her helmet.

He continued speaking. "After all, if a fighter gets sick or injured, then they can't appear in any matches—right? That obviously wouldn't be good for them, so I think Dr. Cthulhy only gave them the very minimum advice necessary."

"Yes, but this situation is different. Miss Tisalia was actually troubled by her losing streak... And there's the risk that not putting horseshoes on her could have lead to an even bigger injury down the line."

The match had started. Tisalia's opponent was a lizardman—a type of monster that, as the name implied, looked like a cross between a lizard and a man. His movements were swift and nimble. However, free to use her lower equine body, Tisalia beat her hooves across the ground, causing a crisp, clear, musical tone to rise as she charged.

Hearing that sound, Glenn knew that the horseshoes he had put on Tisalia had truly come to fit her well.

"That's true, we certainly don't want any more injuries," Glenn agreed.

"In that case..."

"It'd be fine if we became the nagging type of doctor, right?" he said. "We don't have to imitate everything Dr. Cthulhy does... We can do things our own way." Yes, their own way—in the same fashion that they had handled Tisalia's treatment.

While Tisalia's own wishes were important, they also had to properly account for the feelings of Kay and Lorna, who were worried about her. It was probably necessary for Glenn and Sapphee to be discerning like Cthulhy was, but even so, he believed he could attain a better balance by being more hands-on.

The crowd roared. Charging with a flash of her spear, Tisalia dealt a sharp blow to the lizardman. Her opponent fell to his knees. He tried to prop himself up with his fake sword, but the blow—which had caught the center of his body—was serious, and he seemed unable to quickly return to his feet.

The match was settled. There was no trace of the princess horsewoman worrying about poor performance. Standing there was a warrior of the Scythia clan, eminent in both name and deed.

Even Glenn's cold assistant Sapphee was smiling as she looked at Tisalia and said, ""It seems she's already back to form."

Glenn was sure that, in her own way, Sapphee had been worried about Tisalia. There was no doubt that they did not get along well with one another, but despite that, Glenn understood Sapphee's form of kindness—a kindness that he thought made her suited to being a doctor.

With her match over, Tisalia took off her helmet. Wiping the sweat from her brow, she locked eyes with Glenn. He and Sapphee were in the highest seats in the arena. Being able to clearly see the action below meant the fighters could see them clearly, as well. Meeting Glenn's gaze, Tisalia waved her hand at him, a big smile splayed across her face.

Her face was slightly red, perhaps from the elation of winning her match. She had such an appealing charm, holding her helmet under her arm and skipping up and down the arena as she was, that Glenn could see why she had so many fans among the crowd.

He gave a slight wave back to her.

"Doctor," she said.

Raising both her hands, Tisalia didn't stop endearing herself to the crowd. Even while twitching the ears on the top of her head, she was expressing herself with her entire body.

A snake's tail wound its way around Glenn's hand and waved back at the elated Tisalia. The coiling snake scales were pleasantly cool to the touch.

"Surely, you don't have any actual plans to hold a marriage interview with Miss Tisalia, right?" Sapphee asked.

"I don't, don't worry..." Glenn said.

"I wonder..."

Looking at Sapphee's red eyes, it was she clear that she was pouting. Glenn knew that things were going to be rough until they returned to the clinic, and that Sapphee's bad mood could certainly do with being improved.

Tisalia was still waving her hand. Her face was the smiling, grateful one of a centaur who had finally been able to regain her honor. However, because Glenn obviously didn't know just how Tisalia had felt before, he didn't quite understand why she seemed to be thanking him *so much*.

Her freshly shoed hooves sounded on the dry earth each time she jumped up, and loudly echoed through the arena.

CASE 01 : THE CENTAUR OF THE ARENA

A horseshoe was said to be a sign of good luck.

Triumphing over her dislike of horseshoes, Tisalia Scythia could now boldly face any type of arena match or hardship and step firmly down the path of prosperity—though that was all still a long way off for her, of course.

MONSTER GIRL DOCTOR

CASE 02:
The Mermaid from
the Waterways

Saphentite Neikes was an albino lamia and there were many things that albinos had to be careful about in their daily life.

For example, because direct sunlight made them ill and damaged their eyes, they had to avoid the sun as much as possible. Sapphee protected herself by applying sunscreen regularly without fail and by wearing elastic underclothes that protected her skin from the sun. When it came time for her to go outside, she always took out the veil she stored in her nurse's hat and used it to protect her face and eyes. In these ways, Sapphee never failed to deal with the effects of her albinism.

"What did albino lamias do about it long ago?" Glenn asked Sapphee one day. "After all, lamias give birth to albinos quite often, don't they?"

A single gondola, steered by a human gondolier, continued down a canal in Lindworm. Riding in it were Sapphee and Glenn. Sapphee had covered her head with the veil she used for going outside. The specially sewn black veil protected her face from the sun even in the shelter-less canal.

"Yes, they do," Sapphee said. "I've heard that albino-born lamias often avoided the sun altogether and were active at night instead."

"You...can't exactly do that, though."

"That's right. But you're always looking out for me, so it's not a problem," Sapphee said with a smile. Her weak constitution was a thing of the past. Now she passed her days in good health as a pharmacist at the Litbeit Clinic.

Her good health, however, was because of the medicine she had. The sunscreen ointment was particularly valuable. It was made using wax and a variety of different herbs, in addition to purified water. Apart from the other ingredients, the purified water was one of the things Glenn couldn't get ahold of himself. In Lindworm, getting it required a trip to the Merrow Waterways in the northwest district of the city.

"We wouldn't be able to run our clinic if it wasn't for the purified water the mermaids here prepare for us," Sapphee said. "We need to make sure to show our gratitude."

"You're right... Coming out to the Waterways is the only way we can get it," Glenn said with a sigh.

The Litbeit clinic handled a number of different medicines besides Sapphee's sunscreen ointment. Though she was mainly in charge of creating the medicine, they both worked to procure the necessary ingredients. That day, they were out on one of their shopping days for the clinic and had come to the Merrow Waterways to buy various valuable goods that could only be obtained there.

The gondola rocked back and forth as it continued on under the guidance of the gondolier's oar, situated in the back of the boat. While the gondolas were well-equipped, without the skilled technique of the gondolier, Glenn and Sapphee would have quickly crashed the boat into the sides of the narrow canals. Glenn had come here many times, but he always found himself admiring the exquisite skill of the gondolier's rowing.

"I wonder..." Sapphee mused. "When was the last time I was able to have a day out like this with you, Doctor? I'm glad we've been given this opportunity."

"We *have* been pretty busy as of late, haven't we...?"

Even if he was only a general medicine doctor, there were still only a limited number of doctors in the city who could treat monsters. As one of those few doctors, Glenn could have easily argued that closing the clinic and spending the day shopping was a rather extravagant use of their time. True, they were out and about for business, yet despite that, there was still a part of Glenn that couldn't settle down as long as he was outside the clinic.

The Waterways were one of Lindworm's tourist attractions, thanks to its singular scenery and townscape. In addition to necessities like purified water, there were a number of souvenirs and gifts sold there as well, and a large number of tourists from around the continent flocked there in order to procure these items. Merrow glass, in particular, was sold at a high price due to its transparency and unique shades of color.

Coming to such a place meant that their shopping trip also served as a day of relaxation for both of them. To Glenn, however, it seemed that Sapphee's jovial attitude wasn't only because it was a rare treat—as her albino constitution made trips like these few and far between—or that she was simply happy to be outside.

The canal became even narrower, and the water grew more transparent. The Merrow Waterways had been completed under the direction of the representative of the Lindworm City Council—the "Draconess," Skadi Dragenfelt—along with the aid of a large amount of tax revenue.

Upon coming to a canal that looked just barely big enough to fit a single gondola through, the gondolier gently brought the boat to a stop. Without tying it to the side of the Waterway, he hopped out onto the bank of the channel. A gondola without a gondolier!

He removed his hat and politely bowed his head to Glenn. "There will be another gondolier to replace me from here on out, Doctor."

"Okay, thank you for your hard work."

"Please enjoy all the Merrow Waterways has to offer," the human gondolier said in response, bowing one more time. For the remainder of the trip, a human's oar wouldn't be enough. To continue down the narrow channels, a different kind of assistance was necessary.

The gondolier-less gondola once again began to move steadily forward, moving along with neither oar nor gondolier. Sapphee gazed indifferently out at the scenery of the canal as the gondola moved quickly ahead. Oar-controlled rowing simply couldn't manage these types of speeds.

Glenn understood what was going on. Under the bows of the gondolas used to advance through the Merrow Waterways, below even the figurehead decorating the front of the boat, was a long, underwater handle that extended out in front of the boat. The new gondolier that had taken the place of the former held onto that handle and pulled it along as if the gondola were a rickshaw.

If one peered into the clear water of the channel, a number of different things could be seen below the surface. There were mermaids, selkies, scyllas and the like—monsters who had bodies suited for life underwater—all swimming through the vast underwater district that sprawled below.

The bustle of the many-layered cityscape didn't reach Glenn's ears through the thick wall of water separating them, but the lightly swimming figures made Glenn feel how truly lively the Waterways were.

The gondola slowed down slightly and a face popped from the water with a big splash.

It was the gondolier that had come in as a replacement. Naturally, his ability to stay underwater for long periods of time meant there was no way he could be human.

"Welcome to Merrow Waterways!" the new gondolier greeted them cheerfully. He was a young male whose lower body was that of a fish—in other words, he was a merman.

The gondolier pointed out an arched sign underneath the water. Written there in monster script were words welcoming visitors. On the surface of the water, both beyond and before the submerged arch, were humans riding in gondolas, many of them pulled by merfolk.

From here on out they would be entering the true Merrow Waterways—or at least, skimming its surface. For built beneath the water was a city district where aquatic monsters made their home.

× × × × ×

Every year, a large amount of snow fell on the peaks of the Vivre Mountains.

The thickly-piled snow on the steep mountains melted with the coming of spring and formed the Great Vivre River that stretched all the way out to the ocean. The river that flowed through Lindworm was thought to be some of the most limpid on the continent and had become the recreational waters of choice for many aquatic monsters.

Pulling the great river into Lindworm had been one of the undertakings of Skadi Dragenfelt—the woman of influence in charge of building up the independent town of Lindworm, where monsters and humans lived together.

Rebuilding an old unused slum, all of the buildings had been waterproofed. After this followed a civil engineering project on a grand scale, which had diverted the river's flow into part of the slum. The whole northwest district of the city had been submerged in water—thus was the underwater city completed.

It had been an extremely large-scale construction project that used up most of Lindworm's budget. However, it had a worthwhile effect. The underwater district filtered the water that drained into the city, turning Lindworm into a cutting-edge metropolis, complete with equipment for sanitation and sewage. With the crystal clear river already flowing into the city, the drainage was arranged to pass through a completely separate route from the town's inhabited areas, and was dumped outside of the city.

Thus, for the underwater denizens, the Merrow Waterways became an extremely livable district, said to be the best of the best.

"And all because a place for aquatic monsters was needed," Glenn said and couldn't help but give a dry laugh.

A pure and clean flowing water supply, and the latest in sanitation facilities... In order to make those two currents of water a reality, precisely controlling the flow of the Vivre Canal had been necessary. Ultimately, just as Glenn had mused, the complex construction of the canals was all because importance had been placed on making the city livable for aquatic monsters.

Nevertheless, while the environment was optimum for those who lived underwater, it was less so for humans and other monsters that couldn't dive deep into the water. Such beings found it difficult to pass through by boat, as the project had changed the area into a floating labyrinth.

It was because of all this that Sapphee and Glenn had had to change gondoliers in the middle of their journey. Unless one was a denizen of the underwater town, navigating the bizarre and complex waterways was impossible. Steering a gondola with an oar in the narrow canals would have meant immediately bumping into the many other gondolas nearby.

Of course, there were also bigger canals where many smaller boats sailed back and forth, but to get to these area, one had to first go through the small canals—many of which were one-way or off-limits to boat traffic. It was next to impossible for a tourist to reach their destination without a guide. For these reasons, mermen and mermaids acted as gondoliers, joining with the boat as one and pulling it along.

Glenn and Sapphee's gondola left the narrow canals, joining up with one of the major waterways. There, a number of small ships were lined up on either side of the canal. The number of gondolas sailing back and forth far surpassed the area slim channels they had been in but a moment before.

"Oh my!" Sapphee exclaimed. "Dr. Glenn, look there, look at all the Merrow glass! Should we buy some cups for when we make drinks?"

"Come on, Sapphee. Don't forget why we're here."

"Whaaat? But..."

Glenn couldn't hold back a smile. Today, they were only out to buy goods they needed for the clinic. Even so, Sapphee eye's sparkled at all the merchandise on display in the boats.

All of the small craft were street stalls. Using the top of the boat like a display counter, the mermen and mermaid shopkeepers flattered and entertained customers with bright smiles. The merfolk, just as their names indicated, were all monsters with a fish-like lower body. That said, their appearances were quite diverse, as scale pattern, coloration, and fin shape varied greatly from individual to individual. Many of them were quite beautiful, with their multicolored fins and scales.

All in all, the line of merfolk along the Merrow Waterways was dazzlingly gorgeous.

The stall keepers were ingeniously negotiating and enticing the tourists riding along in their gondolas. Being tourists themselves, Glenn and Sapphee were captivated by the sparkling Merrow glass goods. If the stall keepers could get them to start talking about souvenirs, then they would no doubt win them over.

A canal filled with small gondolas darting back and forth, pulled by aquatic monsters; proud stall keepers displaying their souvenirs and gifts; tourists excitedly gazing at their wares—all this constituted the everyday scenery of the Merrow Waterways. It was one of Lindworm's most famous spots to visit, a place where water-bound monsters, land-bound monsters, and people were all woven together.

"Oh my, that perfume bottle over there..." Sapphee said. Her wavering gaze had been drawn in by the canal stalls.

Their gondolier surfaced and looked back at her and Glenn. "Would you like stop over there, Doctor?" he asked, wanting to be sure he didn't let her comment go unnoticed. After all, the gondoliers were also residents of the Merrow Waterways, and were most likely longtime acquaintances with the stall keepers. If a gondolier led their passengers toward a familiar stall, they might thus receive a copper coin from the stall keeper. These types of arrangements were a well-known part of doing business in tourist destinations, and were not at all a rare occurrence.

However—

"Sapphee," Glenn spoke up. "The shopping for the clinic comes first. To Seventh Canal, please."

"Whaaaaat?"

Ignoring her cry of dismay, Glenn gave directions to the gondolier. The suntanned merman accepted Glenn's directions with a cheerful smile.

Unlike the gondolier, Sapphee seemed to be much more displeased about the loss of the sale. She didn't say a word and instead looked back behind the boat, sulking. Not only that, but her long tail trailed behind the boat, as if reluctant to part from the perfume bottle. Glenn thought that if he had left her to her own devices, she would have wrapped herself around the stall's gondola and not let go.

The glassware began with tableware and drinking glasses, as well as a variety of large and small bottles for a variety of different uses. They also sold animal-shaped glass figurines in quite a diverse selection. The multicolored sparkle of the glass really did give one the feeling that they were souvenirs aimed at women.

Although Glenn had told Sapphee they were just visiting for for work, that wasn't actually true. Glenn himself thought their trip would also serve as some relaxation time for the both of them.

"We'll stop by on the way back, Sapphee. Okay?"

"...That's a promise, Doctor," Sapphee said with a pout.

Glenn could only give a wry grin in response, knowing that her expression was exactly why he couldn't refuse her pestering about the perfume bottle.

× × ✖ × ×

At Seventh Canal was a stall Glenn was very familiar with. It was a shop in an area that could be referred to as a back alley, run by a female selkie.

Selkies were a type of monster that wore seal skin on their head and looked exactly like a seal itself. The owner of the stall was no exception; she wore the skin of a seal on her head. As such, Glenn had never seen her natural face. Nevertheless, selkies were a beautiful and good-looking species, and as such the stall keeper's gorgeous looks were without question.

She never said much when Glenn came to purchase purified water from her.

Such water wasn't necessary unless one was a doctor like Glenn. If he hadn't needed the purified water for surgery and making medicines, he could have got along just fine with well or river water instead. With all this in mind, it was likely that selling purified water was probably something akin to a hobby for the selkie shop owner. Glenn often wondered if she was really turning a profit on it.

As usual, the shopkeeper said very little as they made their transaction and then, when they were finished, saw their gondola off. In the back of the boat was now a large amount of bottled purified water, as well as alcohol for sterilization, and vinegar. All of it was pure and high quality. Loaded as it was with a great number of bottles, the boat was undoubtedly heavy, yet the gondolier pulled it along without issue. He was obviously well trained, but even just his ability to steer the boat without fighting the currents was an impressive feat.

With these supplies procured, their shopping duties were done. The amount of purified water they had purchased was more than enough to also help make Sapphee's sunscreen ointment.

The goal of their trip achieved, the lamia assistant now stared meaningfully at Glenn. The gondolier swimming in front of them also cast his dark brown gaze back at them repeatedly.

"...We'd like to purchase some souvenirs. Would you happen to have any recommendations on where we could go to do so?" Glenn asked the gondolier, who then told him not to worry and began to pull them onwards.

Sapphee smiled brightly. Everything that followed was firmly within her realm of control. She kept an eye out for exactly what she was looking for as she carefully perused the stalls one by one.

In a normal marketplace, one could simply buy what they'd like and be done with it. However, though it was gentle, there was nevertheless a current flowing through the Merrow Waterways. And unless a gondola was in a loop or a fixed route, it could only move in one direction—which was why many of the canals throughout the Waterways ended up being one-way. Fittingly, the current in the big canal was strong and difficult to fight against.

All in all, coming across a souvenir you liked was an once-in-a-lifetime chance. While it was possible to stop the boat at one of the stalls, but it was extremely difficult to return to a stall one had already passed by. For this reason, many shoppers felt compelled to buy something they liked as soon as they came across it. It was another business practice particular to the Merrow Waterways and one that tugged on the heartstrings of the tourists who came to visit.

At long last, Sapphee found what she had been seeking.

"I'll take this one, please," she said and bought a perfume bottle made out of red glass. Despite all of the fuss she had made, it was a small, sophisticated yet inexpensive bottle—but all that was very much like Sapphee.

She looked very pleased that she had been able to get a good souvenir. With her shopping complete, Glenn directed the gondola downstream. Having procured so many goods meant they had, quite literally, a lot to carry on their shoulders—thus, they needed to stop the gondola somewhere and have one of the horsemen of Scythia Transportation pull them back to the clinic.

They left the lively main canal and moved into the side canals, which were relatively quiet, and the number of gondolas carrying tourists sparse. The stalls were equally few in number, only a few here and there.

"Not many people heading out yet, huh?" Glenn muttered, as their gondolier surfaced with a splash.

"Yes, that's right," the merman said. "There's a show at night, you see. It's only just past noon, so no one is heading back yet."

"A...show?" Glenn said.

"Precisely."

The gondolier explained that the folk of the Merrow Waterways had been lighting it up with glassware lamps as of late, illuminating the whole main canal. The merfolk played music and danced while doing so, jumping straight up out of the water.

"It's a brand new entertainment show," the merman said, "but it's already a big hit. Would the two of you like to see it as well?"

Next to Glenn, Sapphee's eyes were sparkling with desire and he himself certainly wasn't disinterested in the mermaids' performance. However, he wanted avoid going out of their way as much as possible, what with all the goods they had on their gondola.

"Next time, Sapphee—okay?"

"O-okay..." she said, placated, though she still looked reluctant to let it go. Glenn was thankful that the canals weren't crowded at the moment, and decided that they'd immediately start on their way back.

At long last, an arched stone bridge came into view. Judging by its engravings, it was quite old, which made a certain sense, as the Waterways had a number of above-water buildings—all vestiges of the Waterways' past as a slum. Whatever the case, for a town where the majority of residents could swim, a stone bridge was completely useless, the buildings above the water's surface uninhabited ruins. It made one realize that the urban planning hadn't been entirely thorough.

Beneath the bridge was a single, small boat. It was an undersized gondola. The waterproof coating it had been covered with was peeling off in one section. Inside in the gondola was one of the merfolk.

"Oh!" the sun-tanned mermaid exclaimed. She looked to be a young woman.

The innocent-looking girl suddenly smiled upon seeing Glenn's face. "Hello!" she called. "You two over there, hold on a second!"

"Um... Do you mean us?" Glenn said.

"That's right, that handsome-looking couple over there! Wait a second, hold on! Please come see my shop!"

It seemed to be some kind of invitation to her stall—but her boat appeared to be empty of salable wares.

"Oh my, saying we're a couple like that... You'll make me blush!" Sapphee said.

"You look like a nice, young lamia lady! And a lovely partner, too! Truly an example of the old adage: 'a good wife and wise mother.'"

"Dr. Glenn, let's stop by. This mermaid girl is sweet."

Glenn thought that she had misunderstood the significance of "a good wife and wise mother," but knew Sapphee wasn't going to care after being complimented. Beyond that, Glenn knew it would be impossible to try and prevent her from stopping by the songstress, considering how completely carried away she had become at the mermaid's words.

The gondolier tactfully pulled the gondola toward the side of the canal and found a reasonable place to moor the boat. Thus secured, they didn't need to worry about being carried away with the current.

"Welcome to my shop! I'm Lulala Heine! Thank you for coming."

She spoke with a far-reaching yet cool and refreshing voice. Her brisk way of speaking had a friendly feel to it. She looked to be about fourteen or fifteen years old. Her short hair added to the cheerful impression she gave. The way two of her pointed teeth poked out from either side of her mouth when she smiled was quite charming.

Her suntanned skin was surely a result of her spending most of her time on the banks of the canals. The pattern of her fish tail was beautiful, with black lines blending together with gold and white undertones. The midday sun shining down on the Waterways made them sparkle.

On the skirts at her chest and waist, Glenn could see decorations of glass and shells. She seemed to be young, but she was dressed as if she were a dancer. The sleeves on her outfit were wide, much like the clothes of a dancer—or so Glenn thought, but in fact, they were actually the fins on her arms. They were almost transparently pale and looked like decorative arm sleeves.

"And what type of shop is this, I wonder?" Sapphee had a big smile on her face as she spoke. She seemed to be extremely pleased with the fact she had been called "a good wife and wise mother," although Glenn himself thought she was in fact neither.

"Here is where I advertise my singing," said the mermaid. "One song is three copper coins! How about it?"

It appeared the mermaid girl was in fact some kind of performer.

On the main canal there had been many people advertising their craft—from floating minstrels to acrobatic street performers. It wasn't at all rare for people to advertise their singing, but from Glenn's limited knowledge, he had no memory of ever hearing one of the merfolk advertise their songs.

There were many kinds of merfolk: merrows, mermaids, and sirens, among others. However, their songs were generally reputed to tempt sailors and sink their ships. That was of course nothing more than legend, and their songs were not filled with any strange kind of magic.

In truth, it's that—on their long journeys across the sea—sailors are condemned to deal with extreme exhaustion. In such situations, any man would be enthralled to see a mermaid singing. It was thought that in such situations, helmsmen steer their ship wrong and expose it to danger. In other words, though merfolk may be a primary, but *indirect* cause of a boat capsizing, that didn't mean their singing had any ill intentions...

As for the small songstress, Lulala, her goal certainly wasn't to capsize boats. It was to get coins from tourists.

"How about it? My singing is quite popular in the side canals!" she said, full of confidence.

Despite her claim, judging by the paint peeling off the side of her boat, it seemed that she wasn't making good money. And the decorations she wore felt like they were all she could do to look her best. Not being to able to even spend any money on the tools of her trade was surely a sign of how strapped for coin she was.

A performer so poor certainly suggested something about her relative skill as a singer. However, Glenn's attention had been captured by something else. Lulala's clothes were made up of triangular pieces of cloth which covered her breasts and were tied together with string. The outfit was normal for one of the merfolk, as were what was to be found beneath it: right about where a human's ribs would be located was three crescent-shaped slits. Her gills. No matter the subspecies of merfolk, all of them breathed in two ways—with their lungs and with their gills.

At the moment, Lulala was above the water, so her gills were closed. Underwater, however, was a different story. Submerged, merfolk breathed by taking water in through the mouth and sending it back out through their gills. Above water, they didn't use their gills, so they would usually be tightly closed, but upon closer inspection of Lulala's—

Her gills aren't fully closed...?

From her gill-holes he caught a glimpse of their insides—the internal gill itself. As a doctor, Glenn could tell in his gut that something was amiss.

"Dr. Glenn."

As he stood immersed in his thoughts, Sapphee had brought her face close to his ear, across which flickered a quick, cold sensation. It was Sapphee's tongue. Stretching out longer than that of a human, her lamia tongue licked Glenn's ear and conveyed her anger.

"What in the *world* could you be thinking about, staring so longingly at a tender mermaid like that?"

"Y-you've got it all wrong!" he said. "That wasn't what I was doing!"

"Miss Lulala certainly has quite healthy, tanned skin, doesn't she? Is that more to your tastes?"

"I didn't say anything like that, did I?!"

Indeed, if Sapphee got a suntan or anything of the sort, her life would be in danger. Hadn't they come all this way to the Merrow Waterways to buy purified water in order to protect her skin? Glenn wondered what, exactly, Sapphee thought all the effort they had gone to today was supposed to be about.

For the moment, Glenn put his doctor's intuition aside.

Lulala was still smiling, but it was clear that she was confused by the fact that Glenn and Sapphee had neither paid any money nor hadn't moved their boat. She was surely wondering if they were customers— and whether she should continue promoting her performance or not. She seemed to be struggling to come to a decision.

Or so Glenn thought.

Lulala clapped her hands together. "Oh, that's right, do you two know? The other name of this bridge is the 'Lover's Bridge.' In the middle of the war, a certain mermaid and a certain human man fell in love with each other!" she explained, smiling brightly. "But mankind and monster were enemies. The two decided to elope, so the man held the mermaid in his arms and took this bridge to escape the town. Then, after escaping the town, the two of them committed suicide together! That's why this bridge brings blessings to your love life!"

The fact that she offered up a story that had no way of being proven and used words like "blessing for your love life," gave the distinct impression that it was a made-up story for tourists, but— listening with rapt attention and sparkling eyes was the pharmacist of Litbeit Clinic.

Glenn felt fairly certain that there were no love blessings to be found from such a tragic ending. He also felt that—considering the way she had told it all with a smile— there were a multitude of problems with the way Lulala tried to pander to her customers.

"A daring escape with his lover in his arms... It's so romantic, isn't it, Doctor?" Sapphee said, her tail swaying back and forth as she spoke.

It seemed she was somewhat envious.

It didn't particularly matter to Glenn if she longed for such romanticism, but while carrying a mermaid in one's arms would already be difficult for a human, the idea of carrying a being with a long lower body like a lamia was quite incredible. Well, at the very least, it would have been difficult task for Glenn's slender arms to take on.

"That's just it!" said Lulala. "If you listen to my love song at this bridge, you will definitely find success in your love life. As a couple, you will have a long number of years ahead of you! So how about a song? How about it?"

Somehow, the cheerful mermaid seemed to have interpreted Glenn's silence to mean that he was unsure whether or not he would have her sing for them.

She continued to pile on her sales pitch, while Sapphee—already entirely in the mermaid's grasp—echoed her in a murmur, saying, "Success in love..."

Glenn sighed. It was only just past noon. Surely there wouldn't be any problem for them to listen to one or two of her songs. He stopped Sapphee off as she went to pay, and took out three copper coins from his breast pocket.

"This is my treat," he told her; Glenn wasn't so incompetent as to make a woman pay for a love song.

"Oh, Doctor..." Sapphee said.

"All right then," Glenn said. "We'd like to hear two songs."

"Wonderful, thank you!" said the mermaid. "Oh, but two songs, you said? I'm sorry sir, the amount you gave is a little short..." She looked perplexed, though she kept smiling. The amount Glenn had given her was clearly only enough for one song.

Glenn, of course, had done this on purpose. "No, please sing for us for this amount," he said.

"Are you asking for a discount?" Lulala said, affronted. "My voice isn't that cheap, you know!"

Glenn looked once again at the area around Lulala's chest and said, "I will pay for the rest in a different way."

Just as he had thought, the gills under her breast were unnaturally open. He was a doctor—he simply couldn't let himself ignore a potential disorder.

"The remaining amount I'll pay with my consultation," he clarified.

"Consultation?" Lulala tilted her small head. She seemed to think they were nothing more than a couple of tourists. In the clinic, they were always immediately recognizable, what with his white coat and

Sapphee's nurse uniform. However, the coat he wore for trips outside the office was nondescript—he looked nothing like a healthcare professional when he wore it.

To clarify further, Sapphee gave Lulala a short explanation of their line of work.

Whether it was because they didn't look like doctors, or because she had never seen a doctor before, Lulala's eyes widened in curiosity and surprise upon hearing the explanation.

* * * * *

Lulala sang an ancient monster song loudly.

It was in an old language that went more or less unspoken in the modern age. Glenn thought the language itself probably only survived in the songs of the merfolk. According to some theories, the language's peculiar pronunciation—which required much trilling—had caused it to fall out of use before it became widespread. Glenn, however, had no way to judge whether or not that was true.

The language survived almost exclusively in written documents; only a few monsters were capable of pronouncing it properly. Whatever the reason—whether it because Lulala was singing in that rare language, or for some other reason—Glenn couldn't help but sense something mystical in her tune.

What Glenn *was* certain of was that Lulala's singing voice was relaxed and beautiful.

The songs of merfolk were said to seduce and befuddle the hearts of men. However, Lulala's singing voice seemed to clear one's mind and thoughts, seemed to ease one's mental fatigue and stress. Glenn felt at ease as he listened to her song; it was like he had gotten a whiff of an herbal infusion.

With his mind now refreshed, he progressed with his earlier line of thought. Why was a merwoman with this much skill and artistry doing business on some side canal people took on their way home? She should have had plenty of work to take advantage of. Even imagining her making an appearance in the nightly show didn't seem too far-fetched.

If there wasn't any issue with her voice, then what was the issue— was there some other problem she had? If so, what in the world could it be?

"—Hnk?! Augh... Uckt!"

Glenn's speculations—and Lulala's sonorous singing voice—were interrupted by a hoarse, dry, heaving sound.

Pressing down on her chest, Lulala tried to repress her coughing fit. "S-sorry," she said. "I choked a little... Koff! Koff!"

The coughing didn't stop.

Her harsh hacking continued, but finally Lulala managed to take a deep breath. It appeared she had calmed down somewhat, but tears still rose to the corner of her eyes. Glenn was sure that the coughing fit had been considerably painful for her.

"Forgive me, sir and madam! As an apology, I'll sing one more—"

"No, that won't be necessary."

"What?" Lulala looked at once as though she had been cast aside.

But then Sapphee held out her hand toward Lulala. "Please, come over here."

"Huh? Um... Okay..."

Lulala dove into the water for a second, but was immediately lifted out of it by Sapphee. On top of the gondola, the lamia, the mermaid, and Glenn all sat together in the same boat.

"So, what is this?" Lulala asked.

"I told you, didn't I?" Glenn said. "We're going to give a consultation. Somewhere with fewer people would be better, though... Gondolier, can you move somewhere other people won't come by and see us?"

The young gondolier replied with an "Aye!" and, after undoing the mooring rope, quickly began pulling the gondola. The boat continued on past the "Lover's Bridge." The gondolier's ability to steer through the intricate and labyrinthine canals was truly remarkable. Since he was in the water and pulling from the front, it seemed as if he would neglect to check behind him—however, with boat and merfolk as one, he continued down the watery passage.

At long last, they came out into a big open canal, one nearly as spacious as the main canal. It seemed to be on the edge of the Waterways, and there are was devoid of tall buildings. Even upon looking into the water, there were few monsters to be seen swimming beneath the surface.

"This is the border of the Waterways," Lulala explained. "The currents are swift in this area because the Great River flows directly through here."

It was true that the current was quite fast. The gondolier looked to be doing all that he could to make sure the gondola wasn't swept up by the current. As he had though earlier, Glenn mused that they must be near the suburbs of the Waterways.

"Gondolas don't really come out here," Lulala said. "It's a good spot to watch the sunset though, so there might be a few boats that come to see it...Oh, see? Over there!" Her tanned finger pointed out a single gondola. A young mother and a small boy were in the boat. Waiting for dusk, the tourists had probably come to see the setting sun.

There were no other gondolas around.

"Dr. Glenn," Lulala said.

At his assistant's urging, Glenn nodded. "Yes, that's right." He paused, then said, "Miss Lulala Heine. As we promised, please allow us to examine you."

"Examine...? But I don't have any money! And I'm perfectly healthy!"

"You don't need to worry about payment. I believe I said this would make up for the second song I requested... I can't listen to a songstress's music for free, after all. I just don't believe that you are in good health. However, if you aren't sick, then that itself is something to be happy about, is it not? Now then, will you let me examine you?"

There was something wrong with Lulala, Glenn was certain. With her coughing fits, Glenn didn't doubt that Lulala was aware of it herself, too.

"I-If you don't need any money, then I guess..."

"Thank you very much," he said.

The examination had to take place in the boat. But Glenn knew that if his doctor's intuition was correct, then the examination itself wouldn't last long.

Sapphee picked up on Glenn's intentions and swiftly went around behind Lulala. It was cramped and unsteady aboard the gondola. Glenn moved carefully and knelt down in front of the mermaid.

"Now then, Miss Lulala—please open your mouth."

"Ahhh..."

Lulala did as instructed. Her thin lips and pointed teeth were certainly much like those of a young girl. Considering the cough she had, he suspected that there was probably something abnormal with her throat. If they had been at the clinic, he could have used a tongue depressor to hold down her tongue, but without one on hand, simply looking into her mouth would have to do.

As Glenn thought, it was inflamed, tinged with red. He was surprised she had been able to sing—surely the inflammation was painful. For her to have produced such a beautiful singing voice, while enduring that pain...

"Thank you," Glenn said. "Now, next is your chest."

"M-my chest?!" Lulala said. "By chest, you mean...? N-no way, that's...way too embarrassing..."

"O-oh, uh, no..."

Lulala crossed her hands in front of her chest, her face turning bright red. The way Glenn had spoken to her was partly to blame, but even still her response felt like a bit of an overreaction.

"Dr. Glenn." Sapphee cleared her throat with a cough."Miss Lulala is a young woman—please try to be a little more considerate."

"Th-that's right, my apologies..."

Unable to challenge Sapphee's sound reasoning, Glenn hung his head, reminding himself that telling a young woman to show him her chest was definitely something one would find unpleasant.

Glenn then reconsidered his current position.

He wasn't speaking to a monster that had come to his clinic as a patient. She was simply someone who Glenn couldn't ignore, in the middle of an examination above the surface of the canal. The exam was for medical treatment, yes, but that didn't mean a young woman

CASE 02 : THE MERMAID FROM THE WATERWAYS

would want to show her body to some man she barely knew.

"Please let me listen to your breathing," Glenn asked again, rewording his request.

"B-breathing?"

"I have a stethoscope. Right here." Glenn took a stethoscope out of his bag. It was the only thing he carried around with him, as it was an indispensable item for a doctor.

Due to the complex inner workings behind the stethoscope's casing, they couldn't be mass-produced. What Glenn held was another high quality product the craftsmen at Kuklo Workshop had carefully constructed for him. It was a tool Glenn used often ever since setting up the clinic.

He held the cup of the stethoscope to Lulala's chest. Slipping it under her bathing suit, it began to pick up the sound of her lungs. Since the rubber tubes were long, the stethoscope was bulky. Despite that, however, the Kuklo Workshop product was able to pick up the sounds of her chest with unparalleled precision.

Lulala stretched out her back as she hid her still-developing chest. Trying his best to avoid touching of her feminine areas, Glenn gave her instructions.

"Please take a deep breath."

"Uuuuhhh... Haaaaa..."

He concentrated carefully on the sound coming through the stethoscope. There were none of the sounds characteristic of asthma or other such conditions. He changed the location of the cup to verify, but could find no abnormalities in her lungs.

"Uuuuhhhh—"

If there was an abnormality, it was most likely in her other respiratory organ.

Glenn removed the stethoscope from his ears and put it around his neck.

"Now finally, please let me see your gills."

"Gills? By gills, you mean these?" Lulala asked.

The three crescent-shaped slits below her breast—the gills of a mermaid— opened and closed audibly. Inside a merfolk's throat was a valve used to switch between lung respiration and gill respiration. While they were underwater, this valve adjusted to prevent air from entering the lungs.

Merfolk drank in water from their mouth and pushed it out through their gills; after extracting the oxygen from the water, the fluid was then discharged from the body. This phenomenon had been discovered in the first research study on merfolk, which had been conducted by Glenn's teacher, Cthulhy.

Because of their gills, merfolk could live underwater. Conversely, when they were on land they had to use their lungs to breath air. As such, merfolk could only sing above water.

Glenn nodded when Lulala pointed to her gills. "Yes, those," he said.

"Um, sure, I guess," the mermaid said.

Lulala raised both her arms up. From behind her, Sapphee moved her hands under Lulala's armpits and supported her movements.

Glenn brought his face close to her six gills, split into threes on the left and right sides of her body. Lulala smiled at the ticklish sensation, but just as she had said, it appeared she wasn't opposed to a man looking at her gills.

Glenn began to observe them closely. From the small opening, he could see the mechanism that obtained oxygen from water via a complex fold within the gill. Out of the water, the gills had to be closed, but while underwater, the fold opened and respiration would occur as water pumped continuously through.

On the fold in question, Glenn could see an abnormal redness. It also looked a bit swollen. Indeed, the inside of her gill was just one step short of total inflammation. It wasn't as severe as the inflammation in her throat, but if it got any worse, it was quite possible she would eventually have to deal with pain and breathing complications.

"Is it okay if I touch them?" he asked.

Lulala looked a little unsure, but nodded her head. "It's...fine."

"This might feel ticklish, but please try to put up with it for me."

"Okay."

Glenn felt her gills.

Along with the stickiness of the special mucous membrane, Glenn felt a slight heat. Typically, a merfolk's body temperature was low due to their underwater lifestyle. They felt cool to the touch, much as Sapphee's snake body did.

"How does it feel? Does it hurt?" Glenn asked.

"I-It doesn't hurt, but...it's a little...warm."

"Sorry, please try to put up with it just a little longer."

A human's finger was indeed supposed to feel warm to merfolk. However, palpation was a necessary part of the examination, so Glenn opened up the gill slit and began to gently touch the inner part of the organ with stroking motions.

As expected, he felt swelling.

"Also...um, when you touch there, it feels itchy...sort of."

"Itchy?"

If she felt itchiness more than pain, then there was also a danger of some bacterial infection. Glenn knew that if he didn't treat her immediately, the infection might spread to others besides just Lulala. However, he had already come to realize there was another possibility besides infection.

"Excuse me for a moment, Miss Lulala," he said and suddenly stuck his fingers deeper into her gills.

"Huh...? Hyaaa!" Lulala raised her voice in surprise. Sapphee glared reproachfully, but as it was a necessary step, he just had to bear with her ire. He was sure her surprise had just come from how suddenly he had moved his fingers further into the gills.

"S-sorry. I just wanted to check the deeper part of your gills."

"Hnh... I-It's okay..."

He began feeling the interior of the respiration organ. The gills, composed of a number of folds and mucus, were an evolutionary gift the merfolk had acquired from their long years living underwater. They were capable of complex functions far more advanced than those of normal fish, and with them merfolk were able to live underwater in either salt or fresh water.

"I'll touch them slowly, okay?" he said.

"Nh... Okay."

Glenn continued to feel the inside of her gill. The amount of mucus on the folds seemed to be low.

Typically, they would be covered in mucus much like one's mouth and nose. A shortage of secretions meant her gills weren't protected for life above water. Consequently, inflammation was occurring.

"All right... I'm going to start moving, okay?" he said.

"O-okay...Ah! *Nh*... Oh..."

"Just a little bit more."

"I-I understand," Lulala said. "I'll do my best... Ah! Hngh...!'

As he felt Lulala's mucus, Glenn wondered what had come first. Had it been the inflammation in her throat? Or maybe the bacterial infection caused the inflammation in her throat to spread all the way to her gills? *No*, Glenn thought, *that can't be it*. If that had been the case, then the inflammation should also have spread to her lungs, as well, but he hadn't heard any abnormalities there when examining her with the stethoscope.

The complication in her gills had come first. That was Glenn's judgment. The inflammation of her gills was the cause and had extended up into her throat.

"Thank you," Glenn said. "I'm all done. I'm going to take my fingers out."

"S-slowly, okay?"

Glenn nodded. "Understood." He pulled out his fingers, slimy from the gills' mucus.

Lulala gave a relieved sigh; having Glenn's fingers inserted so deep must have been difficult to bear, after all.

Sapphee immediately wiped down Glenn's mucus-covered fingers with a handkerchief soaked in disinfectant alcohol. She did so as a precaution against bacterial infection, though Glenn was fairly convinced that there was no possibility that there would be any infection.

Sapphee made sure to wipe off Glenn's fingers in a position where Lulala wouldn't be able to see her doing so. Precaution against infection or not, Sapphee took care not to hurt Lulala's feelings by disinfecting Glenn's fingers right in front of her.

Unlike Glenn, Sapphee was a very thoughtful and considerate woman.

"Miss Lulala, may I ask you a question?" Glenn asked.

Lulala tilted her head just a little, but then quickly returned to her businesslike smile and responded brightly, saying, "Sure!"

"How much time do you spend out of water a day?"

"Wh-what...? I wonder... Well, I'm at the foot of that bridge from sunup to sundown every day singing!"

"Huh...? So you're only underwater for a quarter of the day...?"

"If that's what the clock says, then I guess so?"

Such a short amount of time underwater seemed absurd to Glenn. After all, merfolk lived their lives between both the sea and the land. They came on land to sunbathe and regulate their body temperature and swam underwater to eat, sleep, and protect their mucous membrane. However, according to what Lulala had just said, she spent over half the day living above water. Not only that, but she sat aboard a small boat and worked without break as a songstress, overtaxing her lungs and throat in the process.

It was much like if a human stood in the middle of a desert and continued singing nonstop without hydrating themselves. Glenn was not surprised that her gills were as inflamed as they were.

"Wh-why do you work so much?" he asked.

"Obviously it's because I'm broke, isn't it?"

Lulala's boundlessly bright smile was charming—but for just a moment, a serious expression had crossed her face as she replied. It struck Glenn as being Lulala's most honest expression and felt overwhelmed by it in spite of himself.

"You see, my dad ran away, and now I just have my mom!" Lulala explained. "On top of that, I got a ton of siblings! I'm the oldest one of four so I gotta work hard and earn money! There's a lot of chances to make money at the Waterways, so if I can't use my voice to make us money...our lives..."

Lulala grabbed Glenn by the collar as she desperately appealed to him, but as she spoke, she seemed to realize that saying all this to him wouldn't change anything. She quickly let go of him and curled herself into a ball, despondent. For better or worse, the young woman was filled with emotions waiting to be expressed. Was this what it was like for a girl her age?

"Oh... Um, sorry. I..." Lulala started to apologize.

"Don't worry about it," Sapphee said. "Dr. Glenn isn't upset."

"O-okay..."

Sapphee put both her hands on Lulala's shoulders. Having come to her senses, Lulala looked down dejectedly.

At last, Glenn understood. Lulala's enthusiasm for her work came from her impoverished home life. But at this rate, if she continued her life above the water, the inflammation in her gills would progress, and she'd soon find herself unable to breathe underwater.

He was at a loss of how to explain this all to her, but she spoke up before he could even make an attempt. "Oh, but—but, you know! It's okay!"

It seems that, considering her constant cheerfulness, she couldn't handle awkward silences or dead conversations very well. Thus, when everyone grew quiet, she took the initiative and spoke up.

"So, they're building a fountain in Lindworm's central plaza, you know? And I've accepted an invitation from the City Council to sing there! I'll be able to earn more than my work here at the Waterway.

Once the fountain preparations are done, I can start singing there! With it, my number of hours will go down, too!"

"...Is that so," Glenn mused. A reward suitable for her singing voice—and it seemed that the day she would be given that reward wasn't all that far away, either. In that case, what Glenn had to do wasn't that big of a deal.

"Miss Lulala, your symptoms—"

A shrill cry cut Glenn's words off.

"Wh-what?"

There shouldn't have been anyone else around. They had specifically come here to avoid the eyes of others. *No wait*, Glenn thought. *There* was *someone else*. Another gondola, separate from their own.

"Doctor, the child..." Sapphee said.

Glenn could see it too. The child that had come with his mother had fallen from the boat into the canal. The spray of water being kicked up was evidence of his struggles on the surface of the water.

"Someone! Anyone!" the mother shouted frantically.

The currents in the area were swift, and as such it was an area that aquatic monsters rarely frequented. Glenn worried about what would happen to a human child who fell into such a turbulent area.

"Gondolier, can you go help him?!" he shouted.

"If I went, then your gondola would be swept away!"

It seemed the merman was doing everything he could to maintain the gondola's position. Glenn was sure the same would apply to the gondolier of the mother's boat, as well. Their gondolier was a merman who looked to be in his prime, but he too could only look on as the child began to drown, unable to lend a hand to help.

"I'll go!"

"Lulala?!"

"I can swim over to him!" the mermaid said. "I'll grab him and come right back up!"

Glenn had no time to stop her.

Before he could say anything, Lulala's tail smacked the bottom of the gondola and she launched into the air like a dolphin. From there, she dove lithely down into the water. Her beautiful movements made one truly admire the character of the merfolk, but—

"Gondolier! Get us over to that boat!" Glenn shouted, but the gondolier had already begun moving.

While all this was going on, the thrashing water churned up by the drowning child had settled. He seemed to have lost the energy to struggle. Without a fight, he would surely be carried away by the swift current. It was clear as day what would happen to the child.

Glenn's gondola approached the mother's. Sapphee extended her long snake lower body.

"I'm going to bring her to us, doctor."

Using her snake body as a rope, Sapphee forcibly pulled the other gondola toward her and Glenn. The technique required a lot of strength, but it was possible with the hardy lower body of a lamia.

"My child! My child fell, and—"

"It's all right. A mermaid has gone to save him," Glenn said, desperately trying to soothe the mother, who looked on the verge of jumping in herself. Meanwhile, Glenn began to consider the situation. How long had passed since the child went down? If he wasn't struggling any longer, there was a high possibility that he had taken on water, stopped breathing, and slipped into unconsciousness.

If he had stopped breathing, then treating him was a fight against the clock.

Finally—

"Doctor!"

"Yeah!"

The child rose to the surface, a tanned arm wrapped around his stomach. Lulala pushed the drowned child up from under the water and raised him up to the surface. Sapphee once again extended her snake tail and used it to pluck the boy out of Lulala's hands.

Sapphee laid the child on the boat. Glenn quickly took off the child's jacket and got down on his knees next to him.

"Miss, what is his name?"

"Huh...? J-Johann..."

"Johann, can you hear me?! Can you hear me?! It's okay, you're safe now!"

Glenn called out to the limp child, but there was no answer. Glenn put his face close to the child's mouth and looked toward his chest. It was motionless—the boy had stopped breathing. He couldn't feel any breath from the child's nose or mouth, either.

"He's unconscious. Respiration's stopped. Sapphee!"

"He has no pulse. He's in cardiac arrest."

Sapphee was already at Johann's neck, taking his pulse. Then, she tilted his head and cleared his airway.

"I'm going to begin CPR."

Finding the boy's sternum, Glenn placed both of his hands vertically on top of it. Then, he pressed down on it repeatedly, applying pressure.

Glenn was a doctor specializing in monster medicine, but he still had the fundamental knowledge required to treat humans, as well. He certainly had the know-how necessary to perform emergency first aid on a near-drowning victim, as did Sapphee.

Not much time had passed since the boy had gone under. Glenn continued to repeatedly press down on his chest. After doing so over thirty times, he went to perform mouth-to-mouth resuscitation on the child, when—

"Glaugh!"

The boy spit up water with a strong retch.

Glenn got sprayed by the spit-up water, but he didn't mind—what mattered was that the boy was breathing again.

It seemed the amount of water he had taken in wasn't too much after all. Quickly, Glenn tilted the boys head up in order to make sure none of the water the boy regurgitated kept him from being able to breathe.

"*Ugh*... Glaugh!"

"Oh, Johann!" The mother embraced her now-conscious son. The boy sat there stupefied, not sure what exactly had happened.

"He didn't spend much time unconscious, so I don't believe there will be any side effects to worry about. However, just to be safe, I think you should take him to a good doctor to have him examined."

"Thank you so much! Thank you!"

Glenn's treatment had been truly basic first aid. Nevertheless, the biggest achievement behind the boy's return to consciousness belonged to the mermaid who had dove in after him. It was entirely because Lulala had immediately jumped in and brought the child back in such a short amount of time.

"Sapphee, where's Lulala?"

"About that, doctor…"

For a little while, Sapphee had been searching around the gondola. Now, she strained to see through waves, but could see nothing.

"Miss Lulala isn't down there," she said.

"Tch."

Glenn's decision and duty as a doctor of monster medicine had become instantly clear.

✖ ✖ ✖ ✖ ✖

She couldn't breathe.

To merfolk, the water was a sacred place. It enveloped all of life. To them, water naturally surrounded them; they couldn't go without it, just as humans could not go without air.

However, at that moment, things were different for Lulala Heine.

This isn't…right… she thought.

A mermaid who couldn't breathe underwater—it was absurd.

But in reality, Lulala was suffocating. By the time she'd brought the child to the surface, she had already begun having difficulty breathing. She had done everything she could to save the child, but as a result had been swept away in the fast current, and was now sinking further down into the canal.

With her consciousness fading, she couldn't even struggle against the water.

Frantically, she opened and closed her mouth over and over again, drinking in water. To breathe with their gills, merfolk take water in through the mouth and draw oxygen from it by passing it back out through their gills. Just as fish open and close their mouths when they are on dry land, when breathing becomes difficult for a mermaid, they try to drink as much water as possible.

However, no matter how much water she drank, Lulala could not restore her ability to breathe. Her dwindling consciousness began to snatch away her ability to think. As she faded, she thought about a tale of mermaid disappearing into bubbles—the tale of "Lover's Bridge."

That story, which Lulala had told to the doctor and nurse couple, was said to have actually happened long ago. A pair of lovers, a mermaid and a human, trying to escape the war, lamenting that there was no place for them to find peace, held each other's hands and sank down into the water.

The breath of the two drowning lovers became bubbles, and in the end those bubbles enveloped them and they joined each other in heaven.

Lulala wondered if she, too, would turn into bubbles when she died.

However, she was unable to even exhale any bubbles and could do nothing but desperately drink in water.

Someone!

Her voice refused to come out. Like a kaleidoscope, her life turned through her mind.

Her father and mother had gotten married and moved a young Lulala and the rest of her siblings to the Waterways. The war had ended and her father had been enthusiastic to begin their new lives.

However, their life on the Waterways hadn't gone well.

Lulala's father wasn't flexible enough to adapt to the new life and the new city they lived in. The Waterways were brand new, and everyone had been desperate to try and establish a stable existence on the canals. But Lulala's father left them. It was a heavy burden on her mother to look after the children he had left behind and earn enough money for them all to live, so as the oldest child, Lulala had had no choice but to take the initiative and start working.

There had been tough times as she worked in the side canals. There were some customers who would urge her to have sex, mistaking her for a prostitute of some kind, while other customers disparaged her singing voice and refuse to pay for her songs. The kindness of her merfolk neighbors was a small consolation.

But the City Council representative Skadi Dragenfelt had come and scouted her. She was going to be able to sing in the city plaza! It was a chance to finally get by without suffering from the hardships of her difficult life anymore. She'd be able to provide her mother and siblings with good food to eat. She'd be able to get by without having to endure the pain in her throat and forcing herself to sing with a smile.

Not like this... I don't want it to end like this.

Lulala stretched her hands through the water.

The light of the setting sun filtered in from the water's surface. That way was up. However, as a mermaid, the thought of heading for the water's surface didn't occur to her. It was only natural. If she couldn't breathe, she only needed to dive into the water, and breathe with her gills instead. For mermaids, the surface of the water was far more dangerous.

Someone, save me! she shouted into the water. However, with her throat filled with water, her voice wouldn't come out. Thus, her voice shouldn't have been able to reach anyone, and yet—

"I *will* save you."

Underwater, Lulala shouldn't have been able to hear any voice. However, the voice of the doctor was nonetheless calling to her. The man named Glenn had definitely spoken to her—or at least, she thought he had.

As her consciousness faded away, Lulala was positive she could hear Glenn's determined voice speak to her once again.

✕ ✕ ✖ ✕ ✕

Glenn came to his conclusion quickly: Lulala was drowning. Realizing this, he tore off his tunic and jumped into the water. There would be some who would laugh at the thought of a mermaid drowning. However...

There was an example from the past...

Glenn dove into the swift currents of the canal. The eye-catching golden of Lulala's body, the sparkle of transparent glass reflecting sunlight even under the water—both were easy to spot. Finding her was simple.

Instead of swimming against the current, Glenn went limp. It appeared to him that Lulala had already lost consciousness and had been washed away without her swimming at all. Therefore, if Glenn also went limp, and was pulled along similar to how Lulala had been, he would be able to head straight toward her.

In this way, he closed in on Lulala. He caught her in his arms, but she wasn't responsive. Her eyes barely open; her consciousness seemed to be fading. She was opening and closing her mouth. Unconsciously trying to take water into her body.

A mermaid can drown when they're underwater if they accidentally start breathing with their lungs.

As aforementioned, mermaids could switch between lung respiration and gill respiration using a valve in their throats— meaning that they could switch between taking in air and taking in water. However, if elderly merfolk or merfolk suffering from a throat disorder were to experience a sudden accident underwater, it was possible that the valve could fail to switch between the two.

Lulala's case was exactly like that.

Her throat and gills had become inflamed from dehydration. Then, in that same state, she dove energetically into the water to save the child. Now, Lulala was using her lungs and taking water into them.

To make matters worse, when a mermaid's breathing became difficult, they drank water—a common reaction for gill respiration; any mermaid would do so without thinking. However, by accidentally using her lungs to breathe and gulping down water on top of it all, she was only hastening her own drowning.

It was for these reasons that Lulala was drowning and beginning to lose consciousness.

Glenn had read data on drowned merfolk bodies a number of times at the academy. It was precisely because merfolk had both gills and lungs that they would end up drowning.

It's...the only way!

It was clear to Glenn what he had to do. He supported Lulala's body, made up his mind, and took in water.

"Gaugh...Uglh!" He choked, but kept the water in his mouth.

Then he pressed his mouth up against Lulala's.

"Hnh?!"

Her eyes opened. *Good*, Glenn thought. It seemed she was still just barely conscious. Glenn pressed his tongue into her mouth, then forced water from his mouth into hers and down her throat.

While doing all this, he embraced her. He squeezed her back and made it arch backwards. Continuing to pour water down her throat with her body in this position was known as underwater artificial respiration. However, though it was artificial respiration, it wasn't a treatment used for *lung* respiration.

If I can keep going...

Glenn held his breath and carefully checked Lulala's condition.

By arching a merfolk's back, one could clear their body's internal waterway, which connected the mouth to the gills, much like their esophagus acted as a connecting airway. By encouraging a weakened breathing valve to move again, one could revitalize the functionality of a mermaid's gills.

This was the aim of Glenn's underwater artificial respiration.

However, it was not a treatment that a human was meant to give. After all, Glenn could only breathe through his lungs. If he took in water while underwater and poured it inside Lulala's mouth, he himself would stop breathing.

It was a procedure meant to be given to merfolk by other merfolk, but at the time Glenn didn't have any other options. Due to the lack of oxygen, he was beginning to feel dizzy. His vision was going grey, and there was an intense ringing in his ears.

Then Glenn felt water flowing over the arm he had wrapped around Lulala's sides. The gills were open, water was flowing through them—Lulala had regained respiratory function in her gills.

Thank...good...ness...

But that was the end. With his consciousness fading, Glenn didn't have the strength left to carry her back to the gondola. And though Lulala's gill respiration was back to normal, she hadn't immediately regained consciousness. It would still take some time for her to recover from her befuddlement and be able to swim again.

What...should I do...

Glenn's mind—what he considered to be his only redeeming feature—wasn't working. He wondered if there was anything— *anything*, even driftwood would be fine—that he could grab hold of and float up to the surface with.

There! *A fishing...hook?* Unconsciously, he reached his hand out, toward what looked like a white hook. It was emitting a mysterious light, gleaming faintly through the water.

Slithering, the scaled fish hook wrapped itself around both Glenn and Lulala. It was then that Glenn finally realized that it wasn't a fishing hook at all. The world turned upside down as the giant white snake tail lifted the two suddenly from the water, launching them up into the bright, open world.

"Glaugh!" Spitting up water, Glenn was able to breathe again. "Augh... Ug... *Ugh...*" he coughed. Despite his hacking, however, he was very thankful he was to be breathing again.

Sapphee looked frantic as she pulled the two of them out of the water with her tail and dropped them both in the gondola.

"Th-thanks, Sapphee, you saved us..." Glenn gasped.

"Pulling two people up is tough even for me, you know!" Sapphee said. She was also breathing heavily, though she looked relieved. The chain of drownings, starting with the young child, then Lulala, and finally Glenn had been broken by Glenn's reliable assistant. "Honestly, what were you thinking diving in without saying anything?! You need to be more careful with your actions, Doctor—"

"Let's save the lecture...for later," Glenn said wearily and looked at Lulala.

Though she could breathe again, she was shaking, her face a bright red. Glenn thought that she was perhaps plagued with some other abnormality, or maybe suffering from a different kind of trouble, but—

"How long are you going to keep hugging each other?!" Sapphee demanded.

At her reprimand, Glenn once again realized he had made a mistake. The young mermaid songstress in Glenn's arms was trembling out of embarrassment.

✕ ✕ ✖ ✕ ✕

In Lindworm's central plaza, her back to the extravagantly built fountain, Lulala Heine's voice reverberated loudly and cheerfully across the square.

"_____♪"

The bustling humans and monsters all stopped what they were doing and became absorbed by her singing. Lost in the crowd, Glenn and Sapphee, too, were both enjoying Lulala's song.

It had been close to half a month since they had rescued her. The construction of the plaza's fountain was over. The newly completed structure was specially made to draw water directly from the Merrow Waterways. The reason for drawing water from the Waterways simple—so Lulala could swim there directly and situate herself in front of the fountain.

There was a marble seat specially built for Lulala. The stage was

CASE 02 : THE MERMAID FROM THE WATERWAYS

underwater, made to accommodate a merfolk's body. As such, she could sing in a natural position, with her body submerged in the water from the chest down.

"＿＿＿＿＿♪"

The ancient song finished. The song had a mysterious air to it, though it sounded as comfortable and relaxed as ever. Lulala smiled and waved at the audience's applause, every bit the cheerful songstress. Her smile was a bright, full-faced, and radiant, her two small teeth protruding out of the sides of her mouth. *That bright smile really does suit her,* Glenn thought.

"Thank you! Thank you, everyone!" Lulala cried. "I'll be singing here again at noon, okay? I hope you all come and listen!"

With her performances now occurring regularly in the plaza, one no longer had to go to the Waterways to hear the songs of the merfolk. The public interest in her performances was great; a considerable number of people came to listen to her songs. The Merrow Waterways were a very unique tourist attraction and as such, the flow of tourists who paid them a visit was ever strong. However, by singing in Lindworm's city plaza, Lulala was able to grab the attention of a new, larger audience for her concert.

As aforementioned, her performances had come about at the request of the Lindworm City Council itself; the City Council representative Skadi had personally invited Lulala to perform, in order to make the newly remodeled fountain a centerpiece of the plaza. Therefore, Lulala wasn't currently asking the audience for money in exchange for her singing—instead, she received a monthly wage. And because she sang in the plaza's fountain at set times, her job also included telling the time for all of Lindworm.

She wasn't some cuckoo tweeting out the time, but a mermaid who *sang* what time it was.

Her life seemed to have improved greatly for the better; Glenn couldn't see a single cloud on Lulala's smiling face.

"Miss Lulala," Sapphee called in greeting, after the crowd had thinned out.

"Oh! Miss Sapphee... And Dr. Glenn..."

"Hello, Lulala," Glenn said, his hand raised in greeting.

The instant Lulala recognized him, she sank down up to her shoulders in the water. The fins on her arms became drenched with water and expanded out under the surface as if they were shirt sleeves.

Incidentally, the reason Glenn had stopped calling her "Miss Lulala," was because he had been told by Lulala that she didn't feel comfortable when he spoke so formally. Sapphee, on the other hand, continued to refer to her this way, though Glenn figured this was because Sapphee was always polite no matter who she was talking to.

"After everything that's happened, how have you been feeling, Miss Lulala?"

"I've been great!" the mermaid said. "Thanks to the medicine you gave me, my throat's feeling a lot better and my singing has been perfect! I'm definitely not going to drown ever again! I, um... I really caused a lot of trouble for the two of you..."

Lulala glanced hesitantly toward Glenn, but didn't try to make eye contact with him. She would only speak directly to Sapphee.

Well, Glenn thought, *I suppose that's to be expected after what happened and all.*

Although it had been a necessary measure, ultimately Glenn *had* kissed her underwater and held her closely. Thinking about about it from Lulala's perspective, he couldn't imagine her wanting any of that done to her by a man she didn't even have any feelings for. Especially as a mermaid in the full bloom of her youth.

"Are you applying the moisturizer we gave you?" he asked.

"Y-yes," Lulala said. "Um, I put it on my gills when I go on land. And I take a medicated candy before I sing..."

"Good. Then everything's fine, isn't it?"

They had saved Lulala from drowning, but that didn't mean that Glenn's job had been completed. There were still vital treatments she needed for her gills and throat to heal. Indeed, after Glenn saved Lulala, they had returned to the clinic and made medicine. With Sapphee's help, they made a moisturizer to protect her gills from dehydration. And then, in order to curb the inflammation in her throat, made candies from an herbal extract and passed those on to her, too.

Today, their purpose in stopping by the fountain plaza had been to see how she was progressing, yet...

Lulala wouldn't once look Glenn in the eyes. Not only would she not look him in the eyes, but she sank further under the water and blew bubbles at him. Her cheeks were bright red, bright enough to see them even through her golden tanned skin.

"She's angry because you assaulted a young woman," Sapphee declared flatly.

Being reminded of the artificial respiration he had given Lulala, Glenn couldn't deny what Sapphee said.

Lulala shot up out of the water. "Th-that's not it!" she cried. With both of her hands on the marble fountain, she brought her face close to Glenn's and said, "I-I'm truly grateful to Dr. Glenn—it's thanks to him that I can even sing right now, and...that's why...that's why...!"

"More than anything else, I'm just glad you're doing well, Lulala.," Glenn said.

"Hnnnnnnnh!" It appeared that Lulala ultimately didn't know what she should say.

Sinking back into the water with a splash, she then followed the canal and left the central plaza. Now and again her tail and fins, swaying side to side, would peek out from the surface of the water. The canal seemed to be very shallow, and Glenn could clearly see her as she fled.

"She absolutely hates me, doesn't she...?"

"If that's what you think, then I'd say that Dr. Glenn is still lacking in life experience," Sapphee said.

"Why do you say that?" Glenn asked.

"I wonder," Sapphee said, irritably settling the matter in her usual cold manner. "That said, Lulala feels like a younger sister to me," she went on. "Even *I'd* like it if she could get along with you a little better, Doctor."

"...Really?"

"Yes, of course. Just, not *too* much."

The multi-level fountain spouted water upwards and painting the plaza with spray. Sapphee looked on at the complex structure and finally gave Glenn a smile. Unlike the incident with Tisalia, who the lamia seemed to be on bad terms with, it appeared that Sapphee had actually taken a liking to Lulala.

"Hey, Sapphee," Glenn said.

"What is it?"

"I just wondering... Have you ever thought about about why mermaids have lungs when they spend a majority of their life underwater?" There was no longer any sign of Lulala, but Glenn was still thinking about her.

By nature, mermaids had almost no reason to come up on land. It is said that they come up on land to sunbathe in order to regulate their body temperature and kill bacteria—however, doing so was possible even in the shoals and shallow water. There was simply no need for them to have evolved lungs.

"You're talking like Dr. Cthulhy," Sapphee said. "I've never even given it a thought."

Though Glenn's teacher Cthulhy Squele was currently the director of a large hospital, she had originally been a purely academic scholar. She had conducted research into the nature of monsters and how they had evolved into their current forms. The result of her excessive and exhaustive research into the bodies of monsters meant that she was rightly recognized as an authority on monster medicine and treatment.

Glenn wondered... Water and mermaids were inseparable. And yet, at the same time, there was one *other* thing that was inseparable from their lives.

"I'm positive they have them so they can sing," he said.

"Sing?"

In the water, songs didn't reverberate like they did on land. The beautiful voices of the merfolk that tempted and lured sailors were meaningless underwater.

"They have lungs so they can breathe in air and sing with their beautiful voices," Glenn explained. "That must be why, even when Lulala's throat became hoarse, she refused to stop singing."

"That's unusually poetic of you, Doctor," Sapphee said.

Glenn laughed self-consciously. She was right, he thought; it certainly was the typical kind of conclusion he usually came to. Cthulhy would have sneered at him if she had heard such a hypothesis.

"But, I like the idea," Sapphee said. "I think it's even more romantic than the story of the human and mermaid lovers' suicide." She smiled, the scales on the sides of her eyes bending with the motion.

Merfolk were often associated with tragic love, which was why the story was romantic. But sometimes a romantic story without any sort of tragedy wasn't so bad. *Next time*, Glenn thought, *I'll have to tell Lulala about my hypothesis.* He wondered how the still-innocent songstress would react to it. He smiled in anticipation and gazed out in the direction the mermaid had made her exit.

The morning canal's waters sparkled now and then, illuminated by the sunlight. It was as if they were made of the Waterways' famed and translucent Merrow glass.

CASE 03:
The Doctor-Hating
Flesh Golem

Glenn Litbeit had learned a variety of different monster medical treatments. The breadth of his knowledge included many topics.

For example, in order to extend the lifespan of an elderly dryad, he could reinforce their weakening branches with a grafting trick. For an ill slime no longer able to support their shape, he could create a special culture solution to heal them.

Glenn was also well-versed in both botany and chemistry, and his knowledge even extended to the strange fields of alchemy and the occult. Treating monsters—a species quite different from humans—required a wide range of know-how in order to be fit for the job.

Of course, his teacher, Cthulhy, possessed an even more comprehensive knowledge of monsters than Glenn did. As such, he was still inexperienced. No matter how much he studied monster medicine, there would always be more to know—which, naturally, meant there was a limit to what he could know.

One such example was dragons.

Even among monsters, they were quite mysterious, and it was unknown exactly how evolution had brought them to their current forms. Some believed they had been the original monsters, who had now reached the peak of evolution. When it came to this strongest breed of monsters, who could effortlessly transform their colossal wings, arms, and legs into the shape of a human, Glenn couldn't help but admit he was ignorant.

It was for that reason that, when a certain monster arrived at the clinic, all Glenn could do was greet her with a stiff and twitching smile.

"W-welcome to the Litbeit Clinic..."

In the doorway stood was the City Council representative for Lindworm—the most influential person in the city, who had changed Lindworm into the city that it was today, and who still worked hard to manage its affairs: Skadi Dragenfelt, commonly known as the Draconess.

✕ ✕ ✖ ✕ ✕

She had a tiny body and a pair of horns that seemed out of place on her small frame, twisting high from her head.

Her entire form was hidden under a silk robe with decorations embroidered in gold thread. A string was tied between her horns and from it a white veil hung down over her face. With the veil, Glenn couldn't get a peek at her expression, but the tail that poked out from under the bottom of her robe was unmistakably that of a dragon.

It was indeed the powerful political figure that had made Lindworm what it was after the war, Skadi Dragenfelt.

With economic and political strength, as well as her ability to lead, she was in direct control of the Lindworm City Council. While she did have bodyguards assigned to her, there were doubts as to how necessary they even were, as it was hard to imagine there existed anyone foolish enough to attack a dragon.

He had heard her name from a number of different people during his travels around Lindworm, but this was the first time Glenn was meeting her face-to-face. Glenn's teacher Cthulhy was said to be an old friend of Skadi's. In fact, he had heard that it was with Skadi's support that Cthulhy had been able to construct the big city hospital. As she was an investor in his former teacher, Skadi was someone Glenn needed to be extra courteous to and conscientious of.

"U-um...?" Glenn fumbled.

Skadi lingered silently in the doorway of the clinic.

"If you have some business with our clinic, please feel free to come inside." Sapphee said, inviting her inside with a smile.

Skadi, however, did not move. Though she was no taller than a child, she was not someone to be taken lightly. She was a dragon, capable of destroying whole cities and entire nations. While she had no reason to suddenly become violent, just the thought of the tremendous power she was capable of wielding was enough to make one afraid of her.

One day, for fun, Skadi had participated in a match in the arena, but she was so incredibly strong she was banned from ever competing again. As a result, any who had heard of that match were very cautious when dealing with her.

"Excuse me?" Sapphee said.

Skadi's silence continued.

Looking closer, however, Glenn glimpsed faint movement; her lips were very slightly trembling. It seemed that she was saying something or other, but Glenn couldn't catch any of it.

It was hard to believe, but was her voice actually just too quiet to hear?

"Excuse me!" a voice said, as a new figure stepped across the threshold behind Skadi. "This is the Litbeit Clinic, correct?"

"Th-that's right..." Glenn said.

"My name is Kunai Zenow. I am the Lady Draconess's bodyguard attendant."

She was a woman with a penetrating gaze. Her hair was tied up high at the back of her head. Judging by the way her collar wrapped around her neck and the particular cut of her clothes, she didn't seem to be from the central part of the continent. The design of her outfit closely resembled the styles used in the farthest limits of human territory, known as the Far East or the Orient. The sound of her name, Kunai, also had an Eastern sound to it. Glenn was also from the East, so if anything, he was quite familiar with her style of clothes.

However, the patchwork sutures that ran across her entire body stood out more than her clothes, or anything else for that matter. Glenn could even see parts of her that had lost their color and looked like dead flesh, but Kunai herself was completely calm and composed. On top of that, her right arm had been dramatically lopped off at the elbow; a number of stitches hung down from her elbow, dangling where the absent half of the limb would have been.

At the nape of her neck, Glenn could see a scroll typical of the Far East. At first, he had thought it was a strange accessory for tying her hair up, but when he looked at it more closely, the scroll was stuck there, piercing through her neck. It went through the muscle and bone and poked out the other side.

Undead monsters did indeed exist, such as zombies and the living dead. Kunai's face was so poor in color that her face resembled a corpse. Yet, the scroll and the sutures across her body were peculiarities that weren't seen among other types of undead monsters. The undead Glenn was familiar had a slightly difference appearance than Kunai's.

"Um, well..." he said uncertainly.

"I will be conveying my mistress's messages to you!" Kunai announced. "They are words graciously given by the Lady Draconess herself, so listen respectfully!"

She spoke with an extremely overbearing attitude. Skadi Dragenfelt was a very powerful person, but she wasn't someone one should have to prostrate themselves in front of.

"Dr. Glenn," Sapphee said, speaking quietly so that the sutured attendant Kunai wouldn't hear her, "It's a rumor, but...it's said that Lady Skadi's bodyguard is a rather excessively devoted follower of hers."

"You!" Kunai spat. "I told you to listen respectfully, did I not?!"

It seemed like the overbearing attitude was just coming from Kunai herself. Skadi was speaking rapidly in a low voice, but as before, Glenn couldn't make out even a single word of what she was saying. Perhaps she was apologizing for her disrespectful bodyguard.

Glenn hoped that was the case. It was preposterous that Kunai's insufferable attitude might extend to her master as well.

The one-armed bodyguard looked Glenn straight in the eyes and said, "Listen up! These are my lady's words: 'A few days ago, my bodyguard's right arm was wounded in battle with a bandit, and ended up going missing. Therefore, we are searching for her arm throughout the city, and I would like to have you suture it back together with your surgical skills, Dr. Glenn.' The two of you get all that?!"

Glenn had heard everything. He had heard everything, but because Kunai was repeating Skadi's words just as they had spoken, it was difficult to tell who she was talking about. By bodyguard, Glenn assumed that she was talking about Kunai, which meant that Skadi hadn't come to the clinic for treatment of her own—instead, she had come on behalf of Kunai, her bodyguard whose arm was missing from the elbow down.

"There was a battle?" he said.

"As my lady said to me, 'For a while, my bodyguard has been pursuing slave traders hiding in the city. A few days ago, Kunai thought that she finally had them cornered, but she had actually fallen into a trap. She clashed swords with ten opponents as she made her escape, but ended up dropping her arm somewhere during her retreat...'" Kunai paused and then said, "I am utterly ashamed of my defeat, Lady Draconess!"

Glenn wasn't quite sure if Kunai was talking to himself or to Skadi. Nonetheless, he understood the situation. He had wondered what type of medical treatment he might be asked to perform on the dragon, but it seemed that Kunai's arm was the thing that needed treating. With Glenn's surgical abilities, stitching up the wound wouldn't be an issue at all.

A needle likely couldn't pierce a dragon's scales, but sewing Kunai up would be much easier. As far as Glenn could tell from looking at her stitched-up skin, it seemed her body was constantly being injured and damaged.

The fact she felt no pain despite her injuries convinced Glenn that she was an undead monster of some kind. Glenn also was interested in the fact that she had squared off against ten assailants. Escaping a trap, battling through her retreat, and making it out only half an arm was proof of just how skilled Kunai was in battle.

"In her orders, my lady said, 'I have other subordinates searching, but they have yet to find her arm. I'd like you to sew it back on as soon as they find it.' Lady Draconess, how incredibly warmhearted of you!"

Once again, Skadi was inaudible.

"Yes!" her bodyguard exclaimed. "I, Kunai Zenow, am prepared to give my life for you, Lady Draconess!"

Glenn felt her dedication was a bit smothering. It was a mystery to him why Kunai could hear Skadi's voice when it was quieter than a fly's buzzing, but whatever reason, there was no doubt that Kunai's devotion to her was tremendous.

He felt that if Skadi told her to die, then Kunai would have gladly sliced open her own stomach at a moment's notice. Not that cutting open their own stomach would kill one of the undead...

"Miss Skadi," Glenn began, "We of course have the equipment to treat patients here in our clinic. We do everything in our power to treat our patients...but may I ask you a couple questions?"

"'Please ask me anything'—that is her answer! However, obviously that doesn't mean you can *truly* ask her anything. Know where you stand, Doctor!"

Though all she had to do was interpret Skadi, Kunai seemed insistent on adding her own addendum to everything her lady said. Frankly, Glenn found the habit irritating.

"First, why have you come to us?" he asked. "I've heard that Miss Skadi is an old friend of my former teacher, Dr. Cthulhy. Wouldn't it be better to go to the central hospital...?"

"'I went but was turned away before even meeting with her. I was told she has an excellent protégé and I should ask him for help.' That is her answer! How disrespectful, to turn down a request from the

Lady Draconess herself!"

In other words, it was the same reckless behavior Glenn's teacher was known for. Beside him, Glenn could hear Sapphee speak bitterly, saying, "That damn octo-woman."

But for Glenn, he felt that passing on a direct request from Skadi wasn't simply Cthulhy's normal recklessness. After all, they were speaking with the most influential person in the city. Making a connection with such a person would be beneficial for the future of the clinic.

"In that case, I have one more question," Glenn said. "But, um... It's about Miss Kunai."

"Me?" Kunai said.

"To properly conduct treatment, I need to know what she is. Would you be able to tell me what type of monster Kunai is?"

"'...She is not a monster.'" Though Kunai continued to speak for Skadi, her expressionless face had gone stiff, like she was a doll. Combined with her patchwork sutures, it made her look even more like the vestige of some artificial construction.

"'Kunai was originally human,'" Skadi said through Kunai.

"H-human?"

"'She is a flesh golem, made by stitching together human remains. A Far East doctor ripe with ambition experimented with creating life, and she was the result. Kunai was not birthed from a monster, she was built from human corpses.'"

Glenn was speechless. As someone working to treat patients and sustain life, Glenn had never before heard of anyone trying to *create* life themselves. He wondered if such a thing was even allowed.

Though Kunai was a corpse, much like the undead monsters

Glenn had originally thought she was related to, but it appeared she had been created by the hands of a human. From what he could remember, golem creation was a secret and ancient art, created by kneading together mud and clay, and then given orders like a doll to do the bidding of their creator.

Then Skadi, through Kunai, gave him a last word of caution, one that left Glenn with his hands on his head, perplexed:

"'Because of all this...Kunai hates doctors.'"

✕ ✕ ✖ ✕ ✕

Kunai's eyebrows drew together, giving her a lonely visage. *She looks like a cast-out puppy*, Glenn thought.

It was now just him, Sapphee, and Kunai in the clinic. Skadi had many other things to attend to, so she had left immediately after giving Glenn and Sapphee the details of the situation. Without a master to protect, the flesh golem bodyguard didn't speak a word—though she was clearly depressed.

There wasn't a single trace of the haughty and grand attitude she had had when Skadi was at her side.

"Miss Kunai?" Sapphee said. "Is it okay if I call you that?"

"Call me whatever you want," Kunai said. "You're Miss Saphentite Neikes, correct? According to the documents I've seen, you're a lamia well versed in drug and herb preparation—a member of the Neikes family, who have made their fortune selling medicine. It also mentioned that Miss Saphentite is an unparalleled genius in the world of pharmaceutical medicine."

"I've left my family behind, so they have nothing to do with me,"

Sapphee said. "I just have one thing I would like to ask you, Miss Kunai."

"What?"

"While it is certainly true that Dr. Glenn is well-learned in many different fields, golems and other occult matters are not his specialty. He certainly isn't able to use any ancient magic. We only perform scientific treatments, based on observation and clinical medicine... Are you still fine being seen by us?"

"I didn't anticipate a town doctor would be able to do any of that stuff in the first place, anyway."

She gave the nape of her neck a good slap. It appeared that she was pointing to the back of her neck, where the scroll was piercing straight through her cervical vertebrae.

"Written on this scroll are my orders as a golem," she said, a strong tone to her voice. "Right now, I'm moving autonomously, but that is also because there is an incantation inscribed on this command scroll that allows it. The only person who can change what is written here is my mistress, the Lady Draconess. This isn't something that anyone can just have their way with, and I don't plan on letting you touch it."

As there was no question that she had mastered some form of martial art, it was hard to imagine that there was anyone who'd be able to touch the nape of her neck even if they had *wanted* to. She was a dragon's bodyguard, after all, and surely had the strength required of such a role.

"The Draconess is looking for someone to suture me. All you need to do is sew up my body with string. That said, though it is a simple task, it is quite important, especially considering that my mistress herself has graciously appointed you to take care of it. Know that it is an honor."

Glenn thought that it would best if they followed everything Kunai said obediently. He was a complete amateur when it came to making flesh golems—but just as Kunai had said, if all he needed to do was sew her lost arm back onto her body, then that was indeed a job for a doctor. He might have objections to Kunai's attitude, but he had none to the work in and of itself.

"However," Kunai said, glaring at Glenn and Sapphee. "It may go against the wishes of the Draconess, but I have no intention of relying on a town doctor for help. I will sew my own arm back on. In the end, as long as my body is back to perfection, she will be pleased."

"Huh...?" Glenn said. "Wh-what is that supposed to mean?"

"It means I won't be asking for your help. I will search for my own arm and attach it back to me as I see fit. I hate doctors. I can't stand even being in a clinic like this." There was truly no end to Kunai's insolence.

To tell the truth, Glenn wasn't all that surprised by her words. Kunai had only come here as an attendant of Skadi's, after all. Kunai herself didn't have the slightest intention of letting Glenn examine and treat her.

"Sorry for disturbing you," she said and with those words, Kunai exited the clinic and headed off.

Glenn couldn't even try to stop her. It was as if everything had been decided from the beginning. She really did hate doctors and had made Glenn keenly aware of the fact that she wanted to leave the clinic as soon as possible.

"There are always some patients who hate doctors, but..." Sapphee trailed off, resting her cheeks on her hand. She sighed as she rubbed the scales at the corner of her eyes.

"Most of the time, the further a disease progresses, a patient must stay in the clinic whether they like it or not. I suppose it's because they can't handle the pain. But...perhaps it's a little different for Miss Kunai?"

"Does she even feel pain in the *first* place? She was what, a flesh golem? Was that it?"

As far as he could tell from looking at Kunai, her severed right arm seemed to cause her no pain. Even if her head were cut off, she would probably have acted like nothing had happened. Still, Glenn wondered if it was really all right for them to leave her alone.

Kunai had said she would sew her own arm back on. However, was she even capable of performing such a feat? It was clearly a difficult task—keeping the right arm to be sutured fixed in place, all while threading the needle through the flesh...

Besides.

"It must be hard to live her life one-handed," he said.

"Live her life? She's dead, isn't she?" Sapphee said.

Glenn shrugged. "We still need to make sure our patients are healthy. Dead patients aren't all that uncommon anyway, right? Just the other day, Frank—that zombie—came here for some antiseptic, right?"

"Oh my, well now that you mention it..." Sapphee said. As she had been the one to create the antiseptic, however, she was definitely just playing dumb. Sapphee wasn't the sort to tell Glenn that it was fine to leave a patient alone simply because they were dead—and Glenn had no intentions of leaving her alone, either.

"I'm going to head out for a bit," he said. "We have to search for

Miss Kunai's arm anyway, right?"

Putting on his white coat, Glenn quickly prepared to leave the clinic, stuffing the emergency first aid tools he would need into a bag.

"Sorry, Sapphee, but I need you to look after the clinic," he said.

"Leave it to me. The fairies are here, too."

The clinic's fairy helpers were rushing about the floor as if the series of disturbances caused by Skadi's visit hadn't even happened. They were zealous in their work, but had a tendency to be a bit fanatical and didn't always take notice of their surroundings.

Sapphee clapped her hands."All right now, line up," she said

"Line uuuup!"

"Okaaay."

"Is this a new joooob?"

All of the fairies filed into a line. They hadn't been working on any specific task and ran over at Sapphee's orders.

"Dr. Glenn will be stepping out for a house call and surgery. He will be stitching up Miss Kunai Zenow, who's lost the bottom half of her right arm. He anticipates that he will need to perform the suturing at his destination, so depending on the situation he will need disinfecting alcohol, stitching needles, and thread. Also, we need some of you to head out into the city and help Miss Kunai find her right arm, okay?"

"Uuuuunderstood!"

"Goooooot it!"

Having received their orders, the fairies spread out like a blooming flower. Some of them were already rushing out of the clinic. With their superb sense of danger and ability to defend themselves, it was hard to imagine that they would get smashed or run over by a carriage the moment they exited out into the road, but even so, it was a scene that Glenn couldn't help but feel uneasy watching.

"Perfect," Sapphee said. "With this, all the preliminary preparations are taken care of. Now then, Doctor, please be careful."

"Yeah... You're really well prepared, aren't you, Sapphee?"

"Of course." She extended her long tail smoothly. It passed Glenn and was already opening the door to the clinic. "I'm Dr. Glenn's assistant, after all. Even if I can't join you, I will assist you in any way I can."

"You're a huge help... All right, I'm off."

Sapphee brought her tail back to her side and used it to wave goodbye to Glenn instead of her hand. Glenn often wondered why Sapphee tended to use her tail instead of her hands much of the time. Was it out of laziness or for some other reason?

With the preparations complete, Glenn ran out into the street to follow after Kunai. He emerged onto the main southern avenue, where monsters and humans were all jumbled together in the crowd. Glenn scanned left and right, but the patchwork scarred figure of the flesh golem was nowhere to be seen.

Where had she gone? Should he chase after Kunai first or go first search for her right arm?

It was good he had rushed out the way he had, he still didn't know what to do. He thought for a moment. Skadi's underlings and the fairies were all looking for her right arm. Maybe he should chase after Kunai, then. However, he had the feeling that doing so would further provoke her hatred of doctors.

Before he could make a decision, a scream broke into his thoughts.

"*Eeeeeeeeeeeeek*!!!"

Glenn had heard that voice before. Without any hesitation, he ran toward the scream.

× × ✖ × ×

Tisalia was screaming.

A crowd had formed in an alley that continued on toward the arena. Standing in the middle of the crowd was none other than the centaurs' princess. Tisalia caught sight of Glenn and immediately rushed over to him.

"D-Doctor!"

"Whoa!"

Tisalia had a massive, carthorse-like physique. Having someone her size come bounding toward him could only end in injury—or so he thought. Glenn thought he would be run over in the blink of an eye, but a second before she crashed into him, Tisalia came to a sudden, skillful stop. As expected from a fighter in the arena, she appeared to have complete control over her movements. It didn't seem that she would make any mistakes that might cause an accident.

"Wh-what's that matter, Miss Tisalia?" Glenn asked.

"*Sniff*! Doctor, I was on a walk... I just thought I'd buy some vegetables, so I came without Kay and Lorna, but..."

Glenn realized that Tisalia wasn't equipped for the arena. Her clothes were embroidered with a checkered design, and while they seemed to be high quality, it didn't appear to be her best outfit, either. Tisalia appear to be wearing what she might consider normal, everyday clothes.

"Then, I saw... I saw..."

CASE 03 : THE DOCTOR-HATING FLESH GOLEM

"Ah."

Looking at what Tisalia was pointing out with a trembling finger, Glenn understood what had happened.

It was a leg—a patchwork left leg he had seen before. Its greave had fallen off and lay nearby. Kunai had only worn a steel greave on her left leg, so there was no mistaking that it was hers.

Glenn approached the limb. He ignored the sense that the crowd was taking a step as he approached the limb. He gently lifted it from the ground.

"D-Doctor...?" Tisalia said.

"It's seems to have been cut off around the femoral thigh muscles. No, maybe the stitches came undone? Her greaves are dented... The impact of some sort of blunt weapon must have cut the old stitches. It doesn't seem her stitches were made with very high-quality thread, does it?"

"How can you discuss this so calmly?!" Tisalia said. "I-Isn't this a murder?! We need to call the Guard Patrol!"

"If this was cut off during a recent murder, the color of the flesh wouldn't look so poor. Not to mention the fact that there's been almost no bleeding. This is Miss Kunai's left leg."

"Kunai... Kunai Zenow...?" Tisalia trailed off, at a loss for words. She seemed to know Skadi's bodyguard somehow. After a moment, she regained her voice. "You mean the fighter who appeared like a bolt of lightning at the arena five years ago, had an unprecedented win streak, and was scouted to be Miss Skadi's bodyguard based on those achievements? The top ranked arena fighter—*that* Kunai Zenow?"

Five years ago meant that this had happened before he opened up his clinic. Tisalia must have known because she was a fighter in the arena. Kunai apparently had been a fighter, as well. If she was the top ranked fighter, then she had surely been inducted into the arena's hall of fame, a place of honor shared only by the strongest of warriors. It was every fighter's goal, for the top-ranked fighter was renowned as a hero throughout the continent.

Tisalia was a middle-ranked arena fighter, still rank three—in other words, Kunai was even stronger than Tisalia.

"I can't believe someone like her would lose a leg," Tisalia said. "Who could her opponent have been...?"

"Miss Kunai is already hurt," Glenn explained. "Most likely she was targeted because of her vulnerability."

"You're so calm about this, Doctor!"

But of course he was—after all, examining patients was a fundamental part of his job as a doctor. "From what I can tell from looking at her left leg, the threads used for her sutures have already deteriorated quite a bit," he said. "She might have been the top ranked fighter in the past, but right now, I believe her abilities are a bit more limited."

The junctions in the muscles of her legs had been sewn together with thread, which meant that her whole *body* must have been sewn together in a similar fashion in order to create a flesh golem. Glenn was sure that the deteriorating threads and loosening bonds would have an effect on the movements of her body.

The degree of rot differed depending on the flesh in question. Considering the shape of her muscle, it seemed to be sewn together into one piece, regardless of the original sex of the body it had come from. Glenn wondered how her maker had done all that and still managed to create a moving body? Not only that, but the end result was a well-proportioned female leg—how had that come to be?

The more Glenn looked at Kunai's leg, the more he felt like it was something unfathomable, far beyond the current medical knowledge. Surely it was an example of the secret art of gathering corpses together to create a flesh golem.

The ankle of Kunai's leg suddenly convulsed.

"*Eeeeeeeeek*!" Tisalia backed away, her face pale. The crowd that had gathered had already taken flight.

The foot, still wearing an eastern style sandal, was moving slightly.

"Amazing," Glenn said. "It moves even when separated from the body. Does that mean the various parts of her body aren't dead—that each of them has a will of their own?"

"Doctor, how can you be so clinical about all of this?!" Tisalia said in disbelief.

The answer, of course, was simple: in order to learn how to treat monsters, Glenn had examined a large number of patients; during his time at the academy, he even participated in autopsies of human and monster alike. It had all bee necessary in order to acquire the technical knowledge for medical treatments. Looking at a dead body simply didn't frighten him.

Furthermore, now that Glenn understood that it was simply just Kunai's leg that had caused Tisalia to scream, he knew there was no reason to be frightened. However, Glenn was still unsure why her left leg—which had clearly been connected to her body back in the clinic—was now on the ground in the middle of the avenue.

"There are many strange people in this town," Tisalia said, "but... it seems that you, Doctor—that you're actually pretty strange too, aren't you?"

"Oh, sorry," Glenn said. "I lost track of where I was for a moment—
it used to happen at the academy all the time. Scary, huh?"

"Not at all—I've fallen in love all over again!" Tisalia said. Judging
by the restless twitching of the ears on top of her head, there was no
mistaking that she had been charmed somehow or other.

"At any rate, it's not good for me to treat a patient's leg like a
specimen... I have to be careful."

"So it's safe to say this is Kunai Zenow's leg?" the centaur princess
asked.

"Yes. Originally, Sapphee and I were asked to help stitch up her
right arm, but considering the circumstances, it seems her arm isn't
the only thing in need of stitching..."

Tisalia pointed to the greave in Glenn's hand and said, "Let me
look at that, please."

He handed it over.

The greave only protected the shin, but Kunai hadn't been wearing
much armor to begin with—nor did Glenn remember her even
carrying a weapon. Considering that her goal was to protect a rather
important person, one would have expected her to carry at least *some*
sort of small blade. Glenn wondered if wearing greaves only on her
left leg meant Kunai's fighting style put more emphasis on moving
easily than being well armored.

Tisalia stared closely at the dent in the greave.

"It seems this was struck by a mace or some other kind of blunt
weapon. Whatever it was, it didn't have much power. I think it must
have been something that could be concealed under a long coat."

"I-Impressive," Glenn said.

Glenn could inspect the fallen leg, he hadn't the knowledge to guess the type of weapon that had been used simply from looking at the traces of the blow dealt to the greave. Those things were Tisalia's expertise, what with her knowledge of weaponry and combat.

"I suppose this blow was from a surprise attack?" Tisalia mused aloud.

The toe of the leg in Glenn's hand twitched. Was it agreeing with the princess? Although, how a leg without ears could listen in on a conversation was beyond him.

Piecing what Tisalia had just said together with what Skadi had said earlier, Glenn began to work out what must have happened. Kunai had been attacked by someone. Earlier, Skadi and her subordinates had been chasing after slave traders, and Kunai had fought with those bandits directly—the very battle that had prompted her to come to Glenn with only one arm in the first place.

The answer was clear: Kunai must have been attacked by those bandits again.

On top of that, there was a high chance that the culprit that attacked Kunai had slipped back into the crowd with his weapon. Not that Glenn could do anything about the bandits...

"Can this...be healed?" Tisalia asked.

"I believe it will function properly if I sew it back together. It seems the construction of the bone areas is adequate. It should be good as before if I just properly reconnect the muscle together."

If he stitched it together properly with new thread, Glenn thought he might be able to reattach it even more firmly than it had been before. Of course, simply sewing together the dead flesh wouldn't be enough for it to move, but...Glenn was sure that the movement was catalyzed thanks to the secret magic of the flesh golem.

What was really on Glenn's mind were the suture marks. It was understandable that the old suture marks had the loosest seams. Examining her foot made that clear enough. Some of the seams there were sewn with pitch black thread—*old* thread. Glenn figured they were Kunai's first sutures. Had they been sewn by the doctor that "made" her? As a doctor himself, Glenn couldn't help but doubt her creator's suturing skills.

And they had been this bad at stitching, then it wasn't too much of a stretch to surmise that their other skills were likely just as bad. Glenn wondered if the person who had created her had even been a doctor at all.

Tisalia's voice broke into his thoughts, speaking with a strained smile. "It might not be my place to say this, but...stroking a woman's leg like you are, Doctor, makes you look like some kind of abnormal pervert—you know?"

She wasn't wrong—people were avoiding getting near Glenn as they walked by him.

Unsure about how he should reply, Glenn cast his eyes downward and said, "Even with you telling me that, I don't think I'll be able to stop. Just—you definitely can't tell Sapphee I said that, okay?"

✳ ✳ ✖ ✳ ✳

Even when Glenn told her there might be bandits in the city, Tisalia simply smiled at him. She had just been out for a stroll, but had bravely taken on the responsibility of locating the bandits. Given Tisalia's strength, Glenn was sure they wouldn't best her—though on second though, they *had* been able to injure Kunai, so optimism perhaps wasn't the best route.

He told Tisalia not to take any chances, but understood that she wasn't the type of woman to listen to him. At the very least, he wanted her to take proper precautions, and not think it was some carefree task to take up after going for a stroll. After cautioning the enthusiastic Tisalia again and again, Glenn parted ways with the equine princess.

Next, came Glenn's job: he needed to find Kunai, who had to be around somewhere, and perform the stitching surgery without delay. If Kunai had the ability to brawl with ten bandits at once, Glenn had no doubt she could chase after the bandits once she was back in top form.

"Now then... Where could she be...?" he wondered aloud. Carrying Kunai's leg—now wrapped in cloth—under his arm, he continued down the main avenue. He kept a close eye on the end of her foot, which was peeking out from under the cloth, thinking he could use the twitching of her toes to locate the rest of Kunai. He knew he couldn't just carry a bare woman's foot down the street, but he had no idea what else to do with it. Still, if someone happened to look at him, there was no question that he looked like a freak, walking around with a lopped-off half of a leg like he was.

And indeed, there were some humans and monsters who recognized that what Glenn held was a piece of a human body wrapped up in cloth. Half of these people put some distance between themselves and Glenn, while the other half called for the Guard Patrol.

Glenn, however, didn't pay them any mind. Being a doctor, he was understandably consumed with single-minded worry for Kunai.

At last he arrived at the central plaza, where shops and stalls were lined up side by side. All this had sprung up because so many guests had come by to see the newly constructed water fountain. Some time had passed since the water fountain had been completed, but it had turned out to be an ideal date location, so many couples and newlyweds visited the area.

Glenn had arrived there by following the movements of the foot. Its twitching had slowly gotten stronger. He wanted to believe that he was getting closer to Kunai, but—

On the central stage in the plaza fountain, Lulala's loud singing voice rang out, cutting into his thoughts. The audience applauded, leading Glenn to believe that he had arrived right as she was ending one of her songs.

"Oh!" the dark-skinned mermaid said, catching sight of Glenn, staring at her blankly. "Hey! Dr. Glenn! Where have you been? There's big trouble!"

"T-trouble?" he said.

Before, either out of embarrassment or for some other reason, Lulala ran away as soon as she saw Glenn. Today, however, it seemed she had forgotten about all of that and was hurriedly beckoning him over.

With every movement of her arm, their large, wide fins would sway. The glittering light they gave off was mystifying.

"Hey, hey, so there's this rumor that you've been searching all over for a human body for some experiment, you know?" she said.

"What sort of rumor is that supposed to be...?" Glenn said, a bit confused. For starters, it was oddly mistaken about a few key points."It's true I'm looking for a human body, but it's not for any sort of experiment of mine. It belongs to a patient."

"Yeah, I know," Lulala said. "It's Miss Kunai's right?"

"You know her too, Lulala?"

The tanned songstress nodded in agreement. "Yeah—after all, when Miss Skadi came to scout me, Miss Kunai was there, too. She looks a little scary, but she was a really kind lady."

Kunai had been unnecessarily overbearing with Glenn, but it seemed not everyone was given the same treatment. Lindworm was quite big, yet also surprisingly small. It appeared that Glenn's acquaintances were connected in a variety of different ways.

Lulala continued speaking. "That, and I heard that she was chasing after slave traders doing business in town."

"You know about all that, too...?" Glenn asked.

"*Heh heh*. I'm just well-informed, that's all." Lulala chuckled suggestively.

It was just for a second, but on the other side of her cheerful smile, Glenn thought he had glimpsed a suspicious tint to her eyes— Sapphee sometimes wore a similar expression, too. He supposed that in the past mermaids *had* seduced men and pulled them in into water—and that the blood of such water sprites ran in Lulala's veins.

"Anyway, that's why I was searching for you," Lulala said. "Not just you—Miss Kunai or Miss Skadi would've been fine, too—but anyway." With a big splash, Lulala pulled something up out of the water.

It was an arm—a corpse's arm, patched together from different colors of muscle, a sight Glenn had become familiar with. It was, without a doubt, the very thing that Glenn and Kunai had been looking for.

"This was dropped into the Waterways the other day. The guys that attacked Miss Kunai probably just took her arm and threw it away into the canals. Honestly! The canals aren't a place to dump your trash, you know!"

"Oh, okay... I see."

The Lindworm canals weren't like rivers in normal cities, but were in fact the passageways for aquatic monsters and were maintained for that purpose. It was unthinkable that a person from the city who knew this would throw trash into the canals, not when they knew the problems it would cause.

The fact that someone had been so disrespectful was what had Lulala so angry.

Occasionally, one would come across a citizen who was simply indifferent to the people living in the water, but most of the time, the culprits were visitors from outside Lindworm, people who weren't aware that there were monsters dwelling in the canals.

Glenn figured that the slave traders who had attacked Kunai weren't originally from Lindworm—that was why they had thrown the arm in the canals. They would never have expected it to get picked up by a mermaid.

"Thank you," he said. "I've been searching for this... Now I just need to find Kunai herself..."

She had now lost one arm and one leg. Glenn didn't think she could have gotten very far in such a state, though he wondered how he had come so far without seeing anyone that fit her description.

"You know, Lulala, you're pretty calm holding that human arm, aren't you?"

Thinking about how flustered and panicked Tisalia had been, it was surprising to see the younger Lulala completely indifferent to the severed human arm.

"Yeah. I used to live in the ocean, after all."

"The ocean?" he said.

Most merfolk had bodies evolved to survive in both fresh and salt water. As such, it wasn't at all strange for Lulala to have lived in the ocean before—but Glenn couldn't quite see the connection between living in the ocean and being fine with holding a human arm.

"A lot of different things flow through the ocean, you know... It's little different from what we were just talking about, but everyone always seems to think of the ocean as one big garbage dump or something, right?"

"I could see that..." Glenn said slowly.

"Like shipwrecks and stuff!"

That's flotsam, not garbage, was what Glenn wanted to say, but Lulala didn't give Glenn any time to get a word in.

"The next day after a storm is really awful!" she continued rapidly. "The sea is so rough and stormy—and then it finally all clears up! Great, you think, let's go sunbathing! But then a ship sinks right in front of your family's eyes!"

"O-oh..."

"There's nothing you can really do but clean it up, but, you know, there's a lot of people that are on the ship... If they were just bones it would be one thing, but a drowned corpse right before it rots is all fat and flabby, turned completely black and—"

"I-I get it!" Glenn interrupted, flustered. "I don't need to know anymore!"

Naturally he had seen drowned bodies before, and in his role as a doctor, he wasn't opposed to touching dead bodies in and of itself— but it wasn't something to be heard out of the mouth of a young songstress.

The absent-minded and blasé way Lulala spoke about it only made things even worse.

"Well, long story short, I'm totally fine with arms and stuff," she said.

"I understand now..." Glenn felt that he had seen another side of Lulala. She seemed to have suffered in her past, as well.

Whatever the case, Glenn was glad Lulala had found the arm, as he wouldn't able to search for it in the water. After all, there wasn't much someone who lived on land could do to search for something underwater.

He wiped off Kunai's arm with the cloth he held in his arms. It was vaguely cool to the touch, possibly because it had been underwater so long—though its temperature could just as easily been because the limb had come from a dead body. And because the dead flesh had been treated with preservatives, it had been able to maintain its shape even in the lower temperatures of the canal.

The arm was twitching much like the leg. Its fingers moved incessantly, like it was being tickled, as Glenn let the remaining water fall from the arm.

"Wow..." Lulala stared with great interest as the arm thrashed like a fish. Her reaction was truly the complete opposite of Tisalia's.

Now that Kunai's arm was mostly dry, Glenn examined her limb. There didn't seem to be any other injuries. If a finger had fallen off into the canals, then he would have had to scavenge all the waterways of Lindworm to find it, but that didn't seem to be necessary.

Examining the right arm closely, its muscles appeared to be the muscles of a man. The strong girth of it wasn't like that of most females. From what Glenn remembered, Kunai's left arm had been a relatively normal female arm. It appeared a female corpse had been used as a base, but that the other specimens used differed depending on the part of the body.

"Isn't that great, Miss Kunai? If you have Dr. Glenn treating you, I'm sure you'll be fine!" Lulala said, smiling as she spoke to the arm. Glenn didn't know whether it was actually listening, but its fingers did seem to twitch slightly in response.

"Now I just need to find Miss Kunai herself," Glenn said.

"Should I ask some of my merfolk friends?" Lulala asked.

"I'd really appreciate it, if possible..."

"Okay! I'll let them know Dr. Glenn is looking for the owner of a chopped-off arm and leg!" It was another remark that would surely cause people to misunderstand the situation, but Lulala dove into the water before Glenn could correct her.

The fountain in the plaza had canals built on all sides of it, and from there, one could move underwater throughout all of Lindworm. Lulala's message would quickly spread to the denizens of the canals— along with macabre rumors about Glenn.

"I've really done it now," Glenn muttered. "Dr. Cthulhy already has more than enough weird rumors going around..." He let out a sigh and said something that surely would have upset his teacher if she had hear him. "Miss Arm. If possible, would you be able to tell me where your owner is right now?"

The chopped-off arm stayed as it was for a few moments. Then...

"Hm?"

At long last, the index finger bent and pointed toward the southwest end of the plaza. Glenn thought it was just his imagination, but even when he tilted the arm in another direction, the index finger would still point in the same direction, much like a compass. It was indeed pointing to the southwest, after all.

"So this is why the leg couldn't properly make any gestures," he murmured.

Thus, using the arm as a makeshift compass, Glenn followed its lead out of the plaza.

While Glenn was busy looking for the bodyguard, Kunai herself was biting her lip in frustration.

She was missing half her right arm. On top of that, she had now lost her left leg. Losing one leg while she only had one arm meant her movements were limited to crawling. Wanting to escape the commotion that would have arisen if she had been seen by others, Kunai crept into a back alley.

"Dammit..." she sighed, collapsing in the dirty alleyway. The prolonged movement she had made while concealing her body had taken her to the limits of her strength. Unable to move, Kunai desperately tried to catch her breath.

She should have asked someone for help. If she could just get a message to Skadi, her mistress wouldn't hesitate to rescue her exceptional attendant. However, Kunai's loyalty wouldn't allow her to trouble her master. She wanted to avoid the commotion reaching Skadi at any cost.

Thus, she was in her current sad state.

"Hmph, embarrassing," she muttered. Grinding her teeth, she cursed her own powerlessness.

She had found the bandit's gang soon after she left the Litbeit Clinic. As Skadi's attendant, she had prioritized maintaining peace and order, and verifying the bandits' position, rather than focus on searching for her arm.

Kunai simply couldn't allow them to do as they pleased, so she had immediately set out in pursuit. However, it hadn't taken long for the bandits to realize that they were being followed.

They had quickly escaped into a back alley. Kunai followed after and had been hit by an unexpected attack. Her assailant hit her with a self-defense mace. With the threads on her legs tearing loose, she had been unable to counter-attack or chase after the bandits.

She had then crawled after the fleeing bandits. Her torn-off leg had been carried off; she had no doubt it had been ditched somewhere. Kunai imagined it had probably been found by now and hoped it was someone who would realize it was her leg—otherwise they would likely start screaming.

"That bastard..." Kunai growled.

It seemed to her that the bandits had picked up on the fact that her undead body suffered from a number of complications and failures. She had no doubt that it had been for this reason that the her attacker had only aimed for her leg, rather than dealing a final blow. After all, Kunai's body had already become brittle enough to fall apart from a single mace-swing.

"The Draconess must be disappointed, too..." she murmured to herself.

Skadi Dragenfelt had been the one to pick her up when she had nowhere else to go and Kunai thus felt she owed Skadi a great debt of gratitude. It was the only thing that gave meaning to her existence in Lindworm.

Kunai had been created at the edge of the Far East. She didn't know how many years had passed since she had run away from the doctor who created her. A flesh golem couldn't die, but if the dead flesh that constituted its form was pulled apart as was happening to her now, the golem would sooner or later regress back into a dead corpse.

Kunai didn't particularly care whether she lived or died. It was unnatural for a corpse like herself to be moving in the first place. Returning to the earth was nature's providence.

"I always end up thinking about pointless things when I'm tired like this..." Kunai gave a sigh laden with the heavy emotions building in her chest.

The emotions she was struggling against weren't actually her own. All the memories of the various corpses that made up her body sometimes disturbed her own thoughts. Sometimes it was pleasant, but other times it could be annoying—especially during times like this, when Kunai was feeling depressed and seized with a sense of powerlessness.

For example, her right leg had come from the corpse of a certain guard. He had served his master for a long time, and he had died using his own body as a shield, protecting his master from an assassin's blade. Even now, his voice came from her leg. It wanted to serve a worthy master. It wanted to protect someone.

She was missing it at the moment, but in part of her right arm was the muscle from a bloodthirsty killer who used to slice and murder the people of his city every night. He was someone who liked seeing blood and the anguished looks on his victim's faces more than anything else, and would still say to Kunai—*I want to cut people. I want to kill people.* His voice wasn't strong enough to become an impulse, but it took much of her mental energy to ignore him.

The heart of a young maiden beat in her chest. She had been a girl who loved stories and dreamed of loving someone like the people in her stories. However, her own lover was unfaithful to her once, and she hung herself by the neck. She had despaired that that the man she loved wasn't the hero that appeared in her beloved tales and stories. But now, still, the heart of a young girl pining for love beat in Kunai's chest.

"All of you, be quiet."

Kunai's personality was composed of the spirits of the dead people that composed her body. That was the truth, and at times like these, when she was lost deep in her thought, their voices rang in her head.

It was almost like she had a hangover. She wanted to stifle the loud voices echoing in her head and think her own thoughts, but the loud voices of the corpses were unending. They would always be there.

It was the fault of her creator. It was because of that quack doctor, who had committed the taboo of making dead flesh move—

A strange sensation coursed through her, interrupting her self-deprecating train of thought.

"Kya?! Wh-what... Hyah?!"

It was her left leg.

Her twisted her body at the tickling sensation, though she had lost her left leg in the fight earlier.

It didn't take her long to realize that someone was touching her missing leg. Even if her sutures were cut, even if she were separated from one of her limbs, each part of a flesh golem's body was—in a certain sense—alive and interconnected. They shared senses, so any time a part of Kunai's body was touched—even at a distance—that touch was transmitted directly to Kunai herself.

"Who is it, who has my foo—Ah, hnh!"

Kunai covered her mouth with her right hand to make sure her labored breathing didn't escape. She thought that someone might have heard her, but her worries were unfounded, hidden as she was in the isolated back alley.

Nevertheless, Kunai held back her voice. Her face distorted even more in shame. Her cheeks shouldn't have had any blood flowing through them, but she felt them grow hot, as though she was blushing.

It had an illusion, the memories of the dead bodies—just the remnants of the young maiden's love giving Kunai this sense of embarrassment.

"S-sto—!"

Flesh golems didn't feel pain. If their permanently damaged body had been able to experience it, normal life would have been impossible for them. The incantation inscribed on the scroll pierced through her neck made Kunai's body was immune to pain—but she still had a sense of touch. After all, if she'd had no sense of touch, she'd no longer be able to detect injuries or changes in her body.

As a result, despite it being disconnected from her body, she knew that someone was feeling and fumbling the foot attached to her missing leg. As the sensation continued, Kunai tried to hold back her voice, but her voice still escaped.

"Hnh...Ah!"

Was some child playing with her leg as some sort of mischief or joke?

No, Kunai thought, *that's not it*. The hands touching her were clearly those of an adult man. They didn't seem to be trying to hurt her leg. If she had to guess, Kunai would have said it was the limb was being carefully examined—as if the the construction of her foot was being examined.

And not out of some vulgar interest, but with genuine intention and concern—as if it were their job.

"That...doctor?!" she said. "...Hyanh?!"

A sweet voice escaped her lips—one that even Kunai couldn't believe she had made. She wondered why she made such a voice simply from being caressed below her knee. Perhaps her the nerves of her missing body part were especially sensitive.

She would have wanted to kill herself if someone overheard that voice. Unfortunately, for a corpse like Kunai, suicide wasn't something that could be done at a moment's notice. Even having her head cut off wouldn't kill her.

For a while, the strange sensations stopped.

She didn't know what that doctor Glenn Litbeit was doing with her leg, but she imagined that he was probably intending to stitch her back together—which also meant he was looking for her, the body he needed to attach the leg to.

"Dammit... *Argh*... Dammit!"

Kunai didn't know who she should be angry at.

She had put on a strong face in front of Glenn, but in reality she didn't at all think she'd be able to sew her body back together one-handed. To be honest, since she had been taught nothing but martial arts, there was no way she had any sewing skills. She couldn't even sew a blanket—there was no way she could suture a human body.

The odd feeling in her leg was still absent, but now she felt like her right arm was being held. Then, not longer after, it felt like the limb was being wiped with a cloth.

"What's this...?"

She hadn't mentioned it to Glenn earlier, but Kunai *had* suspected that her right arm had been underwater.

Early on, she had considered the possibility that it had been thrown into the canals. There was no other explanation she could think of for the cold feeling that had surrounded it. She had intentionally avoided telling Glenn this, because there would have been no point in arguing against him reattaching the arm if he had found it first.

Yet her cold arm had been pulled up out of the water, and was now being wiped off with some sort of cloth. Then she felt her arm being touched by Glenn's hands.

The arm was being touched.

By a loathsome doctor.

"*Ah! Hngh!* ...*Ah!*"

The way he touched her felt ticklish. She shouted at him in her mind to be more careful—he *was* a doctor, after all. Though he might treat his patients gently, he saw the detached arm and leg simply as things. Glenn didn't understand she could feel his touch even though her limbs were separate from her body—that was why he was touching them this way. That might have been the natural way to regard them, but that didn't mean Kunai had to accept it.

That part of a woman's body you're touching, you know. Be gentle—
"Hnh...Ngh!"

It took all she had to hold her voice back.

Kunai Zenow had once been the top-ranked fighter in the arena and she had no intention of putting up with this humiliation. Her fists had floored countless opponents; with them, she would get payback on the doctor Glenn Litbeit for this humiliation—

"Oh..."

At least, that's what she had determined to do. But then she remembered that her knockout fist belonged to her right arm, which was still being held in Glenn's hands.

With that realization, Kunai once again became overwhelmed by a feeling of helplessness.

✖ ✖ ✖ ✖ ✖

"Miss Kunai!"

When Glenn found Kunai after following the right arm's directions, he first thought he had found a corpse.

Obviously Kunai's body *was* a corpse, but with her body missing its left leg and right arm, she looked like nothing more than a mangled body from afar.

"The doctor, huh..." Her voice was weak.

Glenn noticed that her eyes were watery and wondered why she was on the verge of tears. Of course, he had no way of knowing the turmoil in Kunai's heart.

"I'm glad I found you," he said. "I'll stitch you back up quickly."

"I won't let the dirty likes of you touch me."

Glenn let out a dry, involuntary laugh at Kunai's words. She had told him not to touch her, yet he held in his hand a part of her body. He had already touched her a great deal.

It seemed Kunai didn't have any intention of resisting and only gave him a quick glance as he knelt down next to her. He opened up a dry piece of cloth and placed the right arm and left leg on it. He then began laying out a number of tools necessary for the suturing procedure.

First, a surgical needle and suture thread. Then the needle holders—scissor-like tools used to restrain the surgical needle. Seeing everything lined up in front of her, Kunai's expression changed slightly.

"Hey, Doctor?" she asked.

"Yes?"

"Aren't you going to stitch me up? Why do you have that...small, fishhook-like thing?"

"It's a surgical needle. It's so small because it has to be able to to sew blood vessels together. Wait—you didn't think I was going to sew you up with a sewing needle, did you?"

Kunai nodded. Glenn was dumfounded.

Sutures and stitches were a fundamental medical skill. The quality and shapes of these tools used to sew up injuries in the human body were constantly being refined and improved upon every day. The needle in Glenn's hand had been used throughout all of medical history and honed into its current shape. Not only that, but it was a high-quality item, small but sturdy. It was a surgical needle created by the Kuklo Workshop, which assured Glenn of its quality.

He wondered—did Kunai's reaction mean the doctor who created her hadn't used a surgical needle when he was stitching together her body? He hadn't actually used a *sewing needle* when he made, had he?

Once again, Glenn wondered if her creator had even been an actual doctor.

"...No, wait, Doctor," Kunai said. "Did you say you were sewing blood vessels?"

"I'm connecting the nerves and blood vessels together. It seems that this part of the tissue isn't dead, and I can connect most of the blood vessels together. However, you probably aren't metabolizing at all, correct? The tissue won't regenerate, so I can leave the stitches in."

"The thread or whatever doesn't matter! You don't have to connect the blood vessels! Just connecting the muscles together is enough. I'm a flesh golem, this body operates under a different logic than living things. Stitching them together like that won't do anything."

"Is that so?" he said, then quickly fit Kunai's right arm to the cross section of her elbow. Kunai had told him not to touch her, and yet she held her right arm in place with her left, helping him. With her cooperation, Glenn's surgery would be easy.

Looking at the open wound, he understood the situation better. The portion of her arm in question had in fact been handled sloppily. However, her blood vessels peeked out from the open spaces between the colorless dead flesh. With his skill, Glenn didn't have any problems pulling them out and connecting them together like they had been when the flesh had been living.

He passed thread through the needle and restrained it with the needle holders. Dexterously handling the needle holders, Glenn immediately began stitching, starting with the internal tissue.

"Even if you have no blood flowing through you, even if the movement of your body is driven by a different logic than my own, it's important to link the flesh. If I don't properly connect it all together, you'll remain a body composed of different people, right?"

"Different...people." She repeated Glenn's words in blank amazement, her mind seemingly far off.

During all this, Glenn smoothly slid the thread through her blood vessels, bound them together, then cut the thread. He repeated this again and again, stitching one blood vessel together after another. Not even Sapphee was a match for Glenn when it came to delicate techniques like this. Cthulhy could surpass him in speed, but when it came to the thoroughness of the work, Glenn had surpassed even his master.

"So there are doctors like *you* out there, too, huh..." Kunai mused.

Glenn gave a dry laugh, wondering who exactly she was comparing him to—though he soon abandoned that train of thought. He didn't want to think too hard about a doctor willing to connect one dead body to another dead body.

A silence fell on the back alley.

Glenn focused on his work. He wanted to draw the major blood vessels and nerves together somehow or another. However, that surgery naturally took a considerable amount of time.

"My name. It's Kunai, you see," she said.

It seemed she could endure the silence no longer. She began to murmur quietly and Glenn listened to her, through his hand hand working the needle holders never ceased.

"This seems to be a name only used at the eastern edge, the Far East area of human territory," Kunai told him.

"Yes, I know," Glenn said. "I'm from that area as well."

"...Really? But your name..."

"My name is Glenn. In the Eastern script it's written 'Guren,' meaning 'crimson lotus.' It would be troublesome to continue using that here, so I changed the spelling to match the continent's official language, and made the pronunciation easier for those with a central continental dialect."

At the eastern edge of the world, a culture different from the central continent had taken root. Even after the war was over, many of the people there were still racist, and thus almost no monsters lived in that land.

Kunai continued to speak. Glenn listened attentively to his patient's words while he ceaselessly worked his needle holder.

"Written out, apparently my name says I 'have no suffering,'" Kunai said.

"That's right," he agreed—naturally, he knew that spelling.

"My creator said I was a perfect human, one 'without pain.' And it's true—I feel no pain. I don't suffer. Even as you poke me with that needle, I only feel a slight touch and a sensation of discomfort. That's why, Dr. Glenn, you don't have to move so carefully. I—"

"I've finished up most of the blood vessels. I'll move to the nerves next."

Glenn took a microscope out of his bag. A portable microscope, it could be mounted to his head and looked like a pair of glasses. The nerves—particularly the perineurium that sheathed the nerves—were much finer than the blood vessels. With the microscope, Glenn sutured them together with a needle so tiny it looked like it would be easy to misplace.

The tools had been appropriately sterilized with a bottle of disinfectant alcohol, though Glenn honestly didn't know if there was even any danger of a flesh golem getting an infection or any other type of disease. She had been given preservative treatments, so there didn't seem to be any worries of bacteria rotting her flesh.

Nevertheless, Glenn was a doctor. He tried his best to treat her the same way he would treat a living person.

"...Why are you taking such care?" Kunai asked.

"Because I'm a doctor. It's natural for me to exhaust all my power for the sake of my patients, as the only thing a doctor can do for a dead patient is pray for their spirit in the afterlife, notify their family of their passing, and write a medical report." He couldn't treat a dead patient, after all.

"Besides," he went on. "Someone who doesn't suffer or feel pain wouldn't have such a pained look on their face."

Kunai's eyes opened wide in surprise.

She looked rather lonely, like she was feeling her own powerlessness quite acutely. For someone like her without any parents, her life up until now had probably been lonesome. Glenn was sure she had her own reasons for not being at the side of her creator—they were probably why she was almost excessively attached to her master, Skadi.

No suffering... Glenn wondered what that was supposed to mean. Ever since he met her earlier that day, Kunai had looked to be in constant pain.

Glenn magnified the lens on the microscope and continued to work, sewing the nerve bundles together, now perfectly visible with his eyes. For a normal human, when repairing the nerves, it was necessary for the patient to train the reconnected nerves to move as they originally had. Glenn wondered if the same were true for flesh golems.

"This is second-hand information from my teacher," he said, after a moment of silent work, "but living things need pain and suffering. You feel pain and suffering precisely because your life is in danger. This is true even of the undead patients we get at the clinic. They are all already dead, and don't have any worries about death, but they still come to the clinic with various distresses."

Sometimes, a zombie woman that lived in the clinic's neighborhood would even come by without any real medical issues. Instead, she came by to gossip with Sapphee, who said she was lonely because all of the people she'd been friends with in her lifetime had died. Part of it was also because a weak part of her brain made her mistake Sapphee for her granddaughter.

"Suffering is proof that you're alive," Glenn explained to Kunai. His teacher Cthulhy had said that. There was truth in the words even if one were dead.

Being dead and not being alive looked like similar states, but they were different.

"I think my job—the job of doctors—is to relieve pain and suffering as long as one is alive. We can't take it all away, but we mitigate it as much as we can."

"I see..." Kunai said; she seemed to be lost in thought. Her colorless lips quivered slightly and then still. She appeared to be trying to tell him something that was difficult for her to say. Finally, Kunai relaxed with a sigh, smiled, and said once more, "So there are doctors like you out there, too, huh..."

Glenn didn't know how to answer her. He thought that the fake doctor Kunai was thinking of was the exception, and that there were far more doctors like him than like her creator.

After that, it seemed that Kunai had nothing more to say, and she grew quiet. Meanwhile, she tightly held the right arm being sutured. She seemed to be trying her best not to move at all and assist Glenn with his work.

Glenn normally needed an assistant to perform suturing surgeries. Starting with stabilizing the affected area, there were a number of different things that one needed help with, so no matter what, one person's hands just weren't enough. Indeed, Glenn was performing a job that required incredible skill, but it couldn't be denied that it was taking longer than normal to do. Glenn continued with precision, but also tried to work as fast as he possibly could.

If only Dr. Cthulhy was here...

If Cthulhy, with her excellent suturing technique, had been there, she would have been able to complete the entire surgery without an assistant. Glenn was jealous of that ability of hers.

At long last, he finished stitching the perineurium together, which meant it was time for the last step: the arm's muscle tissue and skin. Originally, Glenn thought he would have to do this part delicately as well, but from what he had seen of Kunai, he knew that if he used thin thread to sew her limbs together, another one of her body parts would end up falling off again. To prevent that from happening, Glenn used a strong needle and thread to tightly piece her muscle and skin together.

Taking off his microscope eye piece, he began sewing Kunai up with a large needle, the sort one would use to sew thick clothing. Kunai, however, didn't seem like she minded at all, and calmly let Glenn treat her. Glenn wondered if her complacent attitude was why she had been roughly sewn together with a big needle—like the one he was currently using—before.

At last, he said, "I'm done. How is it, Miss Kunai?"

Having finished stitching her right arm together again, Glenn wiped sweat from his forehead. The surgery had naturally taken a lot out of him.

"................" Kunai opened and closed her hand, checking the feeling in her right arm. "Hm. Excellent," she remarked.

"Are there any problems?" he asked.

"Not at all. In fact, it feels better than it did before. Great job, Dr. Glenn."

Thank goodness, thought Glenn. He had managed to get by without her telling him it had been meaningless to connect her blood vessels and nerves together.

Even though she had blood vessels and nerves, they didn't seem to be what made Kunai's body move. However, Glenn had wondered if, by firmly and physically connecting her arm together, he could make Kunai's body listen to her mind more closely and fluidly. It seemed that, one way or another, he had been right.

Since he wasn't able to perform any of the secret arts that were used to create flesh golems, this was the only treatment Glenn could properly give her.

"Next is your leg," he said.

"Oh, right. My leg. That still needs doing, doesn't it...?" For some reason, Kunai averted her eyes as she spoke. Her arm suturing had done something, though Glenn wasn't sure what.

Considering the rate at which his work was progressing, he felt confident he could suture up her leg before the sun went down. However, Kunai was strangely against it. However, it didn't seem to be just because she hated doctors. Something else was at play.

"L-listen up," she said. "Be gentle! And get it over with fast! Got it?"

"Yes, of course. It's part of the treatment, but I'll need to lift up your skirt."

"*Hng!*"

Having politely informed her beforehand, he began to lift up her skirt. The sutures in Kunai's left leg had been torn away in the middle of her femoral region and her foreign style of skirt would get in the way of his sewing.

"S-stop, I'll do it myself!" she said. Flustered, Kunai rolled up her own skirt, high enough that her hips were just on the verge of being visible. There wasn't a trace of her warrior-like aspect as she held her skirt up with trembling hands.

"My apologies," Glenn said. "I'll try to finish this as fast as possible."

Her underwear wasn't visible, and even it had been, he had planned on pretending it wasn't. Thus, Glenn felt a little sad that she was so on guard against him.

Quickly, Glenn took the needle holders in his hand and began connecting the blood vessels with the tiny needle.

"Unh!"

When he did, a small voice slipped out of Kunai, one that Glenn hadn't heard up until that moment.

"M-Miss Kunai? Does it hurt?"

"I-It doesn't hurt! It's just a little cold!"

Of course, with the needle being metal, it was natural for it to be cold, but—

"It was all fine up until a moment ago..."

"I-I know that! I-it's probably my legs, or, you know, my thighs... Th-they're sensitive, or something. Dammit, who the hell made this body to be like this?!"

Her arms were okay, but her legs are sensitive, Glenn thought and had a feeling that he more or less understood the meaning behind this. He was really beginning to hate the doctor who created her from the bottom of his heart. This "doctor" had been awful at sewing Kunai's body, but didn't seem to have cut corners when it came to her body's sensitivity.

In short, from what Glenn could tell, Kunai's legs were a delicate area for her.

"Eep, hnh!" she cried.

"I'm sorry, Miss Kunai," Glenn said. "Please try to endure this without moving, if you can. I'll make sure to finish it quickly."

"D-don't be ridiculous!"

Glenn couldn't suture her without his needle and thread. Now that he thought about it, he had been performing the surgery without any anesthesia, as if it had been a matter of course—but if the patient hadn't been Kunai, this was a situation where he would give the patient an analgesic treatment. It was strange that Kunai could get through it with just a tickling sensation, but that was to be expected of someone undead like her.

"Tch...Ahn, hyahn!"

Glenn focused all his attention on the situation, and continued working faster than he had been before. He passed the threaded needle rhythmically through the vascular tissue.

As he worked, Glenn wondered what the operation looked like to Kunai. The cold needle and Glenn's fingers were forcing their way into the inside of her own thigh. And though it didn't hurt, she could feel the temperature of both. Glenn could only imagine what the sensation was like—and yet, Kunai held her voice back, her face twisted in shame and humiliation.

"Dammit, I told you already—be gentler!" Kunai demanded.

"I will finish this quickly," Glenn promised. "Please put up with it

a little longer, Miss Kunai."

"Damn you, your personality is completely different—Hyanh?!"

Kunai's gasps wouldn't stop, but Glenn's fingers didn't stop moving, either. Since he couldn't curb her sensitivity, the only thing he could do was finish the procedure as soon as possible.

"Kya! Ahn! Hnyah!"

"................."

"S-say something, you charlatan! D-don't just stay silent with me crying out like this... Actually, a r-reaction might be wors—Ahn!"

Glenn had reached the limit of his concentration. Only half of the sounds Kunai was making reached his ears, but he couldn't afford to give a reply.

"Damn! Dammit!" she cursed. "I'm won't forgive you, not even after this is over! I'll never forgive you, bastar—! Ah, aaaaahn, hnh-hhhhhhn!"

Not long after, Kunai's leg jumped up for just a second.

For a while after that, Kunai tried desperately to catch her breath and didn't speak to Glenn at all, which allowed him to very calmly immerse himself in connecting her leg back together.

Meanwhile, the flesh golem glared at Glenn with eyes that had lost their light.

✳ ✳ ✖ ✳ ✳

Somehow or another, Glenn managed to finish the suturing before nightfall.

If night had fallen before he had finished, suturing would have been difficult in the poorly illuminated alleyway. If it had come down to it, the main avenue did have the illumination of the street lamps, but even that light wasn't adequate enough light to perform surgery by—not to mention the fact that Glenn couldn't exactly have sewn a corpse together in the middle of the main avenue at night.

If they had returned to the clinic, there would have been sufficient light to work under, but moving Kunai would have been tough while she was missing her leg. Thanks to Glenn's skill, however, the surgery was finished before the sun had gone down.

"...Thanks," Kunai offered with a sort of glum expression after the suturing had been completed. "But d-don't misunderstand anything! I won't forget the embarrassment you gave me today, got it?! It's just, that, well, this way, I won't make Lady Draconess worry any more... So I'll save your punishment for later! Got it?!"

This was the parting Kunai gave Glenn. Her words made it plain just how much she loved and respected Skadi.

By then, night had fallen. Kunai walked down the big avenue and headed toward the Lindworm council hall. Her movement wasn't at all shaky, and even an amateur like Glenn could tell from looking at her that she was a top-class martial artist.

If she had taken revenge on Glenn for the day's forceful treatment (which he had naturally done his best with, though Kunai did not seem to think so), he would have been at his wit's end to try and keep himself from being done in. All he could do was pray that such a day never came and that Skadi would keep a firm grip on her attendant's reins.

"I'm back!" he called as he stepped into the clinic, exhausted from his hard work.

The fairies responded to him at once, immediately pestering him for their reward.

"Welcooooome."

"Baaaaack."

"Heeey, where's the miiiilk?"

"Oh, right. I'll put it out now."

As usual, the fairies they were strict about their payment of milk. They didn't accept early or late payments for their wages and accepted no reward other than milk.

Despite Glenn's skill, he was still dead-tired from the body suturing surgery he had performed on the street. He had given the procedure his full concentration—which was fine, course—but now that it was over, the fatigue he'd been staving off weighed on his shoulders. All he wanted to do was relax for the rest of the night, for if he *didn't* get enough rest, then it would hinder patient examinations the next day.

"Sapphee...isn't here?" he said.

"I'm here, Dr. Glenn," she said and slow, silently appeared from further inside the clinic.

Glenn wondered what she had been doing behind the curtain. The pale doctor would sometimes damper her presence and the noise she made, so that she didn't even seem to be there.

However, Glenn was dumbfounded when he looked at Sapphee's figure.

"...Sapphee?"

"Heh heh—look Doctor."

Sapphee was stroking her stomach. She always wore opaque underclothes that stuck fast to her skin, but apparently she had in the middle of getting ready to go to bed, for she wore a thick negligee over her underthings. That wasn't the issue, however—after all, it was about the time most people retired for the night.

The problem was that the comfortably sized midsection of her nightwear was strangely swollen.

Sapphee had a suggestive smile on her face as she said,"It seems that, somehow or another, I've gotten pregnant."

At these words, Glenn put his hands to his head, completely unsure how to respond.

CASE 04:
The Lamia with an
Incurable Disease

Glenn Litbeit was born to a merchant family at the eastern edge of the human territory.

Glenn's father was an executive of the Eastern Trade Alliance and was a pure, dyed-in-the-wool tradesman, who also ran his own company. The Trade Alliance held and controlled trade routes that went through various regions across the human territory. Controlling everything from land caravans to merchant vessels, they could be counted on to deliver good products to the places that wanted them.

The generation-spanning merchant routes that Glenn's ancestors and the other Trade Alliance executives had established passed through all of the major cities in human territory. When Glenn was born, his father was in a predicament. He had been entrusted with establishing a new prospective trade route by the Alliance, but for him it was a heavy burden, as most of the trade routes that needed to be developed had already been established.

There was the possibility of developing routes to isolated and far-away regions, but even if he invested and developed such routes, he suspected that the profits yielded would not merit the investment. At any rate, there was no way the Alliance executives would give him money for something that would not turn a profit.

A little risk wasn't a problem, however. Glenn's father searched for a trade route that was certain to make back the initial investment and which could bring in profits, as well. Eventually, his search fell upon a certain domain.

It was the monsters' territory.

Glenn's father's answer was foreign trade with the monsters who, at the time, were still at war with mankind. Nonetheless, his father's plan was to pass through the Vivre Mountains and open up a trade route into enemy-controlled territory.

Of course, it was dangerous to do this without any proper plans or idea on how to move forward. Nonetheless, Glenn's father persuaded the executives of the Eastern Trading Alliance, and they decided behind closed doors to boldly construct a foreign trade route—the Alliance's biggest undertaking. At that point, the war had become a mere formality, and no one had any serious intentions of fighting the monsters. If the trade route was constructed and turned profits for both sides, there was the possibility it might even help end the war.

As for Glenn's father, it was unclear whether he was dreaming of an end to the war—he was a taciturn man who never said much. On the other hand, Glenn's mother firmly believed that the reason her husband wanted to develop a trade route with the enemy country wasn't simply for profit; she believed it was driven by his aspiration to bring about an end to the war.

On the other side of the conflict, in monster territory, there were merchants thinking in a similar fashion. They were pharmaceutical salesmen: the snakes of the lamia, who manufactured and sold drugs and medicine. Since they traditionally excelled at manufacturing medicine, they would make it and then made their sales by traveling to wherever medicine was needed. They were highly praised merchants among monsterkind.

Glenn's father secretly got in touch with the Neikes lamia family and prepared the trade route construction.

It was a dangerous gamble. While casualties at the time were fewer in number compared to the height of the fighting, there were still weapons dealers and mercenaries that reaped profit from the war's protraction. If, by any chance, Glenn's father's connection to a monster merchant was discovered, he would likely be convicted as a spy.

And Glenn's father wasn't the only one in danger—the entire Eastern Trading Alliance bore the risk.

The Neikes family was in a similar situation. If they were discovered to be in secret negotiations with the humans, they would be subject to reproach from their fellow monsters, and might even be attacked.

Their biggest fear was of information leaking out. If information spilled out before the trade route was established, everything would be for naught. Conversely, if they could finish establishing the trade route, then it could be a big step toward ending the war—and if the war itself ended, then they wouldn't be traitors or anything of the sort.

For that reason, Glenn and the head of the Neikes family needed to have a strict arrangement to manage the spread of information. So they come up with a hostage proposal.

First, the head of the Neikes family would send their only daughter, Saphentite Neikes, and then later, Glenn's father would send his oldest son, Glenn Litbet, to live in the lamia household. By exchanging hostages, the families would watch over one another, making certain neither betrayed the other.

At first, Saphentite lived in the Litbeit household under strict secrecy. Glenn was six years old at the time, Saphentite was eight. They lived together for close to a year. Saphentite was the ideal hostage. A scandal would surely have been stake if it were discovered that a monster was there in human territory, so Sapphee lived under virtual house arrest. However, because of her albinism, she wasn't able to walk outside during the day, anyway, which made the situation rather convenient.

Living in the Litbeit household were both Glenn and his older sister, who was close to Sapphee's age, which helped Sapphee quickly adjust to her new life. By reading the valuable books in the Litbeit house together, Sapphee and Glenn rapidly deepened their relationship. Glenn even learned the language of the monsters from Sapphee, simple as it was.

Of course, since it was a hostage exchange, it had originally been planned that Glenn would be moved to the monster territory. However, that didn't happen.

Why was this?

Because the construction of the trade route through the Vivre Mountains moved forward smoothly—more smoothly than had been anticipated.

Glenn's father and the head of the Neikes family, having been ready for all of the difficulties they had predicted, rapidly developed the route and began trading goods with one another. The valuable goods produced by the monsters—in particular the Neikes branded medicine, glassware made by the mermaids, and the special textiles of the arachne—could all be sold at a high price.

The Eastern Trade Alliance waited for its opportunity and made it known far and wide that they had been successful in trading with the monsters.

Most of the public were overjoyed. Many knew the high value goods manufactured by monsters had. Conversely, on the monster side, human-made produce and farm products were highly popular. Due to the harsh soil of the western lands, the farming industry there hadn't expanded much. Herbivorous monsters shed tears of joy at the flavor of human-grown vegetables.

Thus, the war ended. People on both sides wanted to live a luxurious life trading goods made by both sides rather than fighting.

Sapphee had been at the Litbeit's home for a year. During that time, because of how swimmingly the new route development had advanced, there wasn't any need to send Glenn over as a hostage.

Thus, Sapphee returned to monster territory and her time exchanging culture with Glenn and his family became memory.

The time Glenn spent sharing cultures with Sapphee became the trigger that drew him into the world of monsters—their customs, and way of life.

Before he realized it, he had read every book on monsters in his house and, as if even that wasn't enough, at fourteen he went to study abroad at the Monster Academy. In all the Academy's long history, Glenn was the first human to ever study there.

There at the Academy, he studied under the renowned Cthulhy Squele, who was an authority on monster medicine. In Cthulhy's research lab, he was reunited with Saphentite Neikes, his upperclassman in the lab. She was—appropriately—learning medicine manufacturing under Cthulhy.

They had been separated from each other for some time, but at a turning point in both of their lives, they became inseparable, always together.

"What a strange coincidence," Cthulhy said to Glenn before he opened up his clinic. "You have a strange bond, and you both get along well. Might as well make use of that and run a clinic together. Don't worry. A place has already been prepared. You can take the supplies you need from my hospital. It's equipped with most of the things you'll need in Lindworm." Cthulhy Squele had announced all this to Glenn rather indifferently.

"There is one condition—you can't use the clinic I've prepared and overseen to do anything audacious. Got it, you two?"

There was a suspicious sparkle in her eyes, hidden by her glasses.

Cthulhy was a frightening teacher to anger, so when the clinic opened, Glenn and Sapphee could only nod quietly in agreement at her words of warning.

* * * * *

Despite all that, there Sapphee was—apparently pregnant.

"That can't be it," Glenn said. After all, he had no memory of doing anything to Sapphee that would have impregnated her. More importantly, if she was pretending to be like this, he'd be chased out of the clinic by Cthulhy.

"But Doctor, look— my stomach's so big."

Glenn couldn't understand Sapphee's thought process behind such a prank. That, however, was something that would soon enough come to light, because—

"First of all," he said, "why in the world would an oviparous lamia be pregnant?!"

"Oh?" Sapphee put her hand up to her mouth and smiled.

It was an extremely contrived gesture. Obviously, Sapphee herself would know better than Glenn that lamia didn't get pregnant.

Still, there were many types of monsters that laid eggs—including harpies, mermaids, and lamia. Glenn served monster patients every day, and was sometimes present as monsters gave birth. If anything, falling for a prank like this would call his fitness as a doctor into question.

"Whatever," he said. "Just let me take a look at that bulging stomach of yours."

"Oh my, Doctor, telling me to strip! How bold."

"I didn't say anything like that!"

Glenn was exasperated. In the past, she had acted like a big sister two years his senior, but recently, while she still politely attended to him as his assistant, these jokes and pranks of hers had grown in number. Joking about pregnancy and other such matters was in especially poor taste.

Sapphee rolled up the skirt of her negligee for Glenn. Glenn's heart skipped a beat, but when he got a better look he saw that, under her negligee, Sapphee was wearing her normal nurse's outfit. Under that was the same opaquely black underclothes, as well.

However, between her negligee and nurse's outfit was crammed a large amount of cloth and a small basket. Just as he had known, Sapphee being pregnant or having some sort of other problem was preposterous. She had hidden these goods under her clothes and used them to pretend she had a bulging stomach.

The basket was tied around Sapphee's body with a string. Sapphee should have known to begin with that her prank would be immediately found out when Glenn noticed her opaque underclothes underneath her negligee.

And as for the inside of the basket, there was something wrapped up in cloth inside it.

"...Eggs?" He gaped.

"The fairies found them a little while ago," Sapphee said. They all scattered across the city to look for Miss Kunai's body, right? Well, they didn't find her body, but they *did* bring this back."

"Well, now."

Sapphee took off her negligee and showed Glenn the basket properly. It seemed she had only been wearing it to hide the eggs. They were quite big, each was about twice the size of a chicken egg. It was immediately clear that they were monster eggs.

"They couldn't just leave them there, after all. I thought maybe if I warmed them up they would hatch."

For a moment, Glenn thought she was joking, but her gaze was serious.

Glenn examined the eggs again. They were different from both the eggs of underwater mermaids and from the soft-shell eggs that lamia laid. If they were indeed a monster's eggs, then it seemed they were most likely harpy eggs.

Harpies were a bird-type of monster with bird-wing arms and raptor-taloned feet. Naturally, there were many harpies living in Lindworm, and they had a colony along the slopes of the Vivre Mountains.

But—even if that were the case, Glenn wondered—had harpy eggs *truly* been dropped in the city?

"Their parents must be searching for them, right?" Sapphee said.

She had a point—if there were harpy children inside the eggs, then the parents would surely be out looking for them. The eggs wouldn't hatch without an adequate amount of heat, and there was a risk of the children inside dying. Taking that into account, Sapphee wrapping them in cloth and hiding them under her clothes had been the proper way to handle the situation.

"Excuse me for a moment," Glenn said to the eggs, picking one up in his hand.

They were distinctly light. Glenn immediately came to a conclusion just from picking them up.

"That's not it," he said.

"What isn't?"

"These eggs aren't fertilized," he explained. "There aren't any babies inside. These are probably just the result of a female harpy's ovulation."

Whether they were actively trying to have children or not, all oviparous female monsters ovulated regularly—Sapphee laid unfertilized eggs periodically, as well.

It wasn't something female monsters discussed lightly with men, but when they were feeling ill or unwell, there were times their ovulation rhythm would be thrown off schedule. There were many women who came to the clinic for a consultation about such situations. Most of the time, the causes were related to stress, hardship, or a disruption in their daily life, so as long as the patients got some rest and ate something rich in nutrients they would suffer no further complications.

"That means they aren't someone's lost children, then," Sapphee said. "I suppose that is something of a relief."

"Still," Glenn remarked, "unfertilized eggs aren't something that should just be lying around by the side of the road."

"Honestly," Sapphee said and took the eggs from Glenn, wrapping them up once more in the cloth.

Even though the eggs were unfertilized, they weren't something to throw out anywhere one pleased. Indeed, Sapphee herself always made sure that Glenn never saw her dispose of her own eggs.

All in all, it seemed only the strangest of things were being left around Lindworm that day—be they arms, legs, or eggs.

Glenn was puzzling over all when he felt a light tugging at the hem of his coat. There at his feet was a fairy, looking up at him with an anxious expression on its face.

Glenn assumed it intended to remind him about their reward—and now that he thought about it, he still hadn't paid them for the work today. But before he could ready himself for them, the fairy declared—

"Outsiiiide!"

"Outside?"

"Outsiiide!"

"Maaaany!"

"Peeeeeople!"

"What...?"

A lot of people outside? Glenn thought to himself. *At this hour?* But the fairies were saying so, which meant it was undoubtedly true. Glenn hadn't noticed, but the fairies had a special sense for such things—he did know, however, that he could trust their word.

"Sapphee, what is this about?"

"It had occurred to me, but..." Sapphee hugged the eggs close to her. "I wonder if the raiders Miss Skadi and Miss Kunai were chasing after were keeping their eye on you, Dr. Glenn."

With her keen gaze, Sapphee looked out the window. Glenn suspected that someone was there, but he wasn't able to confirm whether or not there were any people on the other side of the window.

Lamia, however, had a special organ for sensing temperature. According to Sapphee's description of the way it worked, she could "see temperature." Glenn thought he would probably never be able to fully understand this sense of hers, but that wasn't important.

With this sensory organ, lamia could catch the movements of people or animals even on a pitch-black night. They could also identify where someone had been moments prior by sensing the residual heat a person left in the space they had formerly occupied.

"Wait," Glenn said. "You think they followed me all the way back here?"

"Who knows?" Sapphee said. "At any rate, it's dangerous to stay here. They might surround us."

It was a truly awful situation.

Glenn couldn't possibly go up against the rebels. His life had been entirely devoted to learning—he had absolutely no knowledge of martial arts or one-on-one combat. Fortunately, since becoming a doctor he often found himself running all over the city and had gotten more athletic as a result, but ultimately, he simply had no idea what do to.

As he was racking his brain, the sound of footsteps came from outside the clinic. Then, just as Glenn turned with a start toward the noise, the plain door to the clinic was blown off its hinges.

"!"

In its absence was darkness.

Mixed in with the dark of the night was someone in navy blue attire. His face covered with a piece of cloth, the man swiftly stepped into the clinic. The fairies knew something was wrong and hid themselves with terrifying speed. The man said something in a muffled voice, aimed at Glenn, and rushed towards him, when—

"Doctor!"

This time it was the man's body that was sent flying.

Sapphee's white tail had lashed out. With its whip-like length, Sapphee drove off the bandit that had broken into the clinic.

Lamia's lower bodies were flexible and strong. Able to extend the tip of her tail out like a third hand, Sapphee had used its long reach to pull Glenn out from the water before. With its strong muscles, such a tail could be used to rain down furious attacks on a lamia's enemies.

Such an attack would not likely be possible against a monster, but the man who had burst into the clinic was a human. Without knowing that there was a lamia in the clinic, the bandit was overwhelmed by the entirety of Sapphee's counterattack.

"There are two important things I've realized, Dr. Glenn."

"O-okay," he said shakily.

"First. The bandits probably saw your exchange with Miss Kunai. But before that, they didn't have their sights set on you. Also, they didn't know that a lamia like myself was here, so they thought they'd easily be able to make their attack. Since I'm here, however, we should be fine."

Sapphee was calm; Glenn was glad to have her composed presence in this situation. At the Merrow Waterways, she had shown him her childish grin, but in times of emergency, she was reliable. Of the two of them, it had been Sapphee who was the upperclassmen while they were at the Academy, after all.

"Second. This clinic has been targeted. I think it's time to run."

"G-got it!" Glenn responded quickly.

He threw the medical bag he always had with him over his shoulder. Sapphee cradled the eggs wrapped in cloth and exited through the destroyed door at once. As for the fairies, they had already escaped. They were nimble monsters, good at hiding from the eyes of others, so Glenn wasn't worried about them. It was just he and Sapphee who were left.

"Oh, there's one other thing," she said, just as another bandit rushed them. She blew him away with her tail as he lunged at them. Even in the twilight, Sapphee's vision worked without any difficulty. Utilizing her heat sense to its maximum potential, she rained down blow after blow on the attackers, who—under other circumstances— would have had an overwhelming advantage in the night's darkness.

"Don't worry about treating the bandits," she said to Glenn. "No matter how much of a doctor you may be, your duties don't extend *that* far."

"I suppose you're right," Glenn replied with a dry smile. "I'll just treat them later, after we've successfully made our escape."

"Oh, honestly, Doctor—you really never change." With these words, Sapphee finally smiled at Glenn.

She had seemed on edge since Glenn had returned to the clinic, but she looked at him now with a relaxed expression on her face.

✳ ✖ ✖ ✖ ✳

All told, there were four nighttime assailants, all wearing dark clothes, all with their faces concealed. Having overpowered the two that slipped into the clinic, Sapphee knocked out another as they escaped. She wrapped her tail around the bandit's feet as he pursued them through the city at night and tripped him. Doing this to a human as he was running full speed meant that he went flying face first into the level ground. The bandit let out a small groan before he stopped moving.

Somewhere along their way, they lost sight of their final pursuer. Glenn wondered if the man had concluded it was too dangerous to attack a lamia at night, or if he had departed in order to call more of his companions to join him.

"Where are we running, Doctor? The Central Hospital?" Sapphee asked as she slithered along at top speed. At first glance, her snake body looked sluggish, but with this unique way of moving, she was able to rush through the town with unexpected speed.

The suggestion she had made was the Lindworm Central Hospital—the a large establishment run by Cthulhy Squele, with equipment and personnel that Glenn's small-town clinic simply couldn't hold a candle to. As Glenn's mentor in the city, Cthulhy *did* seem like she would be the natural person to go to for help.

However, Glenn shook his head. "No, I don't want to go to the Central Hospital."

"Dr. Glenn?"

"If we go there while being pursued, we might end up causing trouble for the patients admitted there. We can't do that. Some of the patients there wouldn't be able to escape on their own."

If the bandits broke into a place like that—even if harming the patients there wasn't their objective—there was a risk of casualties. Glenn abhorred the thought.

"In that case, what should we do?"

"Well..."

Glenn's words faltered. He couldn't think of a good plan. *Why did they target me in the first place?* he wondered. Was it because he was an associate of Kunai and her master Skadi? Even so, what would the bandits have had to gain from coming after a town doctor like himself? They should have been chasing after Kunai directly.

Or maybe, he thought, *it has nothing to do with any of that.*

"This is just a thought," Glenn said, looking at the eggs Sapphee held in her arms, "but...could these eggs be what they're after?"

"Wh-what do you mean?" she asked.

"Miss Kunai said she was chasing after slave traders," he explained as he ran, gasping for breath. "But slavery is a system that was long abolished by both humans and monsters alike. In that case, then what is it that they're selling? It's possible that by slavery, she meant illegal trafficking, right?" The more clear-headed he became as he spoke, the more confident he felt in his reasoning.

"Illegal trafficking... They couldn't be trafficking harpies, could they?" Sapphee said.

"That's what I thought at first," Glenn responded, "but that might not be the case. If they're after the eggs...then they might be *selling* the eggs, too. What the fairies carelessly picked up and brought back with them might actually be the bandits' *products*—products they'll try to get back by any means necessary."

"Are unfertilized harpy eggs worth anything?"

"...Yeah, probably," Glenn said, but hesitated to speak further. It wasn't a story he wanted to have to tell Sapphee.

One of the effects of the long war was that both monsters and humans were still filled with prejudices and often discriminated against one another. Both groups harbored antipathy for the other. On the one hand, this extreme dislike manifested in the two groups avoiding one another. However, it also made one group the target of the other's curiosity. Put simply, a certain number of humans treated monsters like they were animals at a freak show.

Such humans were often rich. These people had already had their fill of normal forms of entertainment and had begun dabbling in hobbies that were difficult for others to come by.

During the era when the war was at its most violent, monsters would be taken from occupied villages and kept as slaves by the nobility. It was something Glenn would never breathe a word of to Sapphee, of course, but naturally the slaves had all been beautiful, young, female monsters.

As always, the rich spent their money on their vulgar tastes— what mattered was that they had something to spend their money on. Thus, even if doing so was illegal, it wasn't exactly unexpected that some slave traders would capture harpies, make them lay eggs, and then trade those eggs to such wealthy individuals.

"So, they're after these eggs, then," Sapphee said. She bit her lip and tightly hugged the eggs against her chest.

For a monster like her, Glenn imagined it was a cruel story to hear. As for himself, he couldn't completely scorn those rich people and their curiosity. After all, a similar type of curiosity had driven Glenn's desire to learn about the ecology and physicality of monsters—it was, in part, why he ended up as a monster doctor. He had wanted to know more about monsters, and for both humans, and the men and women who lived completely differently from them, to understand each other. It was a cross between a thirst for knowledge and his own curiosity.

The reason he had hesitated when speaking with Sapphee was because he could understand the feelings of someone who would pay huge sums of money to buy harpy eggs, even if his understanding was only to the slightest degree.

Glenn continued to speak, as if he were trying to shake off his guilt. "It's still hard to say for sure whether they're after the eggs or not... Anyway, let's head to the Lindworm City Hall."

"City Hall?" Sapphee said.

"Security will be tight there, and I'm sure Representative Skadi will be there late. If Miss Skadi is there, then Miss Kunai will be, as well. Let's at least try to get that far."

"That won't be necessary!" barked a voice from behind them.

Thinking it was their pursuers, Sapphee and Glenn stood ready to defend themselves, but instead of bandits, standing behind them was a pale woman with stitches all over her body. Although her dead flesh fit the current situation rather well, Glenn and Sapphee still became frightened when they looked at her complexion.

It was the bodyguard of the Draconess, Kunai Zenow.

"Miss Kunai!" Glenn said.

"There was an eyewitness account of some fairies hauling a basket of eggs around. I had a bad feeling about it and visited the clinic, but the door was already destroyed, the place was a mess... And now, I've finally caught up to you."

Glenn looked closer at Kunai.

In her right arm she held a pinioned form, its arms and legs tied behind its back. It was one of the bandits, his face covered with a piece of cloth. Glenn had thought they'd stopped giving chase, but it appeared that Kunai had still managed to capture one. Tossing the unconscious bandit to the side, she scratched her head.

She had bound an adult man and knocked him unconscious. It appeared flesh golems weren't just well-versed in combat techniques, but also had a significant amount of raw strength.

"We were planning to settle everything by ourselves," she said. "I never would have thought the town doctor would somehow get wrapped up in all this, as well."

"Sorry..." Glenn apologized, though it was really the fairies he'd sent out to look for Kunai's arm who had brought the eggs back to the clinic in the first place.

In other words, it was partly because of Kunai that the eggs had been brought to the clinic in first place. However, Glenn thought that if he told her that now, the truth of the matter would only serve to worsen the doctor-hating flesh golem's mood.

For someone who couldn't fight, like Glenn, fighting strength was certainly a precious commodity.

"I'd like to protect you," Kunai said. "but unfortunately, I can't— and there isn't anyone at City Hall who can, either."

"Huh...?"

"The slave traders realized we had gotten wind of them and are aiming to quickly escape from the city. We've positioned all the City Hall guards to capture them before they can escape. Naturally, I'm heading off to break into their hideout."

It was a bold move—though Kunai was surly capable of capturing them without any trouble. After all, Glenn had personally just sutured her back together. Even if a patient's arm had been severed, as long as a skilled doctor carefully connected it back together, the patient could return to their training and be able to move their arm nearly just as well as before it had been severed—depending, of course on a number of different factors.

Whatever the case, Glenn was positive that Kunai's movements would be far better than they had been when her mended arm and leg had been fit together with sloppy suture work.

"Consequently, as we are all otherwise occupied," Kunai said bluntly, "there is no one who can protect you."

Sapphee looked dejected."That's going to be a problem," she said. "This is your fault to begin with for letting those bandits go free for so long, *right*? 'There's no one here, so we can't protect you'—what kind of logic is that? We're just ordinary people, you know!"

By ordinary people, Sapphee surely meant that neither of them were the sort of people who acted with violence.

"Maybe we could we leave these eggs with you?" the lamia offered. "If we do that, then they'll have no reason to target Dr. Glenn and me."

"If it would set your mind at ease, you may do so," Kunai said. "But there's a chance the remnants of their group might take over your clinic for revenge, you know. I'm won't be responsible for you if you get taken as hostages."

"Miss Kunai!" Sapphee exclaimed. "You're speaking like this doesn't concern you..." Glenn's assistant lifted up her tail, which was trembling violently. The behavior clearly expressed her feelings—some species of lamia even gave a warning rattle when they lifted their tails in such a fashion.

"Hmm. In that case..." Kunai nodded as if she had taken their argument into account, then said, "Lady Draconess and myself are going to raid the slave trader's hideout. Our mission is to circle around the back and rescue the young harpy girls they have captured. If you come with us, I'll protect you." Kunai gave a big grin, an expression Glenn had never seen her make before.

Immediately, he began weighing the risks. They could go back to the clinic, not knowing when they could be attacked—or they could go along with Kunai and Skadi. Not only would the second option allow them to personally witness the bandits' capture, thus allowing them to sleep at night without worry, but they would also be under the protection of both Kunai and an individual of the strongest living species in the world—Skadi Dragenfelt, a female dragon.

"No, thank you," Saphee said. "Something that dangerous—"

"No—we'll go," Glenn interrupted her.

"Doctor?!"

Sapphee looked ready to reprimand him, but Glenn was resolute. "In a battle, there's a risk of people getting injured right? I'm sure they'll need people who can give first aid, Sapphee."

"But..."

"Stop talking in circles. The choice is simple—are you coming or not?"

Sapphee stood for a moment, unsure about what to do, but finally gave a small nod. She seemed to have weighed the risks against her safety, as well.

Kunai appeared to be the practical type—or least, the type who valued saving time and taking action over thinking things through. Glenn thought it must be a habit that had become ingrained in her while working as Skadi's bodyguard.

"With that settled, we'll head to the canals," she said. "We have a boat waiting there."

"Boat...?"

"A gondola. The bandits' hideout is in the Waterways," she explained, then immediately started off. Her personality seemed quick and decisive, indeed. "We're relying on the boat for the raid," she called over her shoulder as they followed her to their destination.

"Heeeey! Doctor! Over here, over here!" a voice rose up from the night-dark canal as they approached; in the dim, Glenn could just make out a figure waving to them as they approached. The person wore glass ornaments that gleamed in the moonlight and by them, he recognized who it was immediately: Lulala.

Her shining golden scales glinted with a unique sparkle underneath the light of the moon. Glenn thought to himself that if she had given a performance in the Waterways light-up show, she probably would have become even more famous.

"Why's Lulala—?" he wondered out loud, but Kunai interrupted him.

"Talk on the way. Hurry up and get in."

At Kunai's urging, Glenn quickly got into the gondola. With Glenn's help, Sapphee slithered in after them.

In the back of the gondola, Draconess Skadi sat shrouded in her robe. She could have been a tourist of some kind, sitting calmly there in the gondola as she was—but of course, that wasn't the case. They were all gathered there in the boat for the same purpose: to raid the slave trader's hideout.

With Glenn, Kunai, and Sapphee all safely aboard, Lulala grabbed the handle in front of the gondola and began to pull. The boat headed out slowly, though it pitched and rolled heavily. Lulala seemed to lack strength compared to the professional gondoliers of the canals.

"Miss Skadi." It was Sapphee, speaking up with a reproachful look in her eyes. Her gaze was clearly filled with anger.

In contrast, Skadi's hidden expression was, of course, inscrutable.

"Why is Miss Lulala pulling a gondola?" Sapphee asked. "Not only that, but why is she pulling this one in *particular*, headed off to expose a group of slave traders? Can I ask you for an explanation?"

"'That was the deal'—is the Lady Draconess's answer." As always, Kunai acted as Skadi's mouthpiece.

"Deal?"

"'I asked Lulala sing in the central plaza—she has a lovely voice, after all. In exchange, we made an agreement that, when the time came, she would pull our gondola to slightly dangerous locations. In particular, we discussed having her pull our gondola to the slave traders' hideout.' Those are the Lady Draconess' words." Kunai then spoke for herself. "The contract Lulala entered into was only made after properly explaining and discussing everything with her."

Glenn could see that Sapphee's expression was growing more and more intense. She was clearly displeased with the answer she'd been given. Her expression wasn't the sulking look she gave Glenn when she was dissatisfied—instead, her eyes were filled with real anger.

"Miss Skadi," she began, but Glenn—thinking that things would likely become difficult if Sapphee asked the question—decided to turn towards the Draconess and ask her directly himself.

"In other words," he said, "what you're saying is that in order to capture the bandits, you're using Lulala—even though she has nothing to do with the situation. Is that correct?"

"Dr. Glenn!" Kunai said. "That's a rude way to talk—"

"I'm sorry, Miss Kunai," Glenn interrupted. "My question was directed at Miss Skadi."

The body guard gave a huff, looking embarrassed.

Skadi remained silent.

While he'd only heard bits and pieces, Glenn understood Lulala's circumstances to a certain extent—including her a meager life on the canals, the invitation from the City Council, and finally, singing in the central plaza—which of course should have been an honor for Lulala Heine. Lulala herself had been delighted; the news had brought a great big smile to her face.

And yet, now he found that it had been part of a deal. In exchange for saving Lulala from poverty, Skadi had given Lulala a dangerous job to perform. True, *someone* had to pull the boat through the waterways—yet the job had been forced on a young girl, still in the prime of her adolescence, almost like she was being taken advantage of...

"_____"

Skadi gave a small nod. It seemed that she had needed some time to conclude whether or not she wanted to confirm what Glenn had said.

"'That is indeed correct, I cannot refute that.' That is the Lady Draconess's statement," Kunai said. The bodyguard appeared to be displeased. Glenn was well aware that Kunai's personality wasn't one that would allow her to calmly listen while her mistress's reputation was being damaged.

"However," Kunai went on. "the fact of the matter is that Lulala is suited for this job."

"What do you mean?" he asked.

"The canals leading to the slave trader's hideout are complex. When the time comes to attack, swift action will be necessary. We wanted to pay painstaking attention to detail in our preliminary preparations. However, meeting with a professional gondolier would have certainly meant that our plot would have been quite easily exposed, don't you think?

"With Lulala working as a songstress, we were able to contact her without raising any suspicions. Giving her a job in the central plaza was a pretext and there were advanced meetings that occurred beforehand. No one would ever expect a tender-aged songstress to be pulling a gondola like this on the canals in the middle of the night. Considering the fact that her reward was an adequate amount of money and goods—not to mention the job she now holds in the central plaza—well... I don't believe it's a bad deal at all."

Glenn couldn't help but admit that he hadn't imagined all of what Kunai had just told them.

Lulula was swimming out in front of the gondola. At one point, she had been on the verge of drowning due to her poor health, and it was still difficult to say whether her dehydrated throat and gills were now completely healed. As a doctor, Glenn wondered—was it really okay for him to stay silent and let her be exposed to such danger?

"Wait a sec, wait a sec! Why's everyone gotten so gloomy?" It was Lulala. She seemed to have sensed the mood aboard the boat and had turned around to speak up herself.

"You know, Dr. Glenn, you're talking like I was forced into doing this, but...I knew everything beforehand, so it's really okay! I talked everything through with Miss Skadi properly."

"But..."

"And she told me to run straight away should any danger come up. I'm not a child, you know! *I'm* the one who decides what work I do! And it's my responsibility to make sure everyone gets through the Waterways!"

Now that Glenn thought about it, even when Lulala had been singing under the bridge at the Waterways, she had been serious about her job. She hadn't had much money to spare, but still retained her dignity.

"...I understand," he said. "If what you say is true, then there's nothing more for me to say, either."

"Right?" Lulala said.

"Please just be careful, okay?" he said.

"Okay!"

Thinking back to her close brush with drowning, Glenn couldn't say he was entirely convinced, but in the end, all he could do was pray that Kunai and Skadi would properly protect her.

The gondola swayed back and forth as they continued on. The bumpiness of the ride was most likely due to the fact it took all of Lulala's strength to control the boat, what with four people riding in it. It was only natural that she was struggling, considering the fact that she was a professional gondolier.

"All right, I'm going to explain our strategy," Kunai said as they entered a narrow canal. "The bandit slave traders have about ten harpy girls imprisoned and are selling their eggs to collectors. In short, they're disgusting scum."

"Why is their base of operations here in this city?" Sapphee asked, though she appeared to have a rough idea herself.

"It's obvious," Kunai said. "They capture orphaned harpy girls, make them lay eggs, and sell them to humans far and wide. Their business crosses both monster and human territory, so Lindworm is convenient because it's in between both."

"So that *is* the reason, then..." Sapphee murmured.

"Incidentally, it's also because Lindworm doesn't have a military," Kunai went on. "Maintaining peace and order is the job of the Lindworm City Council's Guard Patrols. The bandits probably think Lindworm is a city where they can do whatever they want without being subject to the local laws... I'll make sure to teach them just how wrong they are."

Lindworm was managed by the City Council. The members of the council discussed and decided on policies and important things for the city, though it went without saying that their representative Skadi had an influential voice in the decisions. It wasn't like other cities and towns, where an aristocratic lord governed everything, but that didn't necessarily mean that the city was unsafe. The capability of the Guard Patrol, which fell directly under the council's power, played an important role in maintaining law and order throughout Lindworm.

"So, their hideout is in the Waterways," Glenn said.

"They couldn't possibly be aquatic monsters, right?" Sapphee said.

"Of course not," Kunai said. "All of the bandits are humans. The Waterways were originally made by submerging an existing town, right? The underwater portions were heavily remodeled to accommodate the monsters who would live there, but most of the parts still above the water are the same as when everything was sunk— though navigating that area is pretty complicated, with a lot of dead ends and buildings only reachable by boat. The slave traders picked one of the houses on the water's surface to be their hideout."

"There *are* quite a number of abandoned houses..." Glenn mused, as Kunai looked out at the uninhabited town on the surface of the Waterways.

There were some places accessible by bridge, but most of buildings' original entrances were now sunken underwater. The second or third floors of the buildings were as they had originally been, above the surface of the water.

There was a moment of silence, then Kunai said, "Lady Draconess can't help but regret that the maintenance on the Waterways wasn't extended to all the sections above the surface. Because of this, the slave traders were able to make their hideout here. But we'll put a stop to that tonight."

And in order to get there, they had needed Lulala's help, for—as a resident of the Waterways—Lulala would know the area's peculiar and complex geography well.

"Are we the only ones headed there? The guard patrol is coming too, right?" Sapphee asked, and Kunai nodded.

"Of course they will be there. Actually, they are already building a bridge close to the hideout. Ostensibly, it's a part of 'city planning,' but the reality is that they are using the bridge to get into the slave trader's hideout. The plan is that the guards will expose them from the front."

"From the front... So that means we're going in the back?" Glenn asked.

"That's right. When the bastards run, they'll likely try to use boats to avoid pursuit. We're going to free the boats moored in the back and make sure not a single bandit gets away. On top of that, we'll rescue the captured harpy girls. We'll mostly likely find the area where they're imprisoned by first going in through the back," Kunai said, then added, "assuming everything goes well," Kunai added.

After a pause, she went on. "I've been both attacked, and targeted. The bandits have caught on to our pursuit. If they escape, then they'll definitely flee the city. That's why we needed to move forward with the plan to expose them."

"So the rush to reveal the bandits was why you came to me for treatment, then?" Glenn asked.

"If I didn't have my right arm I wouldn't be able to fight at full strength," Kunai said. "On top of that, I'd been attacked again in the middle of the day.Because of that, the Lady Draconess resolved without a moment's hesitation that tonight was the time to put the plan into action."

In other words, tonight's assault had been catalyzed by the trouble Kunai had gotten into during the day when she lost her leg.

Glenn himself had run around in circles to stitch Kunai back up, but behind the scenes, there had been a number of strategies being planned all across Lindworm. Glenn himself, Sapphee, and even Lulala had found themselves wrapped up in these schemes, but...

Glenn glanced over at Skadi.

Just visible from under her veil, Skadi's lips were moving ever so slightly. As usual, Glenn couldn't hear what she was saying, but the word her lips were shaping was one Glenn recognized.

Sorry.

It looked as if she were apologizing to Glenn. And if she was apologizing for getting him involved in everything, then it meant that

Skadi Dragenfelt wasn't the type of person who dragged other people indifferently into something for the sake of her own objectives.

Glenn supposed there was nothing more he could ask for but an apology. However, he did wish she had said it properly, so he could hear her, rather than deciphering her contrition through lip-reading.

"I can move now thanks to your suturing, Dr. Glenn," Kunai said. "The bandits won't be any problem."

"You're going to show us what the former top-ranked fighter is capable of, is that it?" Sapphee's words seemed to have a touch of sarcasm to them, but Kunai didn't appear to take them to heart.

The late-night canals were quiet. The boat stalls that were so lively during the day were closed, the shopkeepers having returned to their houses under the water. There were no tourists around, and the surface of the water was still.

As such, it made a perfect place for the bandits to lie low.

"'Once the bandits are dealt with, we will continue with the maintenance on the Waterways'—so says the Lady Draconess. Her thought is that with more construction work, the tourists will be able to walk over the water as well, and the breadth of business on the Waterways can expand."

Glenn certainly agreed that a thriving Waterways was a good thing. Such was true of the arena as well, but a large portion of Lindworm's revenue came from tourism. This was because monsters and humans, through mutual effort, were making things a reality that were only possible in Lindworm. Glenn was positive that the tourism revenue from the Waterways was linked to the revitalization of the whole city.

"We're almost there!" Lulala said. "We're going to pass under a low bridge, so everyone keep your heads down, okay?"

The canal had already become narrow enough that it was difficult for even a single gondola to pass through. In areas like these, there were sometimes bridges that could treacherous to pass under, depending on the water level.

Still, it was only to be expected that the bandit's hideout would be in an area that was hard to navigate, difficult to reach either by land or by water.

The bridge came into view. Before he brought his head down, Glenn thought he saw a shadow on top of the bridge. The structure was night-darkened, but he had nonetheless seen something move.

"Hit the deck!" Kunai shouted.

Glenn grabbed Sapphee by the shoulder and pulled her down with him—just as Sapphee used her white tail to pull Glenn down. It appeared they had had the same thought.

Pressed into the deck of the gondola, Glenn heard the sound of something flying overhead, accompanied by the snap of taut strings recoiling.

"Archers?!" he said. The sound was clearly that of arrows cutting through the air.

Glenn raised his head and there, standing firmly upright in the boat, was Kunai.

"Miss Kunai!" he said.

"Keep your head down!" she commanded. "More arrows incoming! Lulala, dive!"

From the top of the bridge, arrows flew through the cover of darkness. Kunai was the only person not hiding. She drew a short sword that had been concealed at the base of her left thigh and raised it high overhead. Her skill at warding off the falling arrows was unbelievable. She repelled all of the arrows flying at the boat with marvelous skill. Meanwhile, it was all Glenn could do to keep himself hidden.

"Five people on the bridge!" Kunai said. "Dammit, I didn't expect them to bring out bows and arrows!"

The gondola had come to a halt. Lulala had dived underwater to dodge the arrows, timely and smart decision. However, without her guidance, the gondola would soon be left to the whim of the currents. On top of the that, they were now sitting ducks; it seemed unlikely that the bandits would let such an opportunity slide by. True to form, the archers on the bridge nocked their arrows and fired rapidly at the boat.

As Kunai continued to beat back the arrows, Glenn wondered how these bow-wielding bandits were so well-trained. They were just bandits, yet he felt that they must have been under someone's mysterious command. The fact that they had been able to lop off the arm of a top-class bodyguard such as Kunai—even considering that the attack had been a surprise—meant they must have been more than ordinary criminals at work.

"Here it comes! Get down!"

Glenn was already down in the boat, but the source of Kunai's desperate cry was clear: an arrow was sticking out of her left shoulder. It appeared that she'd been unable to dodge one of the shafts and had been hit.

There was no guarantee that they would be able to continue on safely. Glenn stiffened his body and kicked his brain into overdrive— at least, he had to try to keep Sapphee from getting hurt.

But the rain of arrows had ceased.

The loud clatter of hooves echoed from the top of the bridge.

✖ ✖ ✖ ✖ ✖

"Oooooooooh ho ho ho!"

It was a loud laugh, ringing with confidence—one Glenn thought he had heard before. Indeed, he knew only one person who could possibly laugh in such a way.

There was only darkness to be seen atop the bridge, but it was obvious the shadows that had come rushing in from the side had caused a panic among the startled archers. Moreover, the tall shadow on the bridge, with a large, lower body expanding out behind it, was undoubtedly that of a monster. Matching the shadow to the voice, Glenn was quickly realizing who had appeared upon the bridge.

"This is quite the predicament, Doctor!" the voice shouted. "I tried visiting the clinic to set a date for our marriage interview, but when I got there, it was clear some ruffian had broken in! I set out in pursuit and now suddenly we're up against archer bandits in the middle of the night?! All is well, however—for brandishing their spears before you are none other than the famed warriors of the Scythia clan!"

"You talk too much!" Sapphee yelled back, oddly acerbic. "And marriage interviews have been postponed indefinitely!"

Glenn still couldn't quite make out the person face, but it seemed to him that only Tisalia Scythia would speak out as the monster upon the bridge had done. The ringing of metal horseshoes resounded from the hard, stone arch, and as did the clash of warriors. Glenn glimpsed two other shadows with Tisalia, surely belonging to Kay and Lorna.

"Dr. Glenn!" one of them shouted.

"We'll take care of this for now," said the other.

"How great it is for us to earn the gratitude of City Council Representative Skadi!" Tisalia cried. "I'd say this will end up being quite beneficial for the Scythia business!" It was a calculating thing for her to say, but as she *was* saving them from danger, there was nothing anyone could say in retort to her.

The archers on the bridge were panicking—and understandably so, considering they had been assailed by centaur fighters while aiming at their quarry on the water.

"Now's our chance!" Kunai shouted. "Lulala, go!"

"O-okay!" The mermaid's voice was trembling a little—but even still, she bravely began pulling the boat. The bandits above could no longer spare a moment to shoot at the gondola in the water.

"It's a straight shot to the hideout from here on out. There are no bridges for archers to hide on, so charge right through!" Kunai commanded.

"Y-yes, ma'am!" Lulala said.

The sounds of battle still echoed from atop the bridge and through it all cut Tisalia's loud and high laughter, reverberating brightly across the quiet Waterways. She watched as the swaying gondola continued down the canal. In all honesty, she didn't completely understand the situation. After seeing the ransacked clinic, she had come to the conclusion that Glenn was in a bind and, upon her naturally hale and tireless legs, ran about searching for him. She had sent a message to the fighters she was close with, which meant that the fighting strength of the arena would surely be arriving any minute.

"Kay, my spear," she said.

"Yes, Mistress."

Tisalia took the imitation spear, created for matches in the arena, from her attendant.

There were three bandits. Up until a moment ago, they had been aiming their bows at the gondola on the water, but faced with the centaurs, they now took out their short swords. They had been thoroughly prepared, having armed themselves with the swords in case of close combat. These were clearly not just simple bandits.

The moment one bandit unsheathed their short sword, all the others discarded their bows and assumed a close-quarters combat stance. It was a quick command—one that didn't make any unnecessary noise. They thus got into formation without any orders having been given.

"These don't seem to just be normal bandits," Tisalia muttered. She knew of people who moved like the men in front of her.

The spear she had taken from Kay was her favorite. It was an imitation, but had been decorated for Tisalia specifically, and was a magnificent weapon all the same. Tisalia sighed and rested the long weapon on her shoulder.

"That crest... So you're part of the Scythia, huh?" said one of the bandits. His face was concealed, but he nonetheless seemed to be the commanding officer of the group.

Tisalia was surprised, having assumed that the battle would surely continue in silence.

"You're quite well informed," she said laconically. "I don't believe there is *anyone* who doesn't know the name of the famed military clan of Scythia! But much as I like to brag, I have a feeling you know us for a different reason."

"A family of horsemen, mercenaries by trade," the bandit said. "If

I had to describe the Scythia, it would be that they are—above all else—warmongers."

"That's unfortunate," Tisalia said, sighing again. "We could have discussed this peacefully if you'd said 'transportation business,' instead." She was disappointed that she and her family, as former mercenaries, shared a trade with the bandits. After all, the criminals were illegally selling goods and people, which—in a certain sense—could be considered a transportation business, she supposed, though there was no way Tisalia would really know anything about it.

"If you're horsemen, then what reason do you have to interfere with us?" the bandit asked.

"What? Is there any reason why we *wouldn't* interfere with people who are shooting off arrows in our peaceful city of Lindworm?"

"Weren't you all soldiers? In that case, wouldn't *you* be the ones fighting and firing the arrows and such?"

They aren't bandits, after all, Tisalia thought, considering the man's logic. Instead, they seemed to be rank and file soldiers, trained and given orders—or, at the very least, former archers.

"I have no idea what you are talking about," she said.

"You may be monsters yourselves, but still—shame on you for conspiring with monsters! With the enemy! We're mercenaries, after all—we can't live without war! We sell monster eggs to keep us fed, but we used to be warriors who lived by war! A peaceful age is hell to people like us! Isn't that true for you too, woman of Scythia?"

"Hmph..." she snorted. "Monster eggs, huh?" The bandits wanted Tisalia to understand them, but Tisalia was a monster before all else. There was no way she would be able to empathize with people who spoke idly of illegally turning her kind into a commodity.

Moreover, the phrase "living in an era of peace is hell," wasn't something one said to a member of the Scythia clan, who had worked so hard to survive during the new peaceful era.

"Are you saying it's okay to use monsters for profit just because they're your enemy?" Tisalia asked.

"That's not it," the man said. "If it's discovered that monsters are being sold like products, then this damn peace will finally collapse. Coexisting with monsters is just a fantasy. It's only natural for humans and monsters to kill each other."

Tisalia desperately suppressed her instinctive laughter. *For him to be talking like this*, Tisalia thought, *this man must have lived in Lindworm for a while.* And yet, if that were the case, then what had he even been looking at? Had he been so absorbed with his illegal trading that he had completely ignored the reality of things?

Had he never noticed human tourists enjoying pleasant small talk with the centaurs pulling their carriages along? Or humans listening spellbound to the mermaid's song in the central plaza? Had he never taken note of the human doctor who ran all over the city to heal his monster patients? All that was the day-to-day life of Lindworm, its reality. Had the bandits truly never noticed? Or had they seen it all, but pretended it simply wasn't true? Were they purposely ignoring it, so they could throw around their own self-serving logic?

The only ones wrapped up in a fantasy were the bandits wishing to return to war.

True reality glinted in Tisalia's eyes—the reality of Lindworm, where humans and monsters lived together in a completely natural fashion.

"You all feel the same, right?" the man pressed. "You're suffering without war, right? You can't just simply hang up your spears, can you? Looking at that fake weapon of yours, you must be a fighter. You want to go to war."

"I'll make one thing clear for you," Tisalia said. "During the war, I was a child. I've never hoisted my own weapon and headed off to battle."

"What...?"

The former mercenaries appeared to be convinced she was the same as they were. Yet Tisalia hadn't ever been on a battlefield herself—though she had gone to several battles with her father. At the time of her birth, the war had already been in its final stages; the era for battle had passed.

Even so, with her own specially made spear in one hand, she *had* thrown tantrums about wanting to fight and caused trouble for her parents. Ever since then, she had been a mischievous princess. As a matter of course, she had gotten the two handmaidens she had been assigned—Kay and Lorna—mixed up in her mischief, as well.

"Absolute absurdity," Tisalia said. "I'm the one who should be saying, 'shame on you.'" In her heart, Tisalia had already decided to not to be lenient with these bandits. The same was true of her two handmaidens, Kay and Lorna, standing at her side. Each of them with a weapon in hand, they faced the group of bandits.

"The war is over," Tisalia went on. "It'd be laughable to cling to a peaceful way of life during times of war, wouldn't it? But the opposite is just as true. While everyone else is trying to search for a new way of life now that the war is over, you just keep saying *I want to fight, I want to fight*! How about trying to search for a *new* way to live—in a peaceful society?!"

"You brat," the man growled. "What would you know?! We're proud mercenaries! A world without war is just—"

Tisalia interrupted. "Involving people unrelated to your war and hurting them—that's your 'pride'?!" Take that scummy pride of yours and throw it away. It'll make living in this peaceful society a lot easier!"

Tisalia knew that mercenaries were highly valued during times of war—but the value of things changed with the passage of time. The era when mercenaries were well paid was gone. To still cling to the mercenary way of life despite that change meant they had been reduced to nothing more than bandits. The men in front of Tisalia were a perfect example.

"Allow me to correct you," Tisalia continued. "My attachment to my family's military history and my decision to be a fighter has absolutely *nothing* to do with wanting to go to war."

Did she want to battle?

Did she want to fight?

If Tisalia were to answer these questions honestly, then yes—she did, indeed. That didn't, however, mean she wanted to battle anyone just anywhere. There would definitely come a time when her skills and her lifestyle as a fighter would become necessary even in an age of peace—in fact, her current situation itself proved that very thought.

"I wield my spear in these times of peace so that I may punish wicked people like you!" she cried. "Now then, Kay, Lorna—are you ready?!"

"Of course, Mistress."

"Whenever you are ready."

Her handmaidens were reliable as ever. Kay and Lorna each held their own sword and bow. Both of weapons were made for battles in the arena—the swords wooden and the bows simple pellet bows used for shooting clay balls. Even so, Tisalia thought that what they had to hand was more than enough to put down the bandits.

After all, at the end of the day, they weren't on a battlefield.

"Come now! These villains must to be put to death!"

"You sure can talk, you damn horse!" the leader said and, giving in to his anger, plunged forward with his short sword.

Of course, there was no way an attack driven by emotion could ever harm Tisalia, and the centaur princess coolly sent her riposte back into the man.

As for the rest of the fight, the outcome was simple: having insulted the proud centaur princess, the bandits all fell to Tisalia's spear.

× × ✕ × ×

Around the time Tisalia was beating the archers into submission, the gondola continued down an even narrower canal. Lulala appeared to be having a difficult time steering the boat, but as there were no other gondolas to crash into and no more surprise attacks, they continued onward smoothly.

"I wonder if Tisalia's going to be all right..." Glenn wondered.

"She'll be fine," Sapphee told him brusquely. Turning around, however, she saw that the bridge was already out of sight, and thus couldn't guarantee that what she had said was true.

"They won't have any problems," Kunai said. "That horsewoman had her spear with her. The bandits, on the other hand, had only small swords with them for self-defense. They can't win at that distance, and if they try to fight back with their bows, they'll be stabbed before they can shoot. Either way, it should be the horsemen's victory." As the bodyguard pulled the arrow out from her shoulder, Glenn took some comfort in her words. If a former arena fighter could explain all of that, then what she said was probably true.

"More importantly," Kunai went on, "we'll arrive soon. Stay on your guard."

"U-understood," Glenn said.

"Lulala, once we land, moor the boat and run. You don't need to worry about us."

Lulala raised her hand out of the water to show her assent. Glenn recognized and appreciated Kunai's consideration for Lulala, to keep her safe and not expose her to any more danger than necessary.

"What are we going to do to get back?" Sapphee asked.

"We won't be going back," Kunai declared. "We will bring the enemy's hideout completely under our control. There's currently no need for us to prepare a return boat."

"Wh-what a ridiculous plan!"

"Say what you will."

Kunai wasn't acting like she was putting her life on the line, but Glenn wasn't sure he would be able to share in her readiness to charge down the enemies. He knew Kunai was arbitrarily planning to make reckless, perhaps suicidal, attack—even if it *was* a decision that came from proper planning with Skadi and the Guard Patrol squad.

Finally, the boat came to a halt. They were just a little ways away from what could barely be called a proper docking location—it was little more than a stonework staircase half sunk under the water. If they went up the stairs, they would reach the portion of the building that rose above the water—however, because there was no way to reach the exposed part from land, they had had to travel by boat to get to the building.

There were a number of small boats moored where they had stopped; Kunai cut their ropes with her short sword and began to kick them free of the landing. The boats had presumably been stashed there for the bandits to escape upon, but now that Kunai had cut them loose, the criminals no longer had a way to flee.

Lulala slowly drew the gondola up to the staircase. Just as she did, a silhouette emerged from the dark, directly in their path.

"...Tch," Kunai grit out.

It was an ambush. The bandits from earlier had all been wrapped in standardized navy blue apparel and this one was no different. However, this time around, Glenn had two reasons to be more on guard.

First was the fact that the silhouette belong to just one person. *Why just one?* he wondered. The second was that the gaze peeking out from the cloth covering their face was unusually keen and sharp. Glenn knew nothing of combat, so judging whether or not they were a warrior was beyond him. However, he had seen a gaze such as theirs once before.

It had been during an autopsy of a patient with Dr. Cthulhy. She had dissected the body calmly and indifferently, without a single break in her concentration. The eyes of the bandit standing there alone before them closely resembled Cthulhy's own that day.

In other words—the gaze watching them now belonged to someone who had experience with human dissection.

The boat slowly drew up to the stairs.

The bandit didn't exactly look like he was going to obstruct them. Kunai carefully got out of the boat, followed by Glenn and Sapphee. Then, finally, Skadi disembarked from the gondola.

"You look like the ringleader of the slave traders," Kunai said, readying her short sword.

"I don't remember ever selling any slaves. What we sell is monster eggs. We don't sell or buy monsters or humans."

"So you *are* the leader."

"Yes."

From what Glenn could tell, the man was human.

Despite his status as the bandit's leader, his physique was quite slender. He didn't give off the air of a rough and rowdy type of criminal. If Glenn had had to describe him, he looked like a scout or an undercover agent—like a spy. Or, at the very least, a soldier that pursued that kind of work.

"Illegal squatting in the Waterways, kidnapping and imprisoning harpies, and on top of that, the illegal sale of eggs. There's quite a lot I'd like to ask you," Kunai said.

"All we are doing is protecting monsters that don't have a place to go and raising them," the leader said. "As for the eggs, well—we got to make money somehow, right? After all, in times of peace, former mercenaries have a hard time finding jobs."

"The City Council will work you to the bone. Lindworm is in the midst of redevelopment, to make the city a pleasant place to live in. The construction crews are always looking for workers."

"Oh. And how much is the pay?"

"However much a criminal is deserving of."

The man gave a snort. It seemed he had never intended to accept her offer. Kunai slowly closed the distance between them, while shielding Glenn and the others behind her. In order to make sure of her path on the stone steps, she shifted her position in relation to the ringleader.

"Unfortunately, this is the end of the line," he said. "I won't take your life, but be prepared for some pain."

"How nice of you to say. Well, it's not that I have a life that can be taken, anyway," she said with a chuckle. Then she spoke to Skadi. "Lady Draconess! Now's the time! Glenn and Sapphee—you go, too! I'll deal with this one!"

"You think I'm just going to let you go?!"

The ringleader instantly stepped toward them. In the same moment, Kunai launched herself at him. She held back his arms and tried to push him into the water. They struggled against each other for supremacy, but Kunai twisted her body and secured a path for the Glenn and the others.

"Go! Hurry!"

"Doctor, this way!" Glenn said to Sapphee, as Skadi took the lead and dashed up the stairs. Her dragon tail peeked out from under the hem of her robe. Her golden scales swayed like a guiding light. Relying on it, Glenn and Sapphee followed after her.

As Glenn climbed the stairs, he looked back down at the figures locked together in battle and called out, "Miss Kunai, be careful!"

"No need to worry!" she said.

The two were close, trading blow after blow with their short swords, but Kunai seemed to be doing well enough to be able to give Glenn a proper reply.

"A corpse can't die!" she said. "Thanks to this doctor who sewed me neatly together, my arm is at peak performance! Don't worry—go!"

"Well, then," the ringleader said. "This time I'll make sure to cut you up and sink you to the bottom of the canals!"

Glenn ran up the stairs, guided by Skadi, and entered an abandoned-looking building. He thought absently that fishing the bits and pieces of Kunai's body up from the canals sounded like backbreaking work.

✗ ✗ ✗ ✗ ✗

The ringleader's dexterity was exceptional.

As to be expected of an ex-mercenary, Kunai thought to herself, biting her lip. Before this mission, she had investigated the fact that the slave traders were a former group of mercenaries who had lost their profession with the arrival of peace.

The previous war had been massive in scale, and had lasted many years. Humans and monsters both had individuals who lived and earned their daily bread off of the war itself. In Lindworm, many of the former monster soldiers became arena fighters, but that option hadn't extended to other regions. Kunai could see how selling illegal monster eggs and similar work made use of the bandits' old skills as mercenaries. In fact, they probably welcomed the fighting and violence the work brought them.

Kunai and the ringleader trades blows in the twilight. Kunai could see well at night, but the ringleader seemed to be more accustomed to night battles and easily dodged her attacks.

"You're a nuisance," the ringleader said to Kunai. Stubbornly pursuing the slave traders and discovering this hideout had been Kunai's achievement. Naturally, the bandits had been aware of this, and had attacked Kunai a countless number of times.

"Even if we break off your arm or rip off your leg," he went on, "you calmly just come back to life. It's a shame—I'm sure if there had been soldiers like you during the war, they would have worked for us."

"Well, from what I know, my creator *did* originally make me as a request from the army," Kunai said, aiming a sharp kick with her greaves to break his stance.

The ringleader dodged her blow. He was used to one-on-one battles and fights that took place in dark, cramped areas alike. Breaking his stance from the front seemed like an impossible task for Kunai.

"He wanted to make me into a soldier that couldn't be killed," she explained. "Unfortunately for him, I wouldn't meet his demands—I have no intention of living my life as a soldier."

"And yet you're a bodyguard. Isn't that so, Miss Undead?"

"That's right. Since I'm undead, I can ignore my own body and become my master's shield!"

Kunai raised her sword above her head. Just as she had told Glenn, her body was currently in peak condition. Her movements were far better than the last time she she had faced off against the bandits and it was all thanks to Glenn's careful suturing.

However, the thing his sutures had helped with the most was the one thing that had made her *suffer* the most. The tormenting, all-consuming, grudge-filled voices that stemmed from her various body parts had disappeared almost entirely. The change wasn't such that she could no longer hear them—the parts of her body still told her endlessly of their desires. However, Kunai was now able to brush them aside.

She wondered what had happened. It was like the disparate pieces that composed her body had finally all joined together—like she had finally become her own, unified self.

Kunai slashed downwards with her short sword. The bandit ringleader easily avoided the blow and countered with a roundhouse kick. Kunai's right arm—the one that had been sewn together with nothing but male muscle—took the blow with ease, though she couldn't help staggering a bit.

The ringleader took advantage of her slip and attacked the stumbling Kunai with three flashes of his sharp short sword.

"Hyah!" In the night air, even her breath was like a blade.

He seemed to think that he just had to hit her anyway he could. After all, even if his blows didn't land, he could force her to into the water. Kunai took a step down the stairs—one step more and she would find herself in the swift currents of the canal.

However, even if she fell into the canal, she wouldn't drown. That said, if she fell in, the ringleader wouldn't hesitate to chase after Skadi and the others. She had to keep that from happening—she had to stop this man here, at any cost.

"Hmph!" Kunai let out a sharp breath and stepped forward.

Leading with her left hand holding the short sword, she darted in front of the bandit, prepared to thrust her sword into him. But naturally, right at that moment, a torrent of the ringleader's rage came rushing at Kunai as he swung his sword.

"Fool!" he cried and without hesitation, slashed with his sword.

With a terrible tearing sound, Kunai's left arm was cut cleanly off at the exact middle of her forearm. The shoddy sutures hadn't just come loose—the bone and muscle itself had been torn apart.

Such a blow, being able to cut through bone with just a short sword, made it clear that the man's skills were far from ordinary. On the other hand, quite an amount of time had passed since Kunai's construction—it was possible her bones were just deteriorating. The ringleader kicked Kunai's severed left arm away with contempt.

With a splash, the dead flesh sunk into the canals. Nevertheless, Kunai remained, looking nowhere else but forward.

"Now that you don't have your weapon—!"

"You're the fool," Kunai cut in, never pausing in her forward rush.

She took another step—the final decisive step. By the time the bandit ringleader realized this, it was already too late.

"Did you think a corpse would be frightened from the loss of an arm or weapon?!"

Her right arm, gathered together with the muscle of five adult men—including muscle taken from the corpse of a bloodthirsty murderer—swung upwards and punched the bandit in the chin. An unmistakable knock-out punch.

Since her time in the arena, Kunai's weapon of choice had been her fists—she preferred to fight empty-handed. For the bandit leader, her swooping uppercut had been final. His head shook, and his legs teetered unsteadily.

She had won—and yet, the very moment Kunai thought this, she realized the bandit's eyes weren't empty with death. His sword was in his hand, too.

"Da... Damn you!!" The ringleader's voice rang out, anger and pain intertwined in it together.

Despite everything, his brilliant skill hadn't dulled and now, he was aiming directly for Kunai's neck.

Though even decapitation couldn't kill her, her neck did hold one vulnerability: the scroll at its nape—the command scroll where the flesh-golem-summoning incantation was inscribed. If it were damaged, there was a possibility that her body might completely shut down.

She braced herself to protect the scroll if at all possible when, at that moment—

"Taaaaaaaaaaake this!"

A loud splash resounded, like a rush of gushing water coming down from upstream—at least, that was what it sounded like to Kunai.

"Blugh!"

In an instant, the ringleader's body was thrown sideways. There was nothing he could have done to avoid the attack, which had come directly at him from his blind spot, a direction that neither Kunai nor the ringleader himself had anticipated.

The spray of water drenched Kunai, as well. As for the ringleader, it appeared it had taken the last of his strength to stand up and execute the last attack he had aimed at Kunai. In the wake of the surprise assault, he toppled on the stone staircase, completely soaked and unable to move. Kunai swiftly relieved him of his short sword.

"Honestly!" said a voice from the canal, the direction the assault had come in.

Kunai looked and saw Lulala, her head poking from the surface of the water and her brows furrowed in anger.

"Throwing garbage into the canals is prohibited!" she said. "Honestly!"

Gently, she passed Kunai her lost arm. The bodyguard couldn't repress a wry smile that came to her face at Lulala's blasé attitude towards her severed limb.

It had been Lulala who had launched the water attack.

"That's quite a strange technique you've got there, Lulala," Kunai remarked.

"Huh? This?" she said. "Anyone can do this, right?"

Lulala spread a hand out as wide as she could on the surface of the water. As she brought her fingers together, the membranous webs between them shut tightly. Then she drained the water into her hand and squeezed it out with great force, launching forth an unbelievable amount of water.

"Can humans not do this?"

"Well, they can shoot water if they put their hands together, but... it doesn't come close to that much power."

"Hmmm. I get it, then—it's because I have webs that I can shoot out so much water. None of it leaks out, either."

That must be why, Kunai thought.

The bandit ringleader had resisted Kunai's blow, initially. And though he had ultimately fallen unconscious due to the crushing punch Kunai had delivered to his chin, he had still been teetering for a moment. It had been the force of the mermaid's water blast that pushed him down, just before he slipped from consciousness.

In other words, Kunai had been saved thanks to Lulala's help.

"Thank you, Lulala," she said.

"Eh heh heh!"

"However," Kunai went on, "why are you still here? You were told to run away!"

Holding the short sword in her mouth, Kunai took off the

bandit's mask. The long cloth seemed perfect for tying someone up. She bound both his arms, ensuring he wouldn't be able to move easily even if he woke up. She tied the cloth in such a way that, if he tried to force himself loose, he would break his bones doing so.

"You know how dangerous it is here, right? Both the Lady Draconess and I have already relied on you for help. That's why we don't want to expose you to any unnecessary danger. Got it?"

"B-but, if I wasn't here then you'd be in danger, too!"

"The risks I take on and the risks you take on have completely different consequences. And when I report on the situation, I'll be the one who has to apologize to Lady Draconess and that doctor for putting you in danger."

"W-waaaaah!" Lulala was embarrassed. It appeared that even though she wasn't at all shaken by the chopped-off arm, she *was* scared of Kunai's enraged tone of voice.

"Now then, it's lecture time!"

"Waaaaah! I hate those!"

"Don't be childish!" Kunai said. " Listen, if the worst happened and you got injured, do you have any idea how worried that doctor would be?!"

"Huh...? Dr. Glenn would be...?" When she spoke his name, Lulala's cheeks grew red. Her attitude was distinctly different from just a moment previous.

Watching her, Kunai felt something, as well. Her chest, after all, had belonged to a young girl. Her heart still pined for stories of love, and it sympathized with Lulala. The throbbing heartbeats Kunai felt from within her chest were noisy, though they were nothing more than a trick of her senses. Kunai's heart had stopped beating long before she was created. Even so, the romance-obsessed heart of the young girl had sensed a premonition of love and—still yearning for love itself—refused to stop pulsing.

It had nothing at all to do with Kunai's own emotions. The young girl before her clearly couldn't hide her infatuation at even the mere mention of the doctor's name. But that didn't mean Kunai thought anything of him. Well. Perhaps she felt just the slightest bit charmed.

"After everything's done, you're going to apologize properly to my mistress and Dr. Glenn, got it?" Kunai said.

"Okaaaay!"

In the end, the emotions that had prompted Kunai to give Lulala a long lecture about her actions evaporated. She felt exhausted and plopped herself down where she stood with a thud, letting out a long sigh.

Lulala swam in the canal for a while, but upon tiring, began humming a song. Her form as she hummed along was most becoming of the songstress. The golden reflection of her scales in the moonlight delighted the eyes of Kunai, who sighed.

It had been decades since she had been created. Her appearance aside, Kunai was no longer young—not mentally. But at the thought of the young girl's love, an uncharacteristic smile rose to Kunai's face.

However, there were still pressing matters to be seen to.

After checking the ringleader's restraints once again, Kunai ordered Lulala to flee for good, and then quickly followed after Skadi and the others.

✳ ✳ ✳ ✳ ✳

With Skadi leading the way, Glenn ran through the bandits' hideout.

Besides the ringleader, there were a number of sentries in the hideout as well. But they were all knocked out before they could even brandish the weapons in their hands.

"Hyah!" Sapphee exhaled and wielded her tail.

Lamia were excellent to have around for surprise attacks. The inside of the hideout was dimly lit, but Sapphee swept through it as if they were fighting in the afternoon sun, brandishing her tail like a whip or wrapping it around the bandits' necks and throttling them as she forced them to the ground.

Within, the hideout looked much like the front of a stronghold. Weapons were placed everywhere, and there were sentries posted in the passageways. Knocking out the guards with her tail, Sapphee and the others continued further inside.

"This place is pretty big..."

"It's because the slums were completely sunk under water," Sapphee said. "It's hard to wrap your head around how much excess space there is above the water. So much neglected space shouldn't be the norm... And to make matters worse, the bandits have been using it to suit their own needs."

Glenn seemed to hear an air of irony in Sapphee's words. Running out in front of them, Skadi didn't seem to pay any mind to their conversation as she waved her golden tail back and forth, like a guide telling Glenn and Sapphee where to go.

Turning the corridor, Glenn and the others kept running.

The inside of the hideout had clearly been provisioned and equipped in preparation for an attack from an outside force. The weapons that could be found everywhere pointed to this. On the other hand, however, the number of guards was clearly low. When they heard what sounded like angry voices off in the distance, Glenn figured that the Guard Patrol was moving in with an assault on the front of the hideout.

Because the bandits had their hands full answering the attack in front, they hadn't noticed Skadi coming in from the back entrance of the hideout, via the Waterways. Well, in truth, the bandits' ringleader had noticed, but Glenn was sure he would be kept at bay by Kunai.

When Skadi launched a surprise attack, she also brandished her tail to fight with. Peeking out from under her robe, she rained attacks down on a sentry and knocked him out before he could make a sound. Skadi Dragenfelt, rumored to have no rivals in the arena, had shown him her immense fighting skill. Although her opponents were bandits, Glenn still couldn't help worrying about them.

With the help of the lamia and the dragon, Glenn arrived deep inside the bandit's hideout without difficulty.

"...Is this it?" he asked.

Her face concealed as always, Skadi gave a slight nod. In addition to being unable to read her emotions, Glenn couldn't communicate with her through conversation, so grasping her intentions was proving difficult.

Resolved, Glenn opened the door.

The room beyond was dark. The only illumination came from a lamp that hung from the ceiling. Lacking oil, it was a rather weak light source. The illuminated area was small, and frightened eyes shone on the other side of the darkness.

It was a group of young girls; they stared at Glenn with stiff shoulders. They were in the middle of their teenage years; all of them looked to be either around the same age as Lulala or a little bit younger. At first glance, the monsters looked practically human, but their hands were exactly like bird's wings. The fact that many of them were quite small was a distinctive characteristic of the harpy, as their growth period usually occurs around age fifteen.

According to Glenn's knowledge on the subject, that was about the same time that they started ovulating. They were likely all around the same age, as being of a similar age made it convenient for the bandits to make off with them. It was also possible that the people buying the eggs from the bandits wanted the eggs of girls in the middle of their teenage years.

The thought of it all made Glenn nauseous.

Before he came here, he had been thinking he might have something in common with the type of people who would buy these harpy eggs. But when he looked at the young harpy girls, scared and locked up in this dark room, he felt anger and disgust well up in him. Feeling such fury proved to Glenn that he was still, in fact, a doctor.

Thank goodness, he thought. He could still throw out his chest and declare himself an ally to these harpy girls.

"No need to be scared," Sapphee greeted the girls with a smile. Just as at the clinic, the expression she used to relieve patients calmed the hearts of all who saw it.

"This is Miss Skadi Dragenfelt," Sapphee said. "She has come from the Lindworm City Council to rescue all of you."

Skadi lightly bowed her head, but her face remained hidden. Glenn wondered if the harpies would trust Skadi like this. He was unsure how much the harpies knew about Skadi to begin with, having been kidnapped from distant places and brought here.

As Glenn expected, they still seemed confused. The harpy that appeared to be the oldest among them raised her head slightly.

"You came to save us?"

"Yes," Sapphee said. "Right now, the Guard Patrol is storming in. You're okay now."

In all honesty, Glenn thought that the guards were probably still in the middle of bringing the hideout under their control, and there were likely still bandits around—but there was no need to tell the young harpy girls that.

While Sapphee greeted the harpies, Glenn observed them. He had expected them to be in a far worse state, having been imprisoned, but their clothes appeared to be no different than the clothing most citizens of Lindworm wore. The room itself was perfectly clean, and it looked like the harpies were bathing regularly, as he saw no dirt or grime in their hair or on their skin. They were, after all, in the Waterways, so they could get as much water as they wanted and bathing *was* a necessary ritual for harpies. Keeping their feathers clean was a very important part of a harpy's daily life.

Thus, it appeared that whoever had managed their hygiene had been attentive to detail. Though their kidnappers were bandits, the care they had taken of their prisoners had been thorough. Glenn was, admittedly, a bit surprised.

However, he couldn't overlook the fraying of the harpies' feathers. There was no doubt that the psychological damage from their imprisonment was exhibiting itself physically. They harpies lacked the oils and fats that would normally be secreted into throughout their wings, and as such, the feathers themselves had been damaged.

Even so, though it was all better than Glenn had thought it would be, he nevertheless came to the conclusion that the harpies were not healthy.

The eldest harpy spoke up. "Um, excuse me..."

"Yes?" Glenn asked.

"This girl, she, um, said her stomach hurts..." She made a little room and Glenn saw the she was hiding the younger harpies behind her back, like she was protecting them. He thought the fact that she would tell them this was proof she had put given them her trust.

In the center of where the harpies were huddled together, their bodies rigid, an especially tiny girl was squatting on the ground, clutching her stomach. Her face was terribly pale, Glenn could tell even in the dim light of the lamp. He immediately knelt right next to her to observe her condition.

"Sapphee, bring me the light."

"Okay."

Sapphee lifted up the lamp hanging from the ceiling with her tail. She moved the light source to make it easier for Glenn to examine the girl.

"Ugh...Oww..." The harpy whimpered

"Are you okay?" Glenn asked. "Where does it hurt?"

The harpy had a greasy sweat showing on her forehead. She was biting her lip in pain; her agonized expression was not normal. Glenn could tell that something wasn't right and felt that asking the girl questions wouldn't get him very far. So instead, he directed his questions to the older harpy.

"When did she first complain about the pain?"

"Huh...? Today, a little after lunch... Actually, no—she only started feeling this much pain just a little while ago..."

"Pardon me. I'm going to lay you down for a bit," Glenn said to the little girl.

Among the close observation of the other harpies, Glenn lay the patient on her side. As he did so, Glenn immediately noticed that her abdomen was swollen, as if she had just finished eating.

"Sapphee, cloth!"

"Yes, Doctor... Is a blanket okay?"

"That's fine. Thank you!"

Glenn took the blanket from Sapphee and quickly used it to cover the young harpy girl. At the same time, he took a clean piece of cotton cloth from his bag.

"Bite down on this," he told the harpy.

"Nh... Hnghh..."

Glenn forced the cloth into the harpy's mouth, giving her something she could bite down on, so she didn't bit off her tongue from the excessive pain.

"Sorry. I'm going to feel around your stomach. Raise your hand if you feel any pain."

"Ngh...Nrgh!"

Glenn didn't know how much of what he was saying was getting through to her. She might have been listening, but it seemed she didn't have the composure to answer him.

"Excuse me."

Glenn slid his hands from underneath the blanket that covered the harpy and felt the her stomach.

It was a swelling, after all, and the distention of her stomach felt oddly firm. With it, Glenn was able to confirm that her swelling wasn't caused by an abnormality in her stomach and intestines. The firmness actually felt familiar. It seemed to span from her abdomen, all the way down between her legs.

"Nggggh...Nh! Hgnh..."

"It's okay. It's going to be okay," Glenn reassured her, thinking quickly.

A young harpy girl, taken prisoner, whose eggs were being sold illegally...

Although their living conditions were better than he had predicted they would be, her life in captivity was certainly a great source of stress. The harpies' rough and coarse feathers proved this.

"Doctor? What do you think...?" Sapphee asked.

"I've got it!" he exclaimed. "Her oviduct is blocked. It's become impacted."

At the unfamiliar words, Skadi silently cocked her head to the side. Glenn realized her confused gesture was likely because it was the first time she had seen anything of this sort.

"An impacted oviduct is a condition found in small birds and snakes," he explained. "It's when stress or other kinds of hardship keeps their eggs from coming out smoothly, causing them to build up inside their body. Naturally, the condition can also be seen in lamia and harpies, and other egg-laying monster species."

Dragons were born from eggs, as well—but perhaps because they were such powerful creatures, Glenn imagined that they did not have to deal with impacted oviducts and the like.

"There are a number of symptoms," he continued, "from swelling caused by the blocked oviduct, to intense pain. In the worst cases, the oviduct can rupture, or eggs inside of the oviduct can burst, causing death. It's a very dangerous disorder."

Naturally, during a harpy's normal daily life, they would never experience this sort of stress. Glenn was sure the girl's condition was a result of stress building up in her body, due to her imprisonment. Considering the intensity of her pain, it was clear that Glenn needed to force the eggs to discharge—and immediately. There was no way Glenn could bring patient back to the clinic in her current state. Beyond that, they were on top of the Waterways—even Kunai had said there wasn't any way for them to get back.

"I will begin treatment here," Glenn said.

"Doctor?"

"Sapphee. Keep watch of the area with Miss Skadi."

Without thinking twice, Glenn removed the harpy's clothes. He tried to hide her under the blanket as much as he could, tried not to look at her naked body, yet still removed everything she wore without hesitation, including her underwear. As the patient couldn't move on her own, Glenn had to undress her himself.

"I'm going to massage your stomach," he told her. "It'll be okay. Your body is going to be able to lay eggs properly. Remain calm."

Glenn spread the harpy's legs and made her get into a position suitable for laying eggs, then sat down before her.

With the area between her legs hidden by the blanket from those around her, Glenn slowly touched her bare stomach.

"Breathe in—yes, like that. Now breathe out slowly. That's it. Relax."

"Doctor." There was tension in Sapphee's words.

Outside the room, Glenn could hear men's angry voices and the sounds of numerous feet.

"Doctor, outside—the bandits."

Glenn was too focused to listen to Sapphee's warning. Rubbing the harpy's stomach and talking carefully to her, he was already absorbed with thoughts of how to save her life.

✳ ✳ ✳ ✳ ✳

Some diseases were incurable.

No matter how much of a doctor one was, incurable diseases that absolutely cannot be treated existed. One such disease was death. Treating a fatal disease wasn't within a doctor's power, though there were legends of doctors transcending death itself, and provoking the god of the underworld.

Sapphee was suffering from an incurable disease.

She hadn't told Glenn. It was impossible for Glenn or even their master, Cthulhy, to treat her illness. As such, there was no need for her to say anything about it.

"Hyah!" She brandished her proud tail at the bandits.

It was a confusing melee. The assault from the front by the Guard Patrol had thrown the bandits into a panic. They were planning on running away via the Waterways, but the boats at the back entrance had been set adrift by Kunai. Without knowing this, however, the bandits had broken into the harpies' room to try and bring them all with them as they escaped.

As the source of the bandit's precious commodities, the harpies were important to the bandits. They had come to take back the harpies anyway they could.

"Hmph!" Sapphee swung her stout tail and aimed a blow at the bandits breaking into the room.

In a similar fashion, Skadi threw herself at one of the bandits and sent him flying. She slammed him into the wall with a strength that would be impossible to imagine coming from her tiny frame. Sapphee supposed that nothing less was to be expected from one the dragonfolk.

As Sapphee repelled the bandits, she glanced over at Glenn. He had opened the harpy's legs and was desperately trying to force her to lay the eggs that were trapped inside of her. He was massaging her stomach and dribbling oil in between her legs as lubricant to forcefully discharge the hard-shelled egg.

He wasn't even aware of the bandits charging into the room. Completely and single-mindedly focused on the treatment, he took no notice of his surroundings.

Of course, this meant that he was completely defenseless. Sapphee was sure that if she and Skadi weren't there, he would have quickly been stabbed by one of the bandits' short swords.

Dr. Glenn...

Sapphee lithely dodged a bandit's slash.

The bandit's movements were shrewd. Surely because he knew his opponent was a lamia, he refused to let down his guard. He launched another attack with his short sword. Sapphee batted the blade away with her palm, and with the bandit's stance thus broken, she launched an attack by shoving the heel of her palm into his stomach.

As he collapsed, unable to endure the assault, Sapphee struck him with her tail for the finishing blow.

She wondered what Glenn would think, looking at her flowing series of attacks.

...Dr. Glenn!

From behind her, she sensed an intent to kill—to kill Glenn!

The bandit probably thought he would take Glenn by surprise, but Sapphee had realized what was happening. She immobilized the bandit's wrists with her bare hands and coiled her tail around his wrists. She hefted the bandit up, twisting her tail, and slammed him against the floor.

Her movements were clearly not those of an amateur. She could tell that, next to her, Skadi was looking at her in surprise. Even through her veil, the dragon had probably recognized that Sapphee's movements were those of a warrior—and not just that, but that she was a warrior who excelled in battles where she was outnumbered.

As she fought, Sapphee thought back on the reason that she was able to drive back the group of bandits.

The Neikes family was known among monsters to be a family of famous pharmacists. The lamia had been well-versed in drug preparation for generations. But, from another perspective, it meant that they also excelled at making poisons.

Many people considered poison and medicinal drugs to be separate things entirely. However, drugs and medicine essentially had the same basic structure. If just one step went wrong in the creation process of a drug, it could easily transform into something toxic and harmful. Even proper medicine could become toxic if the dosage was too high.

Most medicinal herbs used in anesthesia were associated with a high risk of dependency and addiction. A drug could become a poison simply by changing the way it was used. Being proficient with medicine thus meant one was also proficient with poison.

The Neikes family wandered across the monsters' territory creating medicine and selling it—but they also carried out missions to murder important people as assassins, using their poison.

Medicine traders on the surface. Assassins behind the scenes. Such had been the Neikes family's business for generations.

The lamia's unique ability to sense people by their body temperatures in dark places, and the silent, ever-changing, and versatile qualities of their serpentine form (which even made it possible for them to lie in wait in ceilings) were all distinct physical characteristics of the lamia that made them well suited to being assassins.

As a matter of course, while Saphentite learned from her mother the knowledge of the Neikes family's specially made medicines, she was also taught how to handle the poisons and hand-to-hand combat techniques used by assassins.

When the war was at its most intense, the lamia of the Neikes family would use their medicine-peddling work as a cover to wander from battlefield to battlefield, secretly assassinating people essential to the human war effort. No matter how big an army was, the death of its commanding officers and famous generals would greatly diminished its fighting strength.

Saphentite herself had practically never utilized the assassination techniques she had been taught. The war had come to an end while she was still a child.

There was only one occasion when her assassination techniques were necessary—but even then she ultimately hadn't used them.

In the past, when her family was exchanging hostages with the Litbeit family, she had been sent off to the Litbeits as a hostage only on the surface. Ostensibly, the exchange had been a part of the negotiations between the Neikes family and the Litbeit family to establish a trade route.

However, the reality of the situation was different.

If the negotiations had failed, Sapphee's role would have been to kill the humans of the Litbeit family, in order to erase all evidence that any negotiations had ever taken place. In the end, everything had moved forward, and she never had to use her skills as an assassin, but...

Sapphee wondered. Even if her skills as an assassin actually had become necessary, would she really have been able to kill the humans of the Litbeit family? Suffering from her incurable disease, would she really have been able to do that?

One of the bandits rushed right up into Sapphee's space, short sword in hand.

"Too slow!" she said and, using her own tail as a shield, she blocked the attack. The proud white scales on her tail could stop an attack from the likes of a small short sword. The blade did cut into her scales a bit, giving her Sapphee a slight twinge of pain—but at most it was like the ache one got from being stabbed with a splinter under one's nail. Sapphee didn't worry about the attack and conversely swung a counterattack at the bandit with her tail. He recoiled as his sword was snatched in her grip.

The bandit was easily dropped with a swift blow to the head.

"Was that...the last of them?!" she wondered aloud

No, she thought, *it's not over*.

The bandits came in one right after the other. Sapphee didn't know exactly how many bandits the hideout held, but she and Skadi had dealt with close to ten of them already, yet more were still coming through the door.

However, at that moment, Sapphee felt her vision shake violently. "Eh?!...Huh?!"

She was sure that she hadn't been hit with any attacks.

And yet, her strength had left her body. She tried to say something, but her tongue was numb and wouldn't move.

Sapphee glanced down at the sword still piercing her tail. The blade was coated in something—a fact that she hadn't realized until just then.

Crap...! It's covered in poison!

For their battle in the cramped hideout, the short sword-wielding bandits had coated their blades in poison.

It was an assumption that should have come to her naturally. With her consciousness growing faint, she desperately reached out her hands. Glenn was just beyond her reach, fully focused on treating the harpy girl.

Glenn Litbeit.

Ever since being sent to his family as a hostage, Glenn and Sapphee had been linked by fate.

Doctor... Run!

Glenn was desperate to save the harpy. No matter how many bandits came into the room, he didn't pay attention to them. Sapphee tried to raise her voice and call out to him, but her needlessly long tongue didn't move in the slightest. She couldn't warn him.

Sapphee wondered if the poison was invading her brain.

Even at times like this, she thought to herself that Glenn looked cool, concentrated fully on the treatment with that earnest expression of his. As the color faded from her mind, Glenn's form burned into her retinas right up until the moment she lost consciousness.

CASE 04 : THE LAMIA WITH AN INCURABLE DISEASE

There were two illnesses that even a doctor cannot cure.

The first was a fatal disease. The other was a fever brought on by love.

Of all the many skilled doctors that had existed throughout the world, there hadn't been a single record of anyone treating lovesickness. Sapphee knew very well that the intense fever that Glenn brought about in her was an illness that even he would never be able to treat.

But that was fine. She didn't want to be cured.

MONSTER GIRL DOCTOR

EPILOGUE:
The Doctor in the City of the Dragon

A pair of snake eyes opened with a snap.

Many people associated snake eyes with wide, tapered, slit eyes—but that really depended on the type of snake. Some kinds had wide, round eyes.

The snake eyes looking right at Glenn had cute, crimson pupils.

"...Doc...tor...?"

"Good morning, Sapphee. You had gone cold," Glenn said and sighed.

He understood why she had coiled herself up under her blanket. Most likely she had done so to try and compensate for the drop in her body temperature from the poison.

Glenn couldn't believe that Sapphee had been done in by poison, considering how deeply knowledgeable she was of both medicines and poisons.

"Doct...or...I...was poisoned, and..."

"That's right," he said. "It was a paralysis poison made from mandrake. For humans, it instantly causes difficulty breathing and leads to death by asphyxiation. If the bandits had had more of it, I imagine the Guard Patrol would have been in a lot of danger, but thankfully they didn't have much. I guess it was their last trump card."

"I..."

"It has no effect on lamia," Glenn said. "All it does is cause drowsiness."

Sapphee's eyes opened wide in surprise.

"You...knew...?" Sapphee said, the ability to speak slowly returning to her.

"If I hadn't, I wouldn't have ignored you while I treated the harpy girl, you know."

"You...noticed?"

"I tried to keep an eye on what was going on."

Massaging the harpy's stomach, Glenn had somehow coaxed her to lay the egg. Of course, he had also been aware of Skadi and Sapphee defending them all from the bandits that had forced their way into the room. But he'd had to be careful as he goaded the egg out of the harpy, as he didn't know if the oviduct would rupture.

"Just by looking, you knew what type of poison it was...?"

"Those soldiers didn't seem prepared to battle monsters, so it stood to reason that they would use human poison? And I figured it wouldn't work too well on a lamia, what with your high tolerance to poison."

"Oh..."

"Besides, I thought they'd use some sort of paralyzing agent, though in actuality, you instantly fell asleep after you were poisoned, but...if anything, that made me relieved. I was worried it might give you spasms or convulsions, but it appeared you had no symptoms like that at all."

As he treated the harpy, he kept an eye on Sapphee, but had given priority to the patient he was treating, as he was confident he understood the lamia's condition.

"Things were looking desperate for a while there, but the harpy girl was able to safely lay her egg. I don't think there is any problem with her oviduct either."

"...I see."

"Skadi let us borrow a room in the city hall. The clinic is still a mess, after all." Glenn sighed. Before they could reopen, they would have to clean up the ransacking the bandits had given the place when they broke in.

Taking on the repairs wouldn't too bad if they could get assistance from their helper fairies, but after the fright they'd been through, Glenn thought they probably wouldn't approach the clinic until it was back to normal. They were a very skittish and cautious kind of monster.

The room that Skadi had prepared for them was very quiet. The only thing that could be heard was the conversation between Glenn and Sapphee. In a separate room somewhere, the harpy girls were resting and relaxing in their newfound freedom.

"In that case," Sapphee said slowly, "what you're saying, Doctor, is that you weighed me against the harpy girl and gave her priority."

"Don't say it like that—her life was on the line."

"I know. I know, but..." Sapphee pouted, covering her head with the blanket. Her tail poked out from under it and swayed back and forth, standing up on end.

"Then...you saw it, didn't you?" she said.

"Hm? Saw what?"

"Me. My fighting."

Glenn nodded. "Yeah. For the most part."

Pouting against, Sapphee averted her eyes from Glenn's face. "I've kept quiet to you about it, but I've learned assassination techniques," she muttered from underneath the blanket.

"That does seem to be the case, doesn't it."

"Back when I first met you...back when the Litbeit family was taking care of me, I was entrusted with an assassination mission. If the negotiations for the trade route didn't go well, I was tasked with the assassination of the head of the Litbeit family...your father... since it's harder to be on guard around a child...and..."

Glenn sighed.

He still remembered when Sapphee first arrived at his house. She had been embarrassed at first, but to Glenn, she was the first monster he had ever met in his life.

Together, they taught each other their languages, and borrowing books on monsters, they talked about many different things. Glenn's sister had been more attached to Sapphee than Glenn, but in any case, the cultural exchange the children had shared them was profound.

"I'm sorry for hiding it from you... Ever since we were reunited at the academy, I thought I would have to tell you someday, but..."

"Yeah."

"I thought that...if you knew that my family had been assassins for a living, that... that you might end up hating me, and—"

"Yeah, I knew that."

"That's why I——Huh?" Throwing aside the blanket, Sapphee's round, red eyes pierced through Glenn. They had a vacant look to them and Glenn thought that it had been a while since he had seen Sapphee make this sort of expression.

"What did you say, just now...?" she said.

"I knew. Or I should say, my father knew. He knew the Neikes family secretly worked as assassins."

"Wh-why...?! Only a few know that, even among monsters!"

"He did exhaustive research. The poison-fanged pharmacists of the Neikes family. Now and again it would show up in old documents. When dad was negotiating with your family, he had sent for piles of old monster documents and literature."

"Th-this was supposed to be my big confession..."

Even though Sapphee had thought she'd kept it hidden, Glenn had found out her secret.

Ultimately, it wasn't common to have a deep knowledge of medicine and drugs. Since he took part in creating treatments himself, Glenn knew very well that poison and medicine both had similar origins. And if one were making poison, of course they had to know very well how to handle it.

Following that line of thinking, it seemed obvious that eventually someone would end up using said poison for its intended purpose: poisoning and assassinating others.

"Incidentally, the Litbeits also thought of something similar."

"What...?"

"You came down with a fever while you stayed with us, right? A servant of ours acted of their own accord and laced your food with poison. The poison didn't work on lamia, so you got away with just a fever, but...they thought if you became sick then the negotiations with the Neikes family might move forward more smoothly."

"Both sides planned the same thing—is that what you're saying, then?" Sapphee was dumbfounded.

Indeed, both sides had been thinking the same thing. Glenn

thought that since both families were deceiving their allies and communicating secretly with the enemy, it was probably appropriate that these sorts of schemes had been swirling about.

However, young Glenn wasn't convinced at the time. Although he was young, he stayed by and nursed the fevered Sapphee, and after doing research in old monster documents, he found an effective herb to combat the type of poison that had been used, and gave it to her. At the time, he had stayed at her side day and night, but Sapphee had been in a haze, so Glenn was sure she didn't remember.

At the time, Glenn didn't know that it was a servant that had acted independently to poison Sapphee. He thought that, whether it was his brother or his father or someone else, there was definitely someone involved with the negotiations that had administered poison to Sapphee with the intention of killing her. Suddenly, Glenn found himself looking at everyone as if they were a suspect.

Thinking back on it...

Caring for Sapphee during that time had been the first medical care he had ever given. As such, becoming a doctor had been product of his anger instigated by Sapphee's illness, and the passion he had for treating her.

"Hmph... Honestly! So this means you saw through everything, didn't you?!"

"No, I just had a hunch, that's all." Glenn gave a wry smile.

He simply had the thought that if the Litbeit family had their own schemes, it was natural to assume there was something being planned on Sapphee's side, too. That didn't mean that he had understood everything about the situation.

"But, Sapphee, your assassination skills and techniques ended up being really useful, didn't they?" he said. "If you hadn't been there during the fight, we wouldn't have been able to save those harpy children. I'm always grateful to have you around, truly."

At Glenn's words, Sapphee's cheeks grew red. Glenn thought to himself that it was an embarrassing line for him to say—or at least he did for a moment or two.

Faster than Glenn could catch with his eyes, Sapphee's snake tail bound both of Glenn's arms. Then, with her lamia strength she dragged him into the bed.

"Wh-what are you doing, Sapphee?!"

"Oh, Doctor! If you say something like that, I... I won't be able to hold myself back!"

"I'm happy you like me so much, but this is way too aggressive!"

"Well, I've always been like this, haven't I?!" Sapphee had gotten serious.

This is bad, Glenn thought to himself.

"We're in City Hall, Sapphee! If by any chance a rumor spreads and Dr. Cthulhy finds out, we'll be chased out of the clinic!"

"I don't care about that anymore! *Heh heh heh... Heh heh*, that's right, if we can't stay at the clinic, then we can run away together! We'll leave Lindworm and run forever... *Heh heh heh...!*"

"You're way too out of control..."

Without hesitation, Sapphee took off her clothes.

Her underwear, which protected her from harsh light, caused the lines of her body to clearly stand out, though at the moment, the only light in the room came from a lantern. Sapphee coiled her snake tail around Glenn, its white scales sparkling mysteriously in the light.

As far as strength was concerned, Sapphee was overwhelmingly superior. If she seriously wanted to show her love, there wasn't anything Glenn could do about it.

"Hey, um, Sapphee?" He couldn't win with his strength, so all he could do was use his words to try and persuade her. Coiling around Glenn's body, Sapphee leaned over on top of him, looking Glenn straight in the eyes.

"I don't want to leave this city," Glenn said to her. "I still need to stay here and be a doctor. There are still a lot of monsters in this town that need treating."

"I know, you're right... In that case, we can just enjoy each other in a way that won't be discovered by Miss Cthulhy!"

"That's not what I mean!"

Sapphee's eyes were out of focus, as if some of the poison still coursed through her.

No, Glenn thought, *this isn't the poison's fault.* At any rate, her sickness—or rather her strange, out-of-control behavior—didn't seem like it was going to stop.

She had only ever wrapped herself around him like this was when she had been drinking alcohol.

"It's okay," Sapphee said. "That octo-woman is so shortsighted, she'll never find out!"

"That's way too convenient an excuse!"

Glenn had started to think that his chastity was about to be in danger, but—

Sapphee's head lurched forward. She stopped moving, as if she had gone numb. It seemed that all of the poison hadn't left her, after all.

"I thought that might be the case," Glenn muttered.

Sapphee collapsed onto the bed as if in a faint. As soon as the strength had gone out of her tail, Glenn immediately unwound himself from her and got out of the bed.

Glenn was glad most of all that they weren't actually going to get chased out of the city. If she'd felt like it, Cthulhy would have probably destroyed the clinic entirely.

For Glenn, leaving a city like this, filled with monsters, would be truly hard. The city needed a doctor, and professionals that could examine and treat monsters were in overwhelmingly short supply.

"Just calm down and behave yourself. I'll stay right here by your side," Glenn said.

Sapphee nodded at Glenn's words, apparently not completely out of it.

"Doctor...I'm sorry."

"What are you apologizing for?"

With her face red, Glenn was sure that the reason she ducked her face deep under the blanket was to hide her own embarrassment.

"I'm always no help, always inadequate..."

"That's not true at all. Having you with me is a huge help."

"Doctor...? I-In that case, um, I have a request I'd like to make," Sapphee said, her voice coming up timidly from under the blanket. "Can you hold my tail...just until I fall asleep?"

She held out her snake tail modestly.

"Of course I will," Glenn said.

The aggression she had shown up until that moment was nowhere to be found. Gently gripping her tail, the cool scales felt comfortable in his hand. Finding a suitable place to sit, Glenn savored the touch of Sapphee's tail.

"Your hand's warm... It makes me feel very much at ease, Glenn," Sapphee said to him, speaking like she was breathing a sigh of relief.

She said Glenn's name the same way she had when they lived together at Glenn's family mansion—to Glenn, it was a nostalgic address from a childhood friend.

✖ ✖ ✖ ✖ ✖

Somehow or another, they were able to restore the clinic.

The prompt return of the frightened fairies was a huge help. Glenn thought it was going to be difficult to make a guarantee of safety that the scattered fairies would accept, but fact that they returned quickly was a testament to Glenn's natural virtue.

He was delighted that they were able to reopen the clinic without much delay. Then came their first patient.

"I'm sorry for making you do this so much, Dr. Glenn."

"Not at all, it's my job."

It was Kunai, who'd had her left arm cut off by the bandit ringleader.

Unlike before, when Glenn had sutured her together in the street, Glenn was now surrounded by all the proper tools and equipment he needed. It appeared that the blade on the bandit ringleader's sword had been quite sharp, and the left-over cross-section of Kunai's arm was extremely smooth. As such, Glenn was quickly able to continue with the suturing. He even had the composure for small talk.

"After the raid, what ended up happening with the harpy children?" he asked.

"Hmm. We're sending all of those with a place to return to back to their homes," Kunai informed him with a business-like tone to her voice. She had come on her own to have Glenn suture her back to together, so even though she hated doctors, Glenn was positive that she'd had a change of heart.

"Tisalia's cooperating, too," Kunai said. "Scythia Transportation is lending a hand with sending the harpies back to their homes. I'm sure those able to return home have had their minds put at ease, and have started the journey back already."

"Then...you're saying there are some who can't go home?"

"Yeah. Some don't know where their home is. Perhaps some don't have any hopes of supporting themselves even if they did return home and others don't want to go back... Those children are going to be taken care of by the harpy colony in the Vivre Mountains. Harpies live a communal life, so they should get used to it quickly."

It seemed like the futures for the harpies was looking bright. Glenn happened to look to his side and saw that Sapphee was smiling, too. Glenn had risked his life to save the harpy children, so it was a relief to him that they were going to be able to continue to live safely from now on.

"It seems the harpy that you desperately treated in the hideout is going to live with the harpy colony. Turns out she was an orphan, anyway. The chief of the colony is a fine individual, so there shouldn't be any reason to worry."

"Thank you," he said.

"Climbing the mountain is hard work, but it'd be nice if you could check up on her every once in a while."

To Glenn, a doctor, conducting follow-up examinations on patients was only natural. He knew that he'd be dropping in on the harpy colony before long. The colony most likely had no doctors among them, either, so it would also serve as a periodic exam for the whole community.

"Oh, and about the captured bandits," Kunai said.

"Oh...right."

"Presently, they are being forced to work hard labor on the Waterways. The sloppy city planning for the Waterways was the start of this whole incident in the first place. In order to make sure it can't be used by bandits again, the bandits themselves are being forced to renovate the Waterways."

"I don't—"

Know about that.

Glenn couldn't help but feel ill at ease. Escape or misbehavior seemed likely. They *had* been bandits, after all. He wondered if they would really carry out their construction work obediently.

"What?" Kunai said. "They don't have any weapons to stage a revolt. They were originally just people who were out of work when the war ended. They'll work properly if they're given a job. They're a surprisingly serious bunch. Their ringleader is setting a good example for them. "

"So you're saying they're...reformed?"

It sounded to Glenn like they had, perhaps, learned their lesson after getting beaten black and blue.

That, or perhaps when they had been attacked, something had changed within the ringleader's state of mind, Glenn wondered. All he could do, however, was make a guess as to what it might have been.

"What?" Kunai said. "I'm their onsite supervisor. I'm returning to the Waterways as soon as you finish stitching me up. If by any chance there is someone who looks like they're trying to escape...well, then it'll be my turn to show them my skills at arms."

"S-sounds like you've got your work cut out for you."

It should be noted, however, Glenn thought, *that I'm currently reattaching one of the arms you're so ready to show off back onto your body.*

In any event, the series of events surrounding the slaver trader disturbance had come to a close. Glenn just happened to end up with Kunai and Skadi by chance, but with Sapphee's help he had been able to find his way out of the difficult situation.

Glenn was confident that with Kunai keeping watch over them, the bandits wouldn't try to do anything dangerous. Their ringleader was probably the strongest among them, but he had been soundly defeated by Kunai in their one-on-one battle.

Kunai seemed to be in good form since getting stitched up by Glenn, and lately she seemed to be more and more energetic. (Despite the fact that she was a corpse.)

"Right now, the Guard Patrol is pursuing the insolent scum who were buying the harpy eggs from the bandits. I don't know how far they'll be able to trace their movements, but the Lady Draconess wants to punish them, if possible."

"Thinking about it from the monster's standpoint, it's possible humans might be denounced over this," Sapphee chimed in.

"But, if that keeps happening, and it triggers the war to start up again, then..." Glenn trailed off.

"Of course," Kunai said. "The Lady Draconess isn't intending for that to happen."

"In that case, I suppose it's okay, then." The desire to never go to war again was written plainly on Sapphee's face.

Glenn agreed with her. He felt that it would be better if the world never turned into one where Sapphee's skills as an assassin would become useful. Her knowledge and skills were best used for healing others and nothing else.

That was precisely why, for Glenn, this clinic was an important place. It was his duty to protect the place where Sapphee could live in peace and thrive without having to become an assassin.

The clattering of a bell sounded. It was the new bell that had been installed to announce customers. Glenn cocked his head, wondering who had come, when a large silhouette came barging into the clinic.

"Paaaaaaaaaaaaaaaaaaaardon me!"

"The centaur princess..." Sapphee didn't even attempt to hide the scowl that came to her face.

Bursting into the clinic was the ever-imposing and stately Tisalia Scythia—with Lulala was riding on her back. The mermaid gave a wave with her webbed hand.

"Hello, Dr. Glenn!"

"What's the matter, you two?" he asked.

"I heard that Sapphee had gotten hurt... Here, some gifts from the Waterways."

"Oh my!" Sapphee gasped.

Lulala had brought sparkling glass accessories and seashells. All of them were things that had caught Sapphee's eye when they had visited the Waterways on previous excursions.

"My, my, my! I'm so happy, Miss Lulala—thank you!"

"Are you all better?" Lulala asked.

"Thanks to the doctor's treatment, I'm all perfect again!" Sapphee

reached out her long tail and hugged Lulala. The mermaid looked like she was being tickled, and a smile broke out on her face.

"I also brought a gift!" the centaur said. "Here, Lindworm's famous dragon dumplings!"

"Thank you very much, Miss Tisalia. You'll see the exit is that way."

Tisalia didn't take the hint and said, "Now then, Dr. Glenn! Today I will make sure we set a date for our marriage interview! We must find an opportunity to introduce you to my parents!"

"I thought I told you that idea was postponed indefinitely!" Sapphee said.

"It's gotten noisy," Kunai said, sounding exasperated.

"How shameful for our clinic," Sapphee hissed.

"I don't mind, actually," Kunai said. "It's just proof that the people here are energetic and healthy. This might be a clinic, but it wouldn't be good to have nothing but pale and sickly looking people hanging around, right?"

As Kunai had the palest and sickliest face of all, Glenn found himself at a loss for a response. In other matters, he felt that, while Tisalia and Sapphee were arguing with each other as always, he was probably the only one who thought that they both looked as though they were enjoying themselves. Meanwhile, Lulala was stuck in between the two of them with an awkward smile on her face.

"I'll have to tell you everything about how I valiantly drove those scoundrels away!" Tisalia said.

Sapphee raised a critical brow. "So you just came to brag, is that it...?"

"Of course!" Tisalia crowed. "I have to tell the doctor all about it and receive my well-deserved praise from him!"

Glenn couldn't tell Tisalia she had come for a get-well visit or for something else altogether, but either way, the centaur was in perfect form today, too.

"I'm done, Miss Kunai," he announced. He had finished up his work quickly, but neatly.

Kunai appraised her securely sutured arm, opening and closing her fist. "You've done a good job. Thanks."

"That's very kind of you to say." Glenn turned to his assistant. "Sapphee. I've finished."

Saphentite was still glaring at Tisalia, but at Glenn's command, she quickly raised her head towards him. Glenn had been right; she did seem to be in a good mood.

"Who's our next patient?"

"Miss Tisalia Scythia. She's here to have her head examined," Sapphee said dryly.

"Just how impertinent can you be?!" Tisalia exclaimed.

"Now, now, don't take the jokes too far," Glenn admonished.

The clinic had just opened for the day, but—emergency or not—their regular patients had begun to gather. The city was full of monsters and humans all living together—yet had few hospitals that took in monster patients, meaning that Glenn's work for the day wouldn't be stopping anytime soon.

Her treatment finished, Kunai told Tisalia that she would get out of Glenn and Sapphee's way and led Tisalia out with her. Tisalia appeared to still have things she wanted to talk with Glenn about, but considering the busy work ahead of him, he knew he hadn't the time to spend with her.

Lulala cheerfully waved to Glenn and Sapphee, and then the

three left the clinic.

"Honestly... Tisalia's so noisy," Sapphee said.

"You've got a good friend, Sapphee."

"I have no idea what you are talking about." Still, as Sapphee spoke, she seemed to be enjoying herself.

In the clinic that specialized in monster treatment, the small-town doctor rolled up his sleeves and sighed."I wonder how busy we'll be today... Let's do our best, Sapphee."

"Yes, Doctor," she said and, showing more respect than usual, the lamia assistant bowed her head.

✕ ✕ ✕ ✕ ✕

In Lindworm, a city crowned with the name of a dragon, the human doctor who specialized in monsters indeed had a busy day ahead of him. His weapons were neither sword nor spear—just his medical knowledge and technique.

Thusly armed, Doctor Glenn fought on to protect the health of Lindworm's monster denizens yet another day.

AFTERWORD

Hello, I'm Yoshino Origuchi.

This will be my first time appearing in DASH X Bunko. Thank you, everyone—I look forward to continuing to work with them.

I'm finally able to write something related to monster girls.

I've written close to twenty books by now, but since around the time I wrote *Sister Succubus Does Not Confess* for Dengki Bunko, I've been obsessed with doing something with monster girls or some other kind of non-human girl stories.

Because I had a connection with DASH X Bunko, I was fortunate enough to be published there. If you enjoyed the book, then I'm happy.

Incidentally, I wrote the plot while watching the *Monster Musume: Everyday Life with Monster Girls* anime.

I wrote the book itself while listening to the *Monster Musume* anime character songs.

I revised it while listening to the *Monster Musume* radio CD.

I went over the illustrations while playing *Monster Musume Online*.

And now, I am writing this afterword as I play the *MonMusu Harem* social network game.

Jeez—guess I'm totally devoted to monster girls, aren't I?!

"Monster girls" are something new.

Conceptually, however, the category of moe—which it belongs to—existed before monster girls became a thing. I'm sure that many men among us has had their heart skip a beat at the women monsters that show up as enemies in RPGs. Depending on the game, the female-bodied monster enemies can almost be too sexy and make you hesitate to defeat them, right?

Through the new "monster girls" term, the concept was defined, and its moe spread worldwide. The anime adaptation of *Monster Musume: Everyday Life with Monster Girls* is the most extreme example, I think. Tsundere was the same way. A concept becomes fixed to a certain shape by associating it with a particular word.

I think that monster girls are a type of moe that have a long way to go.

However, the existence of lamia and mermaids comes from the age of myth. Isn't that proof itself that inside a primitive part of mankind, there exists an instinct that attracts us to these monster-girl-related stories?

From here on out, I think that I would like to cherish monster girls, both as part of my instincts and as a gentleman.

Now, then, to give my thanks.

To my editor, Hibiu-san. With your prompt, accurate, and splendid work ethic, you've made my work extremely easy to complete. I truly want to thank you. I'm truly grateful that you told me to write whatever monster girl-related project that I wanted to work on.

I really did indulge in my monster girl interests when writing this... Are you sure it was all right to let me do that?

To Z-ton-san, who provided the book with their illustrations! Thank you so much for not only undertaking the project, but for drawing a wall scroll illustration, as well. Because you provided me the illustrations early on in the project, I was able to experience writing the book while looking at the character rough drafts for practically the first time ever. Thanks to this, I feel I was able to portray them with a deeper root in their designs.

I have the wall scroll hanging in my room. Boobs, wonderful boobs!

To Okayado-sensei for his comments on the Japanese edition's obi strip—thank you very much! I can't believe I got feedback from Okayado-sensei himself... I will take this opportunity to work even harder and to connect the world with monster girls.

Or rather, if anything, I'd like to inject myself with monster girls, Sensei.

To all the monster-girl-loving creators who always hang out with me: thank you for going along with my morbid stories in our LINE chats. I expect I will continue to talk about nothing but monster girls from here on out, but I hope that you will still continue to entertain my stories.

Other than that, I would like to give my utmost gratitude to my family for always casually giving me suitable material for my stories, to my proofreaders for perfectly pointing out every last little detail, and lastly, more than anyone, to all of you for reading this book.

Oh, if there is another volume, a big-breasted glasses monster girl is going to make an appearance, as well (or at least, that's my plan). Please look forward to it.

Yoshino Origuchi

Contents

Kunai Zenow

Saphentite Neikes

Tisalia Scythia

Lulala Heine

Skadi Dragenfelt

Glenn Litbeit

MONSTER GIRL DOCTOR

1

BY YOSHINO ORIGUCHI
ILLUSTRATED BY Z-ton